T0063274

Ice Dance

Ice Dance

On The Ice

Kent Castle

authorHOUSE®

AuthorHouse™ LLC
1663 Liberty Drive
Bloomington, IN 47403
www.authorhouse.com
Phone: 1-800-839-8640

© 2014 Kent Castle. All rights reserved.

No part of this book may be reproduced, stored in a retrieval system, or transmitted by any means without the written permission of the author.

Published by AuthorHouse   08/27/2014

ISBN: 978-1-4969-2946-4 (sc)
ISBN: 978-1-4969-2947-1 (e)

Library of Congress Control Number: 2014913437

Any people depicted in stock imagery provided by Thinkstock are models, and such images are being used for illustrative purposes only. Certain stock imagery © Thinkstock.

This book is printed on acid-free paper.

Because of the dynamic nature of the Internet, any web addresses or links contained in this book may have changed since publication and may no longer be valid. The views expressed in this work are solely those of the author and do not necessarily reflect the views of the publisher, and the publisher hereby disclaims any responsibility for them.

www.KentCastle.org
www.KentCastle.net
amazon.com/author/kentcastle

Author's Note

This is the second book in the *Ice Dance* romance novel series, which tracks the adventures of a US pairs figure skating team from their rocky startup through their entire career. *Book Two – On the Ice* covers the early contests and their struggles getting ready for them, as well as a number of their off-ice activities. Later books take them through all of their later contests and adventures. The story is fiction, but the references to the artistic sport of figure skating are accurate.

The chapters are organized in chronological order, and they contain subheadings to serve as guideposts for the reader. Numbered notes at the end of the chapters explain technical terms and historical events. Maps located at the end of the book show the locations where much of the story takes place.

Book Two begins with a synopsis of Book One to orient the reader to the story. It ends with a look to the future.

Chapter 1

Introduction — Book One

Dean Steele was a 26-year-old computer programmer when Millie Foster tracked him down at the Lone Star Ice Palace in South Houston, Texas. He had won the bronze medal at the US National Figure Skating Championships eight years earlier, after which he retired. Millie's daughter, Shannon, had won the silver medal at US Junior Nationals the previous year, and was preparing to compete in the Senior Ladies Division in the upcoming season.

Dean worked for a company that sold software for processing radiology images, and he was working on a Master's degree in engineering at night. He lived in a singles apartment house in the Clear Lake City suburb on the southeast side of Houston. Being older and more responsible than most of the other residents, he was the *de facto* assistant manager there. Only a select few of the many female residents had seen the inside of his apartment.

Millie figured that Shannon would not have a chance at a professional skating career unless she won a medal in the Senior Division at the US National Championships. But Millie had her doubts that would ever happen with Shannon competing in the Ladies Division. She broached the idea of Dean skating with her daughter in pairs competition so as to increase the odds of her winning a medal.

Dean was shocked by the idea at first, but he eventually agreed to scout the girl, mainly just to mollify this affluent mystery woman. But he saw great promise in the girl's skating and eventually agreed to postpone his education and go back into figure skating competition with Shannon as his partner.

Since Millie had not discussed the idea with Shannon, Dean had to arrange a "chance meeting" with the girl, make friends with her, then talk her into giving up her singles career to skate pairs with him. Shannon liked the idea at first—until she discovered her mother's subterfuge, at which point she revolted in anger. Dean eventually calmed her down, and she agreed to participate in the pairs skating project.

Shannon lived with her parents, Millie and Fred Foster, in an estate in the exclusive River Oaks section of Houston. Dean had grown up in the middle class, and he had little in common with wealthy people. He particularly disliked

1

pretentious vanity, and he found himself both bored and uncomfortable around Millie's wealthy friends.

Dean's supervising professor offered him a very attractive opportunity to enter the PhD program at The University of Texas, and he decided not to resume skating after all. After Millie exploded in anger, Shannon was able to convince Dean to stick with the pairs skating project instead of resuming his academic career.

The newly formed pairs team had to develop a whole new set of skating skills, and this required endless practice. The Fosters engaged Walt Mason, a public relations executive and a friend of Fred's, to manage the media for them. Walt wanted to maximize their exposure from the start, but Dean objected, due to the toll it would take on their practice time and the additional pressure it would put on their performances. After a tense meeting, they agreed to a more modest media management plan. Walt told Fred privately that his plans included having Shannon published in Sports Illustrated magazine.

Gradually Dean discovered that Millie had been following his career for quite some time, and that her interest in him went far beyond his skating. She had a peculiar fascination with him, and she was both possessive and emotionally demanding of him. Millie was a beautiful, sexy, seductive woman, and Dean found himself severely distracted by her charms as well as by her maneuvering.

Shannon attended a party, but Brandon, her date, got drunk and started his intentions to rape her. Shannon called Dean to come to her aid. After an encounter with some high school football players, he rescued the frightened girl from the wild party. Not wanting to go home early, Shannon persuaded Dean to sneak her into an over-21 club, where he sang on stage while she danced for the audience. After leaving the club, they learned that Brandon had wrecked his car, and Shannon's parents were wading in Buffalo Bayou, looking for her body. After assuring Fred and Millie that Shannon was unharmed, they all met up at the Foster estate, where Millie was quite suspicious about their actions that evening.

Millie eventually informed Dean that she intended to have an intimate relationship with him, keeping it secret, of course, from her husband and daughter. Dean considered the idea foolhardy due to the risks of discovery and the pressure it would put on the skating partnership. Millie, however, was quite persuasive, and Dean found it difficult to maintain his discipline on the face of her seductive maneuvers.

Millie let it slip that she had a private investigator do a background check on Dean. He became upset and forced her to take him to her office so he could read the report. Seeing the file brought back painful memories for Dean regarding the deaths of his parents and his brother, and the loss of his one true love, Sarah Steed. Millie was unable to console him that evening, but she made it up to him the next day.

Shannon often manifested jealousy where Dean was concerned. Not only was she afraid she might lose her partner to another, more accomplished female skater, but she had developed a healthy schoolgirl crush on him as well. The upsets that arose from this situation further stressed the skating project and endangered its success.

Dean and the Fosters attended an ice show in Galveston, after which Dean and Shannon went out with several of the cast members who were old friends from Dean's skating past. One was Elizabeth North, a Canadian champion whom Dean had dated a decade before. Both Shannon and Millie reacted with jealousy toward Ms. North.

Dean accompanied the Fosters to a Halloween party at the River Oaks Country Club. There he met De-de Lindstrom, a very wealthy childhood friend of Millie's. De-de and Millie had long engaged in a playful game of insulting one another, and Dean soon became an unwilling subject in their verbal jousting matches. De-de accused Millie of keeping Dean as a pet, and she offered to buy him. Millie denied the accusation, but only vigorously enough to keep De-de on the scent.

While Shannon was a dedicated skater, she was subject to fits of anger and rebellious misbehavior. On several occasions her disregard for athletic discipline and her teenager's short attention span interfered with Dean's efforts to prepare the team for their upcoming competitions. On occasion he found it necessary to instill discipline by forceful means.

Dean accompanied the Fosters to Fred's boyhood home in East Texas for the Thanksgiving holiday. There Dean met Shannon's grandparents, aunts, and cousins, as well as Ashley, a member of the Kilgore College Rangerettes drill team. Soon after, Dean began dating Ashley.

Dean made a business trip to Dallas to install new software on a customer's computer system. There he happened to run into De-de Lindstrom at his hotel. They had dinner together, with dancing afterward, and she admitted that their meeting had not been by chance. Dean discovered a charming side to the wealthy woman, and she invited him up to her room, where he left her with only a good-night kiss.

De-de eventually confessed her subterfuge to Millie, who then accused Dean of having an affair with De-de. Dean refused to participate in the game of "dueling bitches," or to tell Millie anything about what had happened in Dallas. Millie eventually admitted that De-de had told her the truth, but Dean was not amused.

When Shannon discovered that Ashley had invited Dean to the Rangerettes Christmas party, she maneuvered to get herself invited as well. Then Dean was forced to take Shannon and her date with him to Kilgore for the party. Shannon's jealousy combined with her immaturity to compromise Dean's enjoyment of that trip. He later broke up with Ashley due to the impractical logistics of the relationship.

One of the ice moms asked Dean to skate a number at her daughter's birthday party. The only program he had at the ready was a "bad boy" routine that he used to skate in private. It caused quite a stir at the party, and Millie and Shannon were upset that they were not invited to see it.

One of the young skating club members inadvertently insulted Shannon, and Millie swore to take revenge on her mother by ruining the girl's skating career. Dean objected to her using the child as a pawn to punish the mother, and Millie called him naïve and explained how the game is played. When Dean continued to object, Millie offered to spare the girl if Dean would consent to a clandestine meeting with her. For reasons he poorly understood, he agreed, and Millie appeared at his apartment that night, very much in the mood for love.

Most of the Foster clan came down from East Texas for Christmas in River Oaks. Dean put up Bradley and Boyd, two of Shannon's cousins, at his apartment on Christmas eve night. The two boys sneaked out to attend a party in another apartment and get a taste of life in the big city.

Chapter 2

The Ballet

Bluebonnet Signup

"The deadline to register for the Bluebonnet Open is this week," Millie said.

"We're not ready to enter a contest," Dean replied.

"It's over a month away," Shannon said. "We could be ready."

"We don't have our basics down yet," Dean said. "We'd fall on our butts. We need be getting ready for Sectionals."

"The competition experience would be good for y'all," Millie offered.

"We'll go over to Austin and watch," Dean replied.

"I think we should go for it," Shannon said. "There probably won't be but one or two other adult pairs there. We're guaranteed a bronze."

"It doesn't add anything," Dean said. "It doesn't count toward any championship."

"It'll put one more competition under your belt when you go to Nationals," Millie added. "There's no substitute for competition experience."

"I want to show those bitches in the club we can skate together, In a contest." Shannon said.

"If we start too soon," Dean said, "We'll just show 'em we *can't* skate together."

"Look," Millie said, "Y'all have almost six weeks before Austin. That's plenty of time to get comfortable skating together and work up a short program. Let's enter, and you can withdraw if you're not ready."

"It'll change our focus, Millie. With a contest coming up, we'll have to deemphasize the basics in order to work on a program. The key to winning at Nationals is a strong foundation. We need to get about ten years of experience in the next twelve months."

"I say we sign up," Shannon said. "We can work up a program and still work on basics. I don't see the problem."

"OK," Dean relented, "But I'm not going to let us lose sight of the main goal. If our basic moves don't come together, we're dropping out."

"I'll call Sandy tomorrow," Millie said.

At Shannon's insistence, Millie registered them for not only the Adult Pairs event, but for three of the Couples Dances, and three of the Generation Gap Dances as well. She also registered them both separately for the Adult Artistic Interpretation event.

"You what?" Dean said when he saw what they had done. We can't possibly be ready to skate eight events!"

"Six of them are dances we already know, and the Artistic event is just a gag anyway. You can skate 'Rocket,' or 'Dogtags.'"

"I can't skate 'Dogtags.' They wouldn't appreciate it over there."

"OK, so do 'Rocket.'"

"What are you gonna do?"

"Fancy."

"You'll need a partner for that."

"I've got a partner."

"They won't like it if I skate in your Artistic event. You'll be disqualified."

"OK, you do 'Trashy,' and I'll skate in yours too."

"Rebellious little broad, aren't you?"

An Invitation

"Julie!" Dean called out to a young woman as she was leaving the gym. Julie Harwood stopped and waited for him to catch up, and they walked together toward her car. She was of medium height, with a muscular build and short brown hair. She had changed out of her workout sweats into jeans and a T-shirt that said "Muscle Bitch."

"You were goin' pretty strong on those leg presses," he said. "How much weight were you handling?"

"Well, it's been comin' up slowly. I'm at about 235 now."

"Wow. That's some serious metal. You're a monster!"

She grinned at his flattery. "You're fillin' out pretty well yourself, Sonny Boy."

"Well, I'm still a 97-pound weakling compared to some of those gorillas in the back room." They stopped and stood beside her car. "Listen" he said, "My skating partner's parents are taking me to the Houston Ballet Friday night. Would you like to accompany me?"

"You're asking me out? To the ballet?"

"That's about the size of it."

"I'm not exactly a regular at the ballet, Dean."

"Nor am I," he grinned. "I just thought a little culture might do us both some good. You know … give meaning to our workouts."

She laughed. "So you got roped in to the ballet, and you want me to share the pain?"

"I was hoping you wouldn't figure that out." He grinned.

"I'm not sure I'd fit in with your fancy friends from River Oaks."

"They're not fancy. They're just regular people who have way too much money."

"I don't usually date guys from the gym. It gets kinda messy."

"I know. Me neither. But we could run this like a CIA operation. Your secret would be safe."

She gazed at him. "Invited to the ballet by Dean Steele. Who would have ever guessed that would happen?" She grinned.

"Truth is stranger than fiction! I'm totally shocked by it, myself."

"OK, Dean. I'll give it a shot. I guess I can stand a little culture … and an evening with you."

The Ballet

Fred hired a stretch limousine to take Millie and Dean and Julie to the Houston Ballet. Shannon's date was a boy named Kyle. After that the six of them went out for ice cream. At one point Dean got up to go to the men's room, and Kyle followed him.

"Do you think Shannon likes me?" Kyle asked as they were washing their hands.

"She seems to," Dean said, "But I'm not very good at reading her."

"I was hoping maybe," he paused, "Maybe you could put in a good word for me, you know, with her." He looked at Dean hopefully.

"I'll do what I can, Kyle, but I don't think I have much influence over her … in matters of the heart."

"She's really cute, and sometimes I think maybe she likes me, but other times I don't know."

"Well, she's sixteen, and at that age, girls don't actually know what they want. They're just experimenting with guys like us. I suggest you just hang in there and ride out the rough weather. She'll probably give out a lot of mixed signals before the truth finally comes out."

"So, how do you handle it … with girls, I mean?"

"You mean with someone like Shannon?" He realized the boy was seeking advice.

"Yeah."

"Well, from what I read, guys only need to be clean, well-groomed and funny to be successful with women. That's based on research into which guys get the most sex, but I suppose it translates into other aspects of relationships as well. Shannon's a sharp girl, and she likes to laugh at situations." Kyle was listening intently. "Do you have a baseball cap?"

"Uh, yeah."

"Can you turn it around so the bill faces forward?"

"Uh, sure, I guess so."

"I advise that. I've heard her complain about the backward-ballcap set. And it helps if you ask her opinions on things. You know, like if you see a movie, you could ask her if she thinks Mel Gibson should have shot the bad guy or just shot the aquarium, see?" Kyle looked puzzled. "Just keep her talking. It puts her in a good mood. Ask her how she feels about things. And don't be in a big hurry to tell her about yourself. Let her friends do that. Get her to tell you about her. You'll make a friend out of her." Kyle pondered what he had heard. "Women have to get to know a guy," Dean continued. "With us, Hell, we can tell with one glance if we like 'em. But for a woman, it's not so easy. She's basically looking for a longer term relationship. She doesn't want to start something up with a guy and then find out he's a jerk. She needs time to find out what he's like first. And I mean, what he's really like, not just a bunch of braggin', you see?"

"Yeah," Kyle said. They joined the others, and then Dean and Julie left together.

Julie's Place

"Would you like to stop off for a cup of coffee?" Dean asked.

"I have coffee at my place," Julie said. "Let's just go there."

"OK," Dean said as a grin curled up slowly on his face.

"What is it, Smartass?" Julie inquired.

"Well, I'm just surprised, and, I must say, honored to receive such an invitation. I thought it was your policy not to date guys from the gym."

"Who says I'm gonna date you, dickhead? So far I've only offered you coffee."

"Quite true. But there is always the possibility that things will ... escalate."

"There's always the possibility you'll get your head caved in if you try anything with this muscle girl, you puny little wimp."

"You know," his grin widened, "If it gets out that I've been ... intimate with you, the guys at the gym will hound me to death."

"About what?" She was keenly interested.

"About whether you do steroids or not. Most guys can't believe you got that muscle-bound without a little help from Aunt Diana[1]."

"You plan to riffle through my medicine cabinet?"

"No. It's just that … anabolic steroids are analogs to testosterone. They have a masculinizing effect on the body."

"Oh, you're gonna look for shaving cream?"

"No. Your facial features are still delicately feminine, your boobs are … substantial, and your voice is soft as summer rain. But there is a more sensitive indicator. Something physiological that happens before that."

She eyed him with a suspicious grin. "And what is that?"

"Well, most female bodybuilders who use hormonal supplementation notice … a certain enlargement … in areas of the anatomy that must remain nameless in polite conversation."

"Ha!" she laughed. "So the retards at the gym are laying odds that my clit hangs out, right? I can't believe it!"

"I have heard some … speculation." He suppressed a grin as best he could.

"What do they say, that my dick is as big as yours?"

"Nobody has speculated quite to that extreme."

"So, you're on a mission to check out the size of my clit and report back? Is that why you invited me to the ballet?"

"Not at all. If that were the case, I wouldn't have mentioned it, now would I? I merely desired your charming company for an evening of cultural growth and expansion. If I should stumble upon any such private information, I shall take it to my grave." He gave her a pious grin.

"So, my clit is a topic of intense interest in the men's locker room?"

"Well, I wouldn't say intense." He replied, grinning smugly. "And other organs were mentioned as well."

"Well, it looks like you just blew any slim chance you ever had of getting lucky tonight, Stud."

"Life can be so … tedious sometimes," They were both grinning. Dean sensed that this brief conversation had excited, rather than alienated the woman, despite her voiced objections.

They arrived at Julie's apartment, and she made coffee, then changed into a nightgown. "You're a nice guy, Dean," she said after serving him, "But your little skating partner's a 14-carat brat, and her mom's a card-carrying bitch." She looked at him, grinning. "No offense."

"None taken," he said, sarcastically.

"Both of 'em took me aside for a little chat tonight." She looked at him knowingly.

"Oh, yeah? About what?"

"About their boy, Dean. They both wanted to know what there is between us."

Dean looked closely at the woman. "So would I! What did you tell 'em?" He grinned. "What is there between us, you muscle-bound cunt?"

"Well," she said, taking his jab as a complement, "I told Shannon that you and I are very close, that we share our private feelings, and we understand each other's deepest thoughts."

"Julie," he said, "You're not helping, here. That's not what she needs to hear!"

"You should have seen her face. It was hilarious. She looked like someone had just taken her toys away from her."

"You're cruel, Harwood." Dean closed his eyes and sighed. "And what did you tell Mama?"

"Oh, I was more candid with her. I told her I couldn't wait to get you alone. I said I didn't think you'd get any sleep tonight because I had the whole evening planned."

"Shit, Julie! You must really enjoy messin' up my life."

"Dean, it's those two women who are messing up your life! They shouldn't be allowed to manipulate you like they do. I mean, you're just her skating partner, for Pete's sake! They think they own you."

"They've got a lot invested in me," he said. "We're part of a team."

"The way they feel about you goes a lot deeper than that. You should have seen what I saw. Just my very presence made their hair stand up. I felt it immediately. I was in a combat zone there. I kept looking over my shoulder all night, waiting for an ambush."

"What we're doing is important to them. There's a lot at stake."

"Bullshit, Dean. Shannon has a crush on you a mile wide, and Millie, I don't know what her problem is, but she's touchy as Hell about you. When I said we were going to come over to my house, I thought she was gonna slip a blade between my ribs."

"I just think she doesn't want me to get distracted right now, while we're working up to the contests. She probably figures it would affect my skating if I were to … get serious about somebody."

"What I saw in her eyes had nothing to do with skating, Dean. She thinks she owns you, and she didn't like having me in there playing with her favorite toy."

"Julie, I think you are reading too much into this."

"Maybe so," she said. "But the signs are unmistakable. Those two women want to run your life. And you're screwin' up if you let 'em do it." She paused. "You even let Shannon record your phone message."

"What?"

"You don't know?"

"Know what?"

"Have you called your number lately?'

"I never call my own number!"

"Here," Julie said, holding out her phone. "Call up Dean Steele."

Dean frowned at her and pressed his number into the keypad. "Hello," Shannon's voice, said, sweetly, "This is Dean Steele's pad. I'm his partner, Shannon. Dean can't come to the phone right now, so leave a message after the beep. And thanks for calling. Bye."

"Shit!" Dean mumbled.

Julie started snickering at him. Dean redialed the number and pressed the star key when it answered. He listened to the menu, pressed another button, then said, "This is Dean Steele. Leave a message." He called his number back to verify the change in outgoing message.

"I told you, Dean. They have you by the balls."

"So, what's your advice, Doctor?"

"Fuck 'em. Fuck 'em both. And let 'em know you're the boss. Women like that have to be controlled. It's the only language they understand. You can't reason with them, you just have to fuck 'em. And stand up to 'em all the time. A little slapping won't hurt either, especially the little bratty one."

"Are you saying … have sex with 'em, literally?"

"No, Dean. I'm not saying make sweet love to 'em. I'm saying lay 'em down and punch 'em as hard as you can! Fuck 'em within an inch of their lives." She grinned. "But not at the same time, of course."

"So, your considered opinion is that I should have simultaneous affairs with both my underage skating partner and my sponsor's wife?"

"Damn right! Have wild sex with both of 'em. Just screw their brains out. It's how a man dominates a woman, and both of those bitches need a good dose of domination."

"I'm not sure I'm quite ready for that." He was chuckling.

"You can handle it, Big Boy. There's enough of you to go around. And it's the only way you can hold on to your dignity and self-respect with those two conniving bitches trying to run your life. You've got to keep the two women in your life in line. Otherwise they'll pull and tug you in all different directions 'till you don't know which end is up."

"Thank you, Dr. Freud, for that elegant and eminently workable solution."

"Come on, Dean. You know I'm right. You can't be that blind to those two. You can't let 'em get away with it!"

"Well, I'll get right to work on it, Doctor. With a little luck, I should be in jail or dead of a gunshot wound in just a matter of days."

She looked at him and sighed. Then she changed the subject. "So, are you going to try to resolve the great mystery of the men's locker room?"

He developed a mischievous grin. "I don't know. I doubt if there is actually anything anatomically shocking here. I think it's probably just an urban legend."

She grinned. "Can't be sure."

"As it is related to me," he began, "That normally small organ can become rather … massive. And should its owner become … aroused … the display can be truly impressive. The problem is, it also becomes incredibly sensitive. A gentle touch, and God forbid that it be from a tongue, can drive the poor girl to the brink of insanity." Julie's face became more serious as her breathing deepened. Dean sensed that this discussion was exciting the woman. "And since it's all just hanging out, so to speak, all vulnerable and totally exposed, an unscrupulous lover can take unfair advantage of the unsuspecting muscle girl, subjecting her to mind-bending pleasures and dissolving her will to resist." The flush on Julie's neck gave away her interest in what he was saying. "It seems a terrible sacrifice," he continued, "She takes the hormones to get ripped[2], and then finds herself a helpless victim of uncontrollable passion, unable to protect her vulnerable area from an unscrupulous pursuer." Julie was beginning to squirm. "Even if she stops taking the steroids, the damage is done. She can never go back. She goes through life exposed and vulnerable, helpless to defend herself against the overwhelming sensation that is so easily administered by a skilled lover."

Julie made no effort to conceal the arousal this discussion had brought about. Dean moved close to her and engaged her in a lengthy kiss. "Why don't you show me what you've got? I'll examine the anatomy in question, in great detail, and then I'll see if it can be used to your disadvantage." He kissed her again, then pressed her back on the couch. She gazed into his eyes as she parted her knees compliantly. Her breathing turned to gasps as Dean slowly and deliberately opened her gown and began to kiss his way down her abdomen.

Morning

The next morning Dean woke up alone in Julie's bed. She was cooking breakfast, which she served on a tray. After they finished eating, she removed her gown and slid under the sheet beside him. She looked at Dean. "Did you solve your mystery?'

"Which mystery is that?"

"About me and the drugs."

"Oh, that mystery!" He grinned.

12

"Yeah. You sure spent a lot of time down there - researching!"

"Well, we scientists have to be very thorough."

"You were thorough, all right!" she grinned, recalling their extended lovemaking session. "I can't hardly walk!" They smiled at each other. "So, what did you find out?"

"I can only say that your superb physical conditioning extends to 100% of your body. Nothing … has been left … underdeveloped."

She gave up an embarrassed grin. "I'm a freak, right? A dick-girl."

"No. You're just a woman with an oversized … fully exposed … hanging out in the open … vulnerability. With most women, their sweet spot is hidden … hooded … concealed … protected. With you, it just kinda sticks out and says, 'Here I am! Come and get me and drive Julie crazy!' It makes a very tempting offer."

"Well, you sure put in a lot of … research on my … vulnerable spot."

"Well, you sure weren't objecting to … my research, as I recall."

"That was pretty good research." she admitted as she recalled how she had lost herself in the passion. "I figured you must have talent somewhere, and I found out it's in your tongue."

"I'm glad you enjoyed it." He was grinning smugly. Julie allowed him his little victory.

"You know," he mused, "You better be careful what you wear at the gym."

"And why's that?"

"Well, if you wear anything tight-fitting in the crotch, the gorillas will be able to see that your camel-toe has a finger in the middle of it."

"You think it would show?"

"I think you better wear loose-fitting shorts over your leotard. The Neanderthals will be watching your reps. You might draw a crowd."

Julie draped her leg over his and began to rub his chest. "You really think they'd look up from their lat pulls?"

Dean sensed that she was becoming aroused. "They'd stand in a ring around your bench, nudging each other and pointing at your twat."

"They are a classy lot, all right," she chuckled.

"But the worst part is, you'd notice the attention you were getting, and that ole grizzly bear would come out of her cave."

"You think I'd get … erect just because they were looking?"

"You couldn't help it! That thing would puff up like an adder, and you'd have a hot dog in your pants. Your secret would be out. And if I were spottin' you, I'd make you lay there and be ogled by the ape-men."

"Jerk! You should save me from such a fate!"

"Well, normally I would, but you'd be enjoying it so much, you might whip my ass if I put a stop to it."

"You think I'd like havin' a bunch of assholes gawkin' my bulge?"

"I'm certain of it! You're not just a freak because your clit grows to the size of a plump, juicy Oscar Meyer wiener. You're a freak because you get hot havin' it scoped out!" His face developed a grin. "And you're hot as a two-dollar pistol right now, just from talkin' about it! I'll bet that thing would make a pup tent outta the sheet right now!"

Julie slid her hand down his front and closed her fingers around his erect organ. "Well, I'm not the only one who got a hard-on in this conversation. You need love, Big Boy!" Her face took on a mischievous grin. "Why don't you get back between my legs and give me a kiss where it'll do the most good?"

"You like havin' that big ole thing licked, don't you?"

"Well, you seem to have a special knack for that duty. Just don't wring me out quite so long this time."

"What's the matter, Muscle Girl? Has that thing got all riled up again? This discussion of your vulnerability has given you a woodie?"

"Maybe you better check," she said, moving his hand to her crotch."

"Oh, my God!" he exclaimed. "Your dick *is* bigger than mine!"

"Then you just better give it a big ole sloppy kiss." She laid back and parted her legs.

After a lengthy and intense love-making session, she said, "So now you'll tell everybody I'm a dick girl, right? And that I'm ... vulnerable?"

"I think you want me to! I think you'd like for your ... overdeveloped feminity, as well as your defenseless nature, to be the talk of the gym."

"Not hardly! I get hit on enough as it is, and none of those muscle-bound jerks are my Prince Charming." A grin developed. "Besides, you wouldn't want me tellin' everyone I made Dean Steele suck my dick."

"Your secret's safe with me, Honeychild. I'm not even going to mention that we went out. I don't want to add any more excitement to our workouts." He paused to inhale "I just hope you don't hit that anabolic stuff too hard. It can be kinda rough on the liver and kidneys."

The Phone

Julie did not respond. "You know," she said after a pause, "I told both of your bitches that I was gonna turn off your cell phone so I could have you all to myself last night."

"Well, they must have believed you," he said, "Cause neither one of 'em has called me."

"Oh, I'll bet they have," she said, grinning slyly.

Dean looked at her, then at his pants hanging on the chair, then back at her. The grin widened. "You little bitch," he said, "Surely you didn't ..." He took the phone out of his pocket and sighed when he saw it had been deactivated.

"Better check your messages, Sonny Boy," Julie said. "Your bitches are probably calling you."

Dean pressed a few buttons and then sat in silence listening to a series of recordings. Finally he put the phone back in his pants. "Millie gave up at 1:10," he said, "But Shannon kept it up 'till 3:16."

"Well, you better get busy, Sonny Boy. You've got a lot of apologizing to do for spending the night ringing my chimes. They'll be seriously pissed!"

"That'll have to wait," he said. "Right now I've got to punish one muscle-bound bitch for pissin' off the women I have to put up with."

"Hey, don't try that domination shit on me! I work out, remember? I'll kick your puny little ass!"

"Hey, my dick's still bigger than yours, at least by a small margin, so I'm gonna rear-end you with it, right now!"

"Hey, none of that anal shit for this girl. That's for queers!"

"But it makes a great punishment. And I'll put out the word at the gym that you have a really tight ass, and you really like it. Get ready for a rectum-reaming, you little bitch!"

"Don't you ever call me little!" she said, grinning and attacking him.

"You're so cute, you petite little thing," he said, fending her off.

"I'll show you petite, you sickly ninty-seven pound weakling!"

"You're so tiny. Just like a little doll!"

"You're dead meat, Steele," she said.

The two wrestled in the bed for a time. Soon Dean pinned her and watched as the girl struggled helplessly. Finally she stopped her writhing. "Better not give up yet," he advised. "As soon as you stop fighting, I'm gonna ream your tailpipe!" She began to relax. "Come on, Hot Shot," he said. "I want you to fight 'till you're completely exhausted. Then I can ream your ass with no effort at all."

The woman took on a seductive look and spread her legs slightly. "I need to save some strength for being taken," she said.

"It sounds like you're resigned to your fate," he responded.

"Can't win 'em all," she grinned. "I guess I'm done for." She parted her knees in a seductive motion. Dean released his grip on her. "There's K-Y jelly in the nightstand," she said, rolling over on her stomach. "If you don't use it, I'm gonna be in a lotta pain."

"You're really giving in to this, aren't you?"

"Well, if I'm ever gonna know what it feels like to be dominated by a man, I'd better not miss this chance. I may never meet another guy who can beat me. And who knows? It might be fun."

"What's this? The fiercely independent jungle girl harbors a submissive urge? A masochistic streak? I'm stunned!"

"You beat me, Dean. You're too big and you're too damn strong. I can't fight you off, and I pissed off your women. So you get to ream my ass." She spread her legs slightly as she lay on her stomach.

"But, Julie," he said in mock horror, "It's the worst kind of male domination. It's humiliating and degrading!"

"So, why don't you just shut up, and degrade me?"

"You want it, don't you? You really want it!"

"Well, I'm not looking forward to having that oversize horse dick comin' in my back door," she replied, "But I think a little male domination, tastefully done, might be an interesting experience. Besides, you beat me fair and square. You can take me, so you're entitled to it. I have no choice but to submit."

"What if we just do it doggie style? Would that satisfy your masochistic urge for submission? I could choke you and pull your hair while I'm doing you. Would that work for you?"

"My asshole would be eternally grateful," she said. "But it's your party. Do what you want with me. You can have my ass if you want it." They had sex again.

Shannon

"Hello," Shannon's voice said.

"Hey Tiger," Dean said. "I got your voice-mail. What's up?"

"Nothing urgent," she said coolly. "It can wait."

"You sure? It sounded important."

"No, it can wait."

"OK."

"Why didn't you answer?"

"Oh, Julie made a call on my phone and then accidentally turned it off when she finished."

Shannon was quiet for a time. "How did you enjoy your evening?" she asked coyly.

"I thought it was great. Looks like the Houston Ballet Company really got it together finally."

"I mean after the ballet."

"Well, the yogurt was pretty good."

"I mean after that."

"Oh, we had fun," he said. "Julie's a kick." Shannon was silent. "That it, then?"

"Yeah," Shannon said, "That's it. 'Bye." The small phone went dead.

The next day, Shannon caught Dean in the parking lot before they went in for their practice session.

"Did you fuck her?" she snapped, with anger in her voice.

"Shannon," he said, looking at her softly, "Let me just be completely open and honest and truthful with you about that." He paused to inhale. "It's none of your damn business, you nosey little bitch!" he said through a clenched jaw.

"She told me you two were gonna spend the whole night having sex. She practically laid it out for me, blow-by-blow."

"Well, either we did or we didn't, and you will never know which."

Shannon pouted. "What do you see in her, Dean? I mean ... she's a smart-ass. She's cynical. And she's not even very pretty."

"But she can squat two thirty-five," he replied, "And that ain't hay!"

"Muscles? Is that what it is? A girl with muscles?"

"She looked good last night, Shannon. And she's a muscle girl. The ground shakes when she walks."

"Oh right! She's a muscle girl. You get all soft and squishy over muscle girls!"

"Everywhere except one spot," he said.

"Well, fuck you, Dean!" she snapped. "Just fuck ... you!"

"If you have something to say, Shannon, spit it out. Otherwise, shut the Hell up! I'm just about an inch away from slapping you senseless!"

Shannon's eyes flashed. "I don't like her, Dean. She's all wrong for you. She'll just mess everything up, I just know it."

"Maybe you could let me decide how to spend what precious few social hours I have every week."

"She's a bitch, Dean, a bitch, a bitch, a bitch!"

"Well, thank you for rendering your thoughtful opinion on the subject, Miss Foster. Now take it and stuff up your ass!"

Shannon pouted. "This is really hard for me, Dean. I have this really bad feeling."

"Deal with it, Foster. You're a competitive athlete. Put your emotions under control. If you can't do that, we're dead meat before we start."

"Is that it, then? You're just going to go on seeing this bitch? Knowing she's trying to ruin our partnership?"

"That's not a fact, Shannon. That's some wild idea you pulled out of the stratosphere." The girl glared at him, shook her head, and then walked into the girls' locker room.

Millie

Dean saw Millie later that morning. "You called last night?" he asked.

"Oh, I just wanted to check on some of the details for the costumes" Millie said. "Last night I got worried that we had left something out. But now I think it's probably all right. Sorry to bother you."

"No problem."

"So, did you enjoy your evening?"

"Yeah, it was fun. That was nice of y'all to take us to the ballet."

"Neither your cell phone nor you apartment phone answered," she said. "I suppose you stayed over at Julie's house." Dean was silent. "She told me, you know, that you two were planning quite an orgy. She was very graphic about it." She paused. "Really, Dean, the girl lacks class in a major way." Dean left silence in the room. Soon Millie couldn't help but fill it. "So, how was she? Is she as talented in bed as she obviously is in the gym? Do all those muscles make it better?"

Dean looked at her intently. "She is remarkably skilled at what she does," he said. "Dedicated to the sport."

"So I imagine you two spent the evening putting your finely honed bodies through their paces, wrapped up in lust like a couple of snakes!"

"Would a detailed verbal description suffice, Millie, or should I just run the video for you?"

"Really, Dean, I have no interest in what you two did last night. If you feel the need to bounce on some trollop, instead of staying in training, that's your business. I'm just responding to a distinct lack of class here. I thought you were made of better stuff." Dean shook his head in frustration and disgust. "So," Millie said, at last, "Is this what we have to look forward to from now on? Mr. Steele comes dragging in every morning, exhausted from an all-night bedroom workout with his new gym partner?"

"I hope so," Dean said. "I certainly hope so."

"Is that all you want out of life, Dean? To screw your brains out every night, with some muscle-bound retard?"

"Retard?"

"Let's face it, Dean, She's hardly your intellectual equal. In fact, I think she's a couple of hot dogs short of a picnic."

"You gauged her IQ from a twelve-word conversation? I'm amazed!"

"I had more than twelve words with that little gutter rat." Millie's eyes flashed. "She was very graphic regarding your plans for the evening. It wasn't difficult to peg her type."

"And what is her type?"

"Not smart, but clever. Conniving, even. Proud of her body. Willing to use it to get what she wants. Totally devoid of conscience." She paused. "It fits the pattern."

Dean refused to allow his face to acknowledge. "Who are you describing?" he asked, "That sounds strikingly autobiographical."

"Her brain is between her legs," she continued, ignoring the insult. "I'm sure she showed you a good time last night. That's her specialty."

"There's a mistake that many people make chronically," Dean said. "They assume that an excess of muscle belies a deficiency of intelligence. It turns out not to be a general truth."

"Oh, come now, Dear Boy. How far did she get in school? It's obvious she's working with limited intellectual assets here." Dean was silent. "But that's not what you two do together anyway, is it? You're not this weak and washed out because you spent the wee hours discussing global economics. You fucked like a couple of snakes!" Her eyes flashed anger. "How many times, Dean? How many times did you let that little slut get you off? Three? Four?"

"I'm sorry, Millie," he said. "I'd have kept a score sheet if I'd realized it was so important!"

She glared at him. "So you admit it. You let her drain you dry. You're spent. You're exhausted. You've got nothing left."

"I think I'll recover in due course," he said, "The male body exhibits amazing resiliency in that regard."

"Disgusting," Millie mumbled, almost inaudibly.

"What is it with you, Millie? Why does it frost your ass so bad that I might have slept over somewhere last night?"

"Because it was cheap and tacky," she snapped. "Shacking up with a common tramp and wallowing in it like a pig in a mudhole! Champions have class, and if you're going to be a champion, you need to show a lot more class than that." She fumed. "I don't care what you did to her," she continued. "It's what you let her do to you that was so disgusting. You let her defile you!"

"Were you there? I don't remember seeing you. How in the Hell do you know what we did last night?"

"I know. I just know. And it hurts me to see you allow yourself to be wasted and degraded that way."

"Well, Madam, I used to have a social life, before I got abducted by the Foster family. I used to even get the occasional piece of ass. I sort of miss that. It's kinda nice to squeeze something soft every once in a while." Millie was silent. "But now, you're the premiere female figure in my life. Some perverse amalgam of my mother, my lover, my employer, my football coach, my drill sergeant, my priest, and my third grade teacher. I can't have sex with you, but you don't want me to fuck anybody else. So excuse me if I get a little bit tense sometimes!"

"But you can have me, Dear Boy," Millie blurted. "That's the answer to your dilemma, don't you see? That's where you should be channeling your excess energies. Not wasting it on some stringy-haired gym rat!" She put her hand on his cheek. "I can fill your needs, Dean. I can keep your hormones under control. You needn't go around frustrated." She smiled softly. "I can keep the savage beast as tame as a kitten."

"You present an interesting proposition," he said. "But there's one slight problem with the plan. It involves adultery for yourself and fornication for me. It's you betraying your husband, and me fucking my partner's mother, and my sponsor's wife, for Pete's sake! All in all, it's a sure-fire formula for disaster."

"Those factors can be controlled, Dean. No one would ever know." They stared at each other.

"I'm sorry, Madam, but I must decline to pursue that particular course of action. It's just a bit too bizarre for me."

"Dean," she said, softly, "I'm sorry if I appeared a bit too forward then. I apologize. But I think there is some … very strong feeling between us, and we would be foolish to deny it."

"I believe 'lust' is what it's called," Dean said. He didn't bother to deny his attraction to the woman.

"No, Young Man. Lust is what you wallowed in last night. It doesn't compare to what I feel for you … or what you feel for me."

Dean regarded the woman intently. "Are you now going to tell me what I feel for you?"

"No," she said, "You'll figure it out for yourself, in time. I'll just wait 'til you come to your senses."

"Fair enough," he said, "But maybe just a hint … if only to put me on the right track." He was interested to learn her viewpoint on this matter.

"You and I, Dean." She paused. "We're not like other people. We have abilities and insights that ordinary people don't have." She looked into his eyes. "We're special, Dean Steele. The ordinary rules don't apply to us."

"I see," he said. "Well, I'm a little short of cash right now. How about we go out and rob a bank, and then you can explain to the cops how the ordinary rules don't apply to us."

"Dean," she said, ignoring his sarcasm, "We're special … and we deserve each other." She gave him a knowing smile.

"Is it just you and me?" he asked, "Or are there more of these superhuman beings in our midst?"

"There are a few," she said. "A very few."

"Anybody I know?"

"One." She inhaled and let out a sigh. "My darling daughter. I recognized it when she was three days old. Someday she'll try to take away everything I have. She's the only one who could." Dean's face registered puzzlement. He wanted to ask another question but didn't know where to start. "Someday you'll understand all this, Dean," she said. "Until then … I'll just bide my time." She blew him a kiss and left.

Shannon's Phone

"Oh, my God, Shannon!" Jenny said. "They took away your phone! What will you do without a phone?"

"What?"

"I just heard that the phone company cancelled your phone! I was about to call you, but …"

"Jenny, what are you talking about? Nobody cancelled my phone!"

"Kelsey said she tried to call you at home, and she got a phone company message that said you had been disconnected!"

Shannon pulled out her cell phone and pressed a button. A dial tone told her it still worked. She dialed her home number. After three rings Dean's voice came on. "You have reached the number of Shannon Elaine Foster in Houston, Texas. Southwestern Bell has determined that Shannon Foster is not old enough, or mature enough, to qualify for residential telephone service, and we have disconnected this line. If you need to reach Shannon Foster, you can call her mommy at 713-555-6641. We apologize for the inconvenience." There was a beep. "Screw you, Dean Steele," Shannon said, inadvertently leaving herself a message.

"That was a shitty thing to do, Dean!" Shannon said when they met for practice at the Texas Ice Stadium.

"What?"

"Putting that message on my answering machine. You're an awful shithook!"

"How do you know it was me? Maybe it was the phone company."

"Because you're an asshole, you jerk. I recognized your voice. It was the most hideously embarrassing thing that ever happened to me in my whole entire life!"

"Kinda like what you did to my phone, right?"

"As if! I put a nice message on yours. You tried to ruin my life!"

"Let's look at your 'nice message,' Precious. Suppose I met some really cheap and tacky woman in a bar and gave her my phone number. She would call up, ready to jump in the sack with me, and hear your cute little voice telling her you are my 'partner.' Notice you didn't say 'skating partner,' just 'partner.' She would think I'm living with someone, and she'd drop me like a hot rock!"

"It would serve you right! You embarrassed me to tears, and you don't need to have trashy women coming over there anyway!"

"But it's my decision, don't you get it? I decide whether trashy women come over or not. Not you!"

Shannon pouted. "You were mad about my message?"

"You must be psychic!"

"I don't see why. I thought you'd think it was cute."

"It was presumptuous. It leaves the impression that I've shacked up with somebody."

"Poor Dean! He's worried about his reputation," she said sullenly.

"Listen, Bitch, my reputation is what it is, and I don't need any help from you making it worse. You're just my skating partner, for Pete's sake! Why is my life suddenly dominated by an overdose of Fosters?"

Shannon rolled out a pitiful face. "OK, Dean, if you don't like me, I'll just stay out of your life. We'll skate together, and then we'll just go our separate ways. You'll never hear a word from me except on the ice."

"Is that a promise?"

"Yes!"

"Will you sign a contract?"

"In blood! I never want to see you again, except to skate! You're old and mean and cruel, and I hate you!"

"Good! I think we have the basis of a deal here. Why don't we start right now? Get in your car and haul ass!"

"With pleasure!" She stomped into the girls' locker room.

When Shannon got home she pressed the "play announce" button on her phone to hear Dean's outgoing message again. Instead she heard a telephone company tone and a woman's rather cheery voice saying, "We're sorry. The number you have dialed is not in service. Please check the number and dial again. Or ask your operator for assistance. Houston, 713, 555." Dumbfounded, Shannon called her home number on her cell phone. She got the same response.

"Dean, you shit!" Shannon said when Dean answered his cell phone. "What did you do to my phone?"

"Oh, hello, Princess, and a very good day to you too."

"You made it make that weird message. I know you did!"

"I'm sure I don't know what you're talking about."

"Damn you, Dean! You make me so mad!"

"Sorry, Precious."

"I'm gonna change it back, and don't you ever mess with my phone again, you slimy shit!"

"Goodbye, Princess."

Shannon pressed the code to record the outgoing announcement, but the machine rejected her password. She tried it three times before she called Dean back.

"OK, Mr. Smarty Pants. What did you do to my phone?"

"I thought we went over that."

"No, now it won't let me change the message."

"Use your password."

"It won't take it."

"Then maybe you're using the wrong password."

"You changed it, you shit! It's always been 000."

"Then change it back."

"I can't change it if I don't know the new one! Damn you, Dean!"

"Then you kinda gotta problem, don't you?"

"Dean, don't do this! All my friends will think my phone's been disconnected when they hear that message. I'll never get any calls!"

"Now there's a modern American tragedy!"

"Dean, please! Tell me what the new password is. You can't possibly be this mean!"

"It's a three digit number, Shannon. There are only a thousand of 'em. Try 'em all."

"I am not gonna try 'em all, you asshole! Tell me what it is!"

"Tell you what I'll do. I'll make a telephone service call tomorrow afternoon and see if I can fix it."

"I'll miss a hundred important calls by then!"

"Ain't life just a bitch sometimes?"

"Screw you, Dean Steele!"

"And 'good day' to you too, Princess."

Dean arrived at the Foster home about 2:30. He accompanied Shannon upstairs to her bedroom. "Tell you what I'll do," he said. "I have prepared the script for a new announcement. If you'll put that message on your phone, and let it stay for 48 hours, then I'll give you the new password."

Shannon took the piece of paper he was holding and read it. "I'm not sayin' this!" she snorted.

"OK, then. The message stays as it is." Shannon fumed for a while, then relented. Dean pressed the passcode into the phone without letting Shannon see it. "Start reading at the beep," he said.

"This is Shannon Foster," she began. "I'm Dean Steele's skating partner. He's a total jerk, but I'm a perfect angel. Leave a message."

"Close," Dean said, "But no cigar. Do it right." He pressed the buttons again.

"This is Shannon Foster. I'm Dean Steele's skating partner. He's a really cool guy, but I'm an insufferable brat. Leave a message."

"You got the words right. Now do it with feeling. Convince me!"

Shannon read the message again, and Dean was satisfied. "Now leave it connected for 48 hours. I'll be making random checkup calls. At the end of the period I'll give you the new password."

Two days later Shannon called Dean. "OK," she said, "It's been 48 hours. You have to tell me my password."

"What's your birthday?"

"March 27th."

"There you go."

"327? Is that it?"

"Guaranteed."

She tried the code, and it worked. Two days later she replaced the message, after making sure all of her girlfriends had a chance to hear it.

---

1.   Aunt Dianna – a reference to dianabol, an anabolic steroid sometimes used by bodybuilders to enhance muscle growth.

2.   Ripped – having good muscle definition.

Chapter 3

Dogtag Two

"So, tell me, Shannon," the girl said as they packed up their skate bags, "Have you slept with your new pairs partner yet?"

"What?" Shannon was incredulous.

"Oh, come on, Shannon," another girl said as they walked out of the girls' dressing room. "You don't have to be coy with us. Has he gotten you in the sack yet?"

"Are you crazy? We're skating partners, you idiot, not lovers!"

"Shannon, everybody knows Dean Steele won't skate with a girl unless she sleeps with him. It's part of the price you pay to have him as a partner ... but I guess you know that already." She grinned knowingly.

"What, was it in the paper? I must have missed it!" Shannon was angry.

"Just look at it, Shannon, Dean Steele can have any girl skater he wants, and he's a man, you know, an older man. He's not very well gonna pick a girl who won't put out, now is he?" Shannon was so angry she couldn't formulate a response. "OK, Shannon. If you don't want to talk about it, we understand. If he's already got you this quick, well, it makes you look like a pushover. If he hasn't pinned you to the mattress yet ... then it looks like maybe you're not very attractive or something. I'll ask you again later." She smiled sweetly and left.

"Fuck you, Muffy!" Shannon yelled after her. The girl waved back without turning around.

Teasing

"You know what the girls are teasing me about, Dean?" Shannon asked when they met in the parking lot.

"I couldn't possibly imagine."

"They're asking me if I've slept with you yet. They say you won't skate with a girl unless she ... you know..."

"So?"

"So, what?"

"So, take off your clothes. I haven't got all day."

25

"Dean! What are you saying?"

"You're way overdue for the payoff here, so get naked and spread them legs!"

"I can't believe this! You don't actually think I'm gonna just ..."

"On your back, Bitch. Time's a-wastin'! I'm a busy man."

"Dean!" She was wide-eyed.

"What?"

A quizzical frown took its place on her face. "Are you teasing me?"

"What do you think?"

"Well ..., maybe you are."

"Well, there you go!"

"Bastard! That was mean! For a minute there I thought I had a pervert for a partner."

"You do have a pervert for a partner!"

"I mean a child molester."

"I've molested children."

"No, you haven't!"

"Sure I have! Why, just this morning I wrestled a piece of bubble gum away from a six-year-old. Boy, was he pissed!"

"OK, Mr. Smarty Pants. Be a shithook if it fills a need. Just don't expect any ... sexual favors from your skating partner!"

"No offense, Princess, but I wouldn't touch your tender tush with a six-foot Swede."

The girl's face fell. "Really?" she asked. "I'm not sexy?"

"No, you're very sexy." He paused for effect. "I just don't like you!" He broke out laughing.

"OK, Smartass. This is the part where I kill you!" She attacked him with her fists. Still laughing, he grabbed her in a bear hug to protect himself. He held her until she stopped struggling.

"So, what do you tell them?" he asked, releasing her from his grip. "I mean, when they ask you if we're sleeping together."

"Well, I tell them ... I kinda ... I don't say." She offered a sheepish smile, embarrassed to admit that she didn't simply deny it.

"Fine. They won't believe what you say, anyway. If you say 'no,' they'll think you're hiding it. If you say 'yes,' they'll think you're bragging. No answer is probably the best way to handle it."

Shannon was relieved that Dean was not upset about how she handled it. "What do you say ... when they ask you, I mean?"

"Nobody asks me," he replied.

"Why not?"

"Because nobody in his right mind would think I have the slightest interest in you … sexually, I mean."

"Liar! You just admitted you think I'm sexy. What's the real reason?"

"They probably think I'd smash their face."

"Would you?"

"No. But I wouldn't answer, either. It's just not a fair question. And in my case the answer is easy anyway. It has to be 'no,' since 'yes,' is a felony in the Lone Star state."

"But doesn't it bother you that they pester me about that?"

"It's just something you live with, Kid. People will do that. Don't take it personal."

"But I don't know which way I'd rather have them thinking."

"It'd be better if they knew we weren't. But curiosity and suspicion is about the best we can hope for."

"They say you sleep with every girl you skate with." She eyed him inquisitively.

"Do tell!" He faked surprise.

"Do you?" Though embarrassed by her question, Shannon still waited for an answer.

"Well, that question doesn't have an answer since I've never skated pairs or dance before. So far I'm 'oh for one,'" he said, "And you're the 'one.'"

"Maybe you've never competed with a partner, but you've skated with girls before. I hear you won't even do that unless she …"

"Remember that first time I skated with you at TIS? Did I ask you to blow me first?"

"No, but maybe I'm the first … because I'm underage and all."

"That could be it."

"So, am I the only girl skater you didn't …?"

"I'd need some time to go over the list," he replied, "But I might find a couple more. After all, I've skated with hundreds of girls. There may have been one or two who …" He looked at her and grinned.

Shannon put on her disgusted look. "You're shittin' me again. Why can't I ever get a straight answer out of you?"

"Because you ask questions you shouldn't be asking, Twerp!"

Shannon wanted to press the issue, but couldn't decide how.

The Performance

Dean had agreed to do his dogtag dance at the next Club Ice. All the women who missed it at Allison's birthday party a few weeks earlier wanted to see it, and the ones who were there wanted to see it again. A few of the Ice

Dads were curious what all the fuss was about. Attendance at Club Ice that night was at an all-time high.

The announcer called all the twelve to sixteen year old girls out on the ice. They collected at the end of the arena to watch Dean's performance. About half a dozen of them wore "455 Rocket" T-shirts and dogtags that Walt had supplied for the occasion. They were joined on the ice by women up to at least thirty-five, some with shoes on. Shannon and Millie were there, but they remained in their seats.

The hard driving music played for about half a minute before the featured skater made his appearance. Most of the assembled females had started to dance to the music by the time Dean skated out looking like a combat soldier in his olive drab undershirt, tight jeans and dogtags. His hair was slicked back and his muscles bulged under the thin outfit.

The girls immediately started screaming and jumping up and down when they saw him. He skated his masculine, sexy routine with disco moves combined with jumps and spins. He would flick a hard sexy stare from girl to girl with the beat of the music. He would occasionally single out one girl and gyrate directly in front of, or behind her, much to the delight of the crowd.

At the end of the number, the adoring fans mobbed Dean. Shannon ran up the stairs looking for her mother, and found her alone in the upstairs lounge. Millie was leaning forward, watching Dean through the glass window as he chatted with his female fans.

"Mom?" Shannon said. Millie looked up at her in surprise. "What are you doing, Mom?"

"Nothing," Millie said, exhaling deeply and collecting herself. "I was just ... watching the show."

"Up here? By yourself?"

"Well, it was quiet. I wanted to get out of the hubub." The girl turned and left.

Millie

"Well," Millie said, "Your dogtag dance was even better than its billing. That was more hip-swiveling than I've seen since Elvis in 1957."

"Thanks, I guess," he replied.

"And that little girl you played with. I thought you were gonna spray her with musk. Her mama will need to get her a pregnancy test."

"OK, Millie. If you ease off now, we can still be friends."

"Don't take offense, Dean! I liked it. It was probably the most intense skating routine I've ever seen. I'm in awe of you. Nobody can put that kind of emotional power into a figure skating program."

"I don't know what to make of your reaction, Millie."

"OK, let me spell it out for you. I'm flabbergasted - overwhelmed by the intensity of your skating. It was masterful. You had forty or fifty women in the palm of your hand, all at once. Every one of them was your lover at that moment. They belonged to you. It's incredible, Dean. It's an amazing power you have."

"OK," he said. "And what did it do for you, personally?"

"If you must know," she paused coyly, "It gave me this wild urge to get down on my knees and start ripping away at your belt buckle, right there in front of God and the Figure Stating Club."

"My God, Millie!"

"Are you shocked?" she asked.

"Wasn't that the point?" he asked. "To shock me?"

She looked pensive. "Shannon walked in on me at a very inopportune time today," she sighed, changing the subject.

"What happened?"

"I went up to the VIP lounge to be alone while I watched you skate," she said. "By the time your little dance was over, I was pretty well worked up. Anyway, after you finished, I was … entertaining myself, just to relieve the pressure a bit. Force of habit, I suppose, after spending so many private afternoons alone with your videos, and now finally seeing you live. Anyway, Shannon walked in. Her timing was almost perfect. A minute earlier and she would have witnessed her dear old mom in the throes of passion."

"Is your obsession still a secret?"

"Fortunately, she doesn't know the awful truth. But it was a close call. You really make my blood boil, you naughty boy!"

"Sorry," Dean grinned.

"No, you're not! She grinned back at him.

Shannon

"Your routine was really good," Shannon said. "Everybody liked it. All the girls are going around, singing '455 rocket,' and giggling at each other. I hear that Kathy Mattea CD is sold out all over Houston now."

"Yeah, they run up behind me and yell "Rocket!' or 'Biggest block alive!' and giggle a lot."

"They're bitches, Dean."

"It won't be long. Tiger, 'till we're doing our routines together. That's gonna be the really big deal."

"I know. But still it's fun to have you do that cool stuff. And everybody knows I'm your partner. It makes me real proud."

"So, you're not jealous, like last time?"

"Yes! You think I like you dangling your dork in front of all my friends?" she grinned.

"Nothing dangled, Shannon. Watch your mouth!"

"No, your jeans were too tight to let anything dangle."

"Watch it Kid!"

Club Censorship

"Did you hear what happened at the skating club meeting last night?" Millie asked.

"No," Dean replied. "Was it on ESPN?"

"That little ninny," Millie continued, ignoring his joke, "Sue Ann McAlister, proposed that we establish guidelines for what is appropriate for Club skating events. She said we don't want any 'bad influences' on our young skaters. She was obviously referring to your dogtag number."

"Oops! What was the reaction?"

"Well, I was just about to reach across the table and claw her eyes out when Sandy said she was thinking about hocking her jewelry so she could pay Dean Steele to skate at her daughter's birthday party. Then Mary Ann said she'd trade her Mercedes for one of your ice dances. It kind of went downhill from there, with each one trying to top the last one. It got a bit raunchy. I ended up keeping totally quiet. Needless to say, Sue Ann's motion died for lack of a second."

"Lucky me," Dean said. "I'd hate to get censored by the Figure Skating Club."

"Dean, you're gonna be a Hell of a lot bigger than this pompous little club! They're just lucky to have you."

He smiled.

Chapter 4

Queen's Visit

The first time Millie came over to Dean's apartment to work on choreography and costume design, she was very well-behaved. Conservatively dressed, she was polite, friendly, and strictly business. She was a charming guest, and Dean was amused and entertained by her company. He enjoyed working with her, and they got a lot accomplished.

A Second Visit

They made a second appointment a few days later, and Millie showed up at the door on time. This time she was not so conservatively dressed. She wore a thin clingy minidress that did very little to conceal her voluptuous form. Her breasts protruded menacingly underneath the soft, pale blue cloth. Her formidable derriere stretched the thin cloth tight when she moved, revealing her feminine shape. Her hair was immaculately done, as was her makeup. She moved in a cloud of soft scent.

"My goodness," Dean exclaimed as he saw her. "Is this my regular co-worker?"

"The very same," she replied, grinning at the look on his face. "I just didn't have time to dress like a dowdy ice mom before I came over."

"You are anything but dowdy, Your Majesty," he said, regaining his composure. "You are truly a vision."

"I'll take that as a compliment, Young Man," she said, waltzing confidently into his home.

They worked on ideas for skating programs and costumes, and they listened to samples of music that might work in competition. Dean found himself frequently distracted by the woman's bulging breasts, her luscious hips and thighs, and the scent of her fluffy blonde hair.

During the meeting her conversation was more intimate than it had been the last time. She occasionally gazed into his eyes, and she often smiled softly at him, as if she had something unspoken to say. A few times he found himself confronted with bulging boobies or a well-rounded derriere in his face.

Dean found himself unable to ignore her sexy presence. Self-conscious at first, he tried to avoid staring at her, or even letting his thoughts dwell on how attractive she was. After a while, though, he became less uncomfortable with the situation, and allowed himself to indulge in the occasional opportunity to admire her beauty.

Dean reasoned that she couldn't possibly have simply found herself dressed like that, with inadequate time to change into something less conspicuous. Surely she had done just the opposite. She must have changed into that outfit immediately before coming to him. If so, it belied a deliberately flirtatious intent. The Ice Queen was teasing him with her considerable feminine charms.

Dean was both amused and puzzled by that realization. He wondered what purpose it served in the Ice Queen's plan to so openly display her femininity before him in this way. He did, however, appreciate the opportunity to enjoy having so well-endowed a female body in his presence. Her beauty, though distracting, provided a thoroughly enjoyable visual experience that made the work more pleasant.

It was even fun, he realized, to be the target of the Ice Queen's teasing. Whatever her game was, he was the quarry, and that make for an intriguing puzzle. There are worse fates than being manipulated by the Ice Queen.

After they had reached a stopping point, Millie turned to him softly and put on a coquettish face. "You know, Dean" she began, "I work hard for you and Shannon."

"You are the wind beneath our wings," he replied.

"And I don't ask for much in return," she continued. She looked up at him with a pouty, little-girl face. "I just need a little encouragement every once in a while."

"And what is it that encourages you most, Madam?" he inquired.

"Sometimes I just need a little hug to keep me going," she said, her voice soft and vulnerable. She looked at him with pleading eyes. "Can you spare a hug for the hard-working Ice Queen?"

"Such a reward is richly deserved," he said as a grin broke out on his face. To see this powerful and strong-minded woman play the pitiful waif was humorous indeed. "Let's give the poor Ice Queen the recognition she so desperately requires."

The two came together in an embrace. Millie pressed herself against him and began to melt visibly. Dean could feel her warm body through the thin dress. He could smell the intoxicating scent of her hair. He could feel her pneumatic breasts pressing against his chest. He held her for a moment and then yielded to the urge to slip his hand down across her hip.

Coupled with an afternoon of watching her voluptuous body wiggle and writhe beneath that thin blue dress, this additional stimulation began to take its toll on the young man. He became aware of an expansion inside his pants. He was not surprised. In fact, he had been lucky it had waited this long to happen, given the circumstances. He knew he would soon embarrass himself if he did not break off the embrace.

But holding the soft woman was so pleasant, that he savored the moment for a while. Long enough, in fact, that Millie pulled back and said, "My goodness, Dean. I believe something has come up between us." She grinned mischievously as she savored his embarrassment.

Dean realized that the helpless waif he had taken into an embrace was gone, replaced by the haughty Ice Queen. She could feel the bulge that had developed in front of him, and she was holding him accountable for it. He was showing manifestations of desire for her, and she was enjoying it immensely.

"Is that a skate guard in your pocket, or are you just glad to see me?" she joked, grinning. "Does hugging the Ice Queen give you naughty thoughts, Dean?"

Dean had no comeback to her teasing. She had him cornered, and she was making the most of it. He was embarrassed by his involuntary response to her presence, and by the fact that he had allowed her to play this game with him and win. She was taking great satisfaction in his discomfort.

"I noticed you ogling the Ice Queen all afternoon," she chided him. "Shame on you, naughty boy!"

He reasoned that being sexy was important to this woman, and that teasing a younger man, to the point of undeniable arousal, must be very satisfying to her. There had been a good-naturedly competitive aspect to their relationship from the very beginning, and she had now won a round in that competition. It was also clear why she had showed up dressed as she was. Dean had no choice but to respect her for the little victory she had won at his expense.

While Dean was pondering the situation, Millie's hand touched his inner thigh and slipped gently upward until it closed around the bulge in his trousers. Dean's eyes widened at the audacity of her move, but he didn't flinch.

"My goodness, Dean" she cooed. "You *are* a big boy!"

"Uh, I believe that's a foul, Millie," he said. "Illegal use of the hands."

"Oh, you don't mind me feeling what you've got, do you, Dean? After all, you did it for me, didn't you?" Her grin was positively mischievous. The woman was savoring her victory. He would have seemed a poor sport not to let her have the equivalent of the medal awards ceremony, he reasoned. He decided not to pull himself free immediately, but rather to scold her verbally instead.

"You're misbehaving, Madam" he said.

"Perhaps," she admitted, "But you don't mind, do you, Dean? Just for a moment?"

"You really need to get away from there, Millie," he advised her.

"My goodness, Dean," she exclaimed, "How big are you going to get? Does the Ice Queen excite you that much?"

Under her soft caress, his organ was continuing to grow, in spite of his embarrassment, or perhaps in response to it. Having this powerful woman gloat over his reaction to her sexuality was strangely erotic for him. Though still not full size, the rebellious appendage had become quite a handful. His involuntary display of increasing arousal significantly deepened his embarrassment, her victory, and the overall intensity of the situation.

"My God, Dean!" she exclaimed softly as she gently squeezed the soft beefy organ, "This is something huge!" There was little Dean could do to salvage the situation. She had teased him into a partial erection, and it was now moving toward full size. He could either break the spell by forcibly pulling her hand away from his recalcitrant organ, or he could let her have the full measure of her victory. As he pondered the situation, the shaft reached full size and began to firm up.

"You're being very naughty," he told her, trying to salvage something from his defeat. "You really ought to keep your mind on skating and your hands to yourself."

Millie simply looked at him and grinned as she felt the organ gradually becoming more firm and rigid with every beat of his heart. Her face showed her amazement as she discovered the true size of the instrument she held. Perhaps this was one thing that dissuaded Dean from freeing himself from her grip. His organ, in the erect state, was well above average in size, and he was curious to see her face when she made that discovery. He wondered how she would respond when she saw the degree of masculinity of which he was capable.

"You are a monster!" she exclaimed. "Shame on you for being such an unrepentant stud!"

Dean stood still as her fingers examined his organ. Now fully erect, it was rigid and firm as her fingertips explored it thoroughly through the soft fabric of his pants.

"I'm ashamed of you, Millie" he said. "What would your girlfriends think of your tacky behavior?"

"Green with envy, Dean. They've never seen anything like this either! I never dreamed you would be so …"

Millie's gushing over his size tended to dissuade Dean from ejecting her from his private area. After all, the damage had been done. Propriety had been breached. Her victory had been won. Somehow he felt compelled to allow her to take a victory lap. He stood in silence as she amused herself at his expense. Surprisingly, he enjoyed her gloating as well as her amazement.

"Don't you think you've had enough fun for one day?" he asked at last. "You've been behaving rather badly."

"Oh, you're just a party pooper," she said, taking her hand away from his pants. She backed away slightly to regard the bulge she had brought to his trousers. "You need to buy a larger size pants, Dean, if you're going to think naughty thoughts about the Ice Queen." She gave him a triumphant grin.

"It had nothing to do with you, Madam," he said, grinning dryly. "It was just a random physiological event."

"Bullshit!' You were ogling the Ice Queen and thinking naughty thoughts about her, and it caught up with you. Your secret is out, Dean."

"And what secret is that?"

"That you lust after the Ice Queen, you naughty boy! That you think absolutely tacky and disgusting thoughts about her. And…," she added with raised eyebrows, "That you get a positively mammoth muscle contraction when you do!"

"And you're disgusted by all this?" he asked, grinning.

"I am in awe. It's a positively miraculous display of masculinity. You have my undying respect." Her admission that she was impressed by his manhood took some of the edge off his defeat. At least the Ice Queen was gracious in victory. "Will you be OK?" she asked. "Will it … go away?"

"Not until you leave," Dean chuckled. "No permanent damage though, but thanks for your concern. I'll be OK in a day or two." They laughed.

Millie gathered her things and prepared to leave. At the door she gave him a kiss on the cheek. "Sweet dreams," she said, grinning. She left his apartment, but not his thoughts.

Chapter 5

Shannon's Fit

Their morning practice began at 7:00 AM. After about half an hour of practicing lifts, Shannon became frustrated. Her exasperation grew to the point that she pulled away and skated over to the boards. After a brief delay, Dean skated over to her.

"What's the matter, Tiger?" he asked.

"It sucks, that's all. It just sucks!"

"I see," he responded. "Anything in particular, or just everything in general?"

"Both!" she replied. "Skating in general and you in particular."

"Makes sense," he mused. "What about skating in general sucks?"

"It's too damn hard, Dean," she said. "We'll never get these lifts down right. They write the rules too hard. People can't do all this stuff."

"Yeah," he said. "Somebody should have mentioned that to Gordeeva and Grinkov[1] before they won the gold." He paused. "And, what about me in particular?"

"The way you do," she said. "The way you treat me, always criticizing me. Whatever I do, it's never good enough." She fumed. "You never fall. You never make mistakes. But you're on my ass all the time. It's like I'm the only one that ever screws up."

"Yeah," he said, pondering her comment. "I've noticed that too."

"What is this, Dean? Is it skating, or is it ... the Marine Corps? Are you some kind of ... drill sergeant or something? Hup, two, three, four..., hup, two, three, four." She marched around in a circle, stomping the ice. Then she stood at attention and gave him a salute. "Private Foster, reporting for duty, sir!"

"At ease, Soldier. This is not the Marines. All those guys are trying to do is learn how to fight a war without gettin' killed. What we're doing here is a lot tougher. We're trying to get to the US National Championships. The marines couldn't do that. We have to fight harder."

Shannon dropped her jaw in a gesture of disgust. "Look at me, Dean! Do I look tough? I'm a girl. I'm sixteen. If you want tough, you better go to the ... Navy Seals, or something."

36

"Nobody said you have to be male, or old, to be tough! Toughness is a state of mind. It's determination. Tough people come in all sizes and shapes." He paused. "Besides … I happen to know you *are* tough. I've seen it." He raised his eyebrows as if telling a secret.

She glared at him for a moment. "You know what it's like, Dean, skating with you? You're Mr. Perfect. And you're old. It's like that girl we saw at the Sugar Land competition[2], skating with her dad in the freedance. She couldn't get a partner her own age, so she had to skate with her daddy. Everybody said, 'Oh, isn't that cute! She's skating with her daddy.' But it sucks."

The girl inhaled as her anger welled up. Dean decided to allow her pent-up venom to drain, vowing not to be poisoned by it.

"You know what they say about me? They say, 'She peaked out at Juniors, so her mom got this old guy to skate with her so she might have a chance in pairs, where there's less competition.' I'm a joke, skating with you, Dean Steele. I ought to be skating with someone my own age." She offered him an icy glare. "You think I actually like skating with you? I only do it to keep peace in the family."

"Yeah, I know," he said, "It's a real bitch, too. Now, if you don't have anything else scheduled for the remainder of the hour, maybe we can get back to work on our routine."

Shannon gave him a disgusted look, turned and walked into the girl's locker room. She stayed in there for several minutes, and then finally emerged. They spent the last quarter of their hour practicing spins. At eight o'clock they traded skating boots for street shoes. Dean finished first, and he was outside, with his car started, before Shannon noticed it.

"Hey, Dean," she yelled as she burst out of the ice stadium doors. "You almost forgot me!"

"You have school, remember?" he said.

"Yeah, but we always eat breakfast together after morning practice."

"We *sometimes* eat breakfast together after morning session," he corrected her. "This morning I'm having breakfast with some people my own age." He regarded her coldly through the open window on the driver's side. "Maybe you should do the same."

Shannon's face fell, then her anger flared. "Screw you, Dean Steele!" she said coldly. The rear wheels of the Mustang began to spin on the asphalt, as he drove away without further comment. Filled with anger and frustration, Shannon walked to her car, cursing her miserable life.

Breakfast

Dean met Kevin, his former boss, and two co-workers at a nearby restaurant for breakfast. They discussed the project he had turned over to Rick, one of the other programmers. Dean enjoyed the technical discussions and the camaraderie with the other computer programmers.

"How's the skating going?" Kevin asked.

"Oh, it's coming along," Dean said." We're just learning the basic moves now, so it's kinda dull."

"What about your partner?"

"What about her?"

"What's she like?"

"Oh, she's a perfect little angel, to be sure!" He rolled his eyes. "I've now decided *never* to have kids." They laughed.

"Will we be seeing you on TV?" Rick asked.

"Probably not," Dean replied. "They don't televise the small contests. About the best we can hope for is to have our names spelled right in the local papers."

When the meeting was over, Dean realized that he had been somewhat distracted by what had happened with Shannon that morning. He knew that what she had said did not reflect her true feelings, and he tried to pass it off as merely the product of a teenager's frustration. But she had said some very cruel and hurtful things. It was the fact that she had seen fit to attack him so viciously that he couldn't get out of his mind – not *what* she had said, but *that* she had said it.

Millie

Dean ran into Millie later that morning at TIS. "No offense, Madam," Dean said, "But your daughter's a bitch." He had little success concealing his exasperation.

"If you're just now figuring that out," Millie replied, "You're a slow learner." She eyed him, only partially able to suppress her grin.

"It's the sheer enormity of the problem that continues to dumbfound me," he replied.

"It's a relatively recent occurrence," Millie said, grinning slyly. "Only in the last fifteen years. She was almost a normal child until she turned one!"

"You could have warned me," he said.

"I *did* warn you, Young Man," Millie reminded him.

"But you didn't impress upon me the full measure of the situation."

"I couldn't! First off, words fail to capture the dimension of the problem. Second, you wouldn't believe me, and third, you'd have run for the hills if you did. I had enough trouble roping you into this as it was."

"So, you admit you conned me?"

"I admit nothing," Millie grinned. "But I do acknowledge that you got screwed."

"Her world only has seating for one," Dean sighed.

"We can press our noses against the Plexiglas, but we can't come in," Millie added.

"It's very trying," he said.

"She's the offspring of two very headstrong people," Millie replied.

"Genetics doesn't go nearly far enough to explain the observed phenomena," Dean responded.

"I'd help you out if I could," Millie said, "But you can see the results of sixteen years of my effort. We can only hope that you can bring new methodology to bear on the problem."

"I have zero child-rearing qualifications," he said, his face showing hopelessness at being given the task.

"Perhaps," Millie said, "But you're in a good position to influence her behavior. She respects you, and you seem to have the required lack of patience."

"If impatience is a prerequisite, I'm well qualified."

"Cheer up, Dean," Millie grinned. "She can be halfway civil at times."

"I keep telling myself that."

"And, on very rare occasions, she's actually nice."

"If you say so." He regarded her skeptically.

Millie grinned softly and placed her hand on his neck. "I don't mean to sound callous, Dear Boy," she said. "It's just that I've been dealing with that problem for a very long time." She paused. "Welcome to Disneyland!"

"If I could just slap the shit out of her, or break her jaw once a day or something, I'd feel a lot better about it. But I have to keep her in good health for skating."

"Use whatever you have to, Dean. Sometimes it takes a heavy blow to get her attention."

"Well, I'm still looking for the right stick to hit her with."

"You'll find it," she said. "Just keep looking."

Shannon

Shannon was lacing her skates for their afternoon practice when Dean walked up. "How was your breakfast?" she asked coolly.

"The bacon was overcooked," he said, "But the eggs were good."

She huffed. The practice session was conducted with a minimum of chatter. They practiced some of the less taxing moves required to pass the USFSA intermediate level pairs skating test. Dean was, if anything, slightly more critical and less patient than usual. There was none of the joking, teasing, and horseplay that normally punctuated their practice sessions.

"This sucks," Shannon mumbled as she stuffed her skates in her bag.

"What sucks?" Dean inquired.

"That was the most exquisitely boring hour of my entire life!"

"Sorry, Kid," he said with a bite of sarcasm in his voice, "But we gotta pass all the tests, one by one."

"It's not that," she said. "It's just …," He looked at her, waiting for the conclusion of her thought. "Forget it!" she said. She left the arena.

The Call

Late that night Dean's cell phone rang.

"You're mad, aren't you?" Shannon's voice asked when he answered. "You're mad about what I said."

"Not about what you said," he replied. "I know it wasn't true. But I am a bit disappointed that you saw fit to say it."

"I was tired and pissed off. You should just ignore it."

"No," he said. "I have to assume you knew what you were doing."

"Why? I was just pissed. Why can't you just forget it?"

"I have to assume that you had your emotions under control."

"Why? Maybe I just lost it for a minute. Shit happens!"

"You're a competitive athlete. I have to assume you can control your emotions. If you can't, we're sunk before we start. If you can't keep your mind focused in practice, you'll never make it under the pressure of a contest. So I have to assume you knew exactly what you were doing with that vicious little tirade you unleashed. And beating up on your partner like that …," He paused. "It just sucks, to use the technical terminology."

"OK, Dean, I was pulling your chain a little. But you should be able to take that. You're a tough guy."

"I shouldn't *have* to take that, you little bitch!" he exploded. "I gave up a rewarding career to skate out your little ice fantasy, and now it sorta looks like maybe I just kinda … screwed up!"

"Dean," she said, "I'm sorry."

"Sorry don't get it, Kid! Sorry is for putting the salad fork on the wrong side of the plate. Sorry is for being five minutes late for practice. Sorry don't cover a deliberate and vicious attack on your partner like that. This goes a lot deeper." He inhaled. "There's something very wrong here," he sighed.

"You're right, Dean," she said. "There is." She paused. "I've been meaning to talk to you about it." She paused again. "You have a bitch for a skating partner. Any other girl would be so thrilled to skate with you that she'd never say anything bad, no matter how frustrating it was. But you got the one girl in the world who can't keep her big fat mouth shut. You got the one girl who'd blow her big chance just because her partner doesn't like her as much as she wants him to. You have a crazy girl for a pairs partner."

"You think that's all it is?" he said, calming down.

"Sure, Dean. It's the luck of the draw. Win some, lose some. You just drew a bad hand, that's all."

"Reckon I oughta fold?"

"That's up to you, Slim. But a good poker player will make the most of a bad hand while he's waitin' for a good one."

"You know a lot about poker?"

"I know a lot of stuff that would surprise you. I've been alive almost seventeen years."

"Whoa!" he mused. "So, what's your advice, Oh wise and aged wizard?"

"Throw the bitch in the dumpster! Get a partner who can appreciate what she's got. You don't have to put up with cheap bullshit when there are ten girls for every boy on the ice. Get yourself a real partner!"

"You make it sound very tempting. What about Katerina Witt?"

"Nope, too old. Get somebody else."

"Liz North?"

"Oh, no, Dean! Bad combination. Your styles aren't compatible. Trust me on that."

"I see. Then what about … Nicole Bobek?"

"Not reliable enough, Dean. Sometimes she's hot, and sometimes she's not. You demand consistency."

"I'm running out of candidates."

"Well, maybe you're stuck with the bitch-kid then."

"Surely there's some alternative."

"Well … maybe she'll grow up someday. Ever thought about that?"

"It seems too much to hope for."

"Miracles happen, Dean. Just wait and see."

"Now this *really is* an ice fantasy."

"Welcome to Disneyland!"

"Uh … what was that you said? I mean about me not liking you very much?"

"I don't know."

"You said something about I didn't like you as much as I should, or something."

"I'm a psycho, Dean. My ramblings don't mean anything."

"It must have meant something. Don't you think I like you?"

"Sure."

"Then why did you say that?"

"I don't know. I just …,"

"Just what?"

"Sometimes I just wish you'd be a little more … cordial toward me. A little warmer, that's all."

"Hey, I criticize your tiniest flaws. What else do you want?"

"I know you do, Dean, and I'm very grateful for that. But sometimes I need a little … personal affection. You know, just act like you like me for myself, not just as your partner."

"I'm not that good an actor."

"Bite me, Dean!" she giggled.

"No, really. Don't I act friendly toward you?"

"Sometimes. You tease me a lot, and that's kinda cool. But sometimes I just wonder if you really like me, if I'm your friend, you know? Or if I'm just the girl you skate with, and you don't care anything about me as a person."

"Ooh, that *is* a tough one," he said.

"Bite me, Dean!" she said.

"No, look. There have been times when I had some really warm, affectionate thoughts about you.

"Name one!"

"Well, give me a minute."

"See there! You don't like me!"

"Sure I do. Just don't rush me to think up a reason."

"Bite me, Dean!" she said.

"Who wouldn't love a girl who's always inviting teethmarks?"

"Come on, Dean. You have ten seconds to remember a time when you liked me."

"Damn! Ten seconds isn't very long."

"It's all you get!"

"OK, OK, OK! Here's one. What about that time I came home and you were sittin' on my steps, like a puppy dog, waiting for me?[3] I thought that was cute."

But, did you like me?"

"Yeah, I think I kinda did. It was like, 'Hey, she's really kinda cool, here.' I thought you looked really cute in your overalls and dual matching dog-ear ponytails."

"You remember what I was wearing?"

"I can see you in my mind."

"Cool deal! What else did you think?"

"Well, I thought, 'She must have more going for her than I thought if she would wait here for two hours to talk to me about working together."

"OK, Dean, I'm coming down there. I'll be there in thirty minutes."

"No you won't! It's too late. You need your sleep."

"You're telling me how cool I am. I want to hear this in person!"

"By the time you get here, I'll be out of the mood."

"No, you won't. I want a hug!"

"Hug me tomorrow. Tonight I need my sleep."

"OK, Dean. Tell me three more things you like about me, and I won't come down there."

"OK, but you gotta give me some time."

"Take all the time you need. Just make it really good."

"OK, here's one. You have this really cute face. Sometimes you get this cute … innocent … puzzled look, like you're trying to figure something out. Your face really glows when you do that."

"Cool! What else?"

"Well, there's that giggle. Sometimes I think up a little joke just so I can hear that giggle."

"You do? Wow! What else?"

"Well, there's the way you walk. Sometimes I lag behind a little so I can watch your ass wiggle when you walk. It's really cute."

"OK, Dean, I'm coming down there. I gotta have a hug!"

"No, you're not! A deal's a deal. Hang up and sleep!"

"Party pooper!"

"Good night, Shannon."

"Really, Dean, you ought to do this more often."

"Good night, Shannon!"

"I'm not kiddin'. I'll bet I'd be as sweet as Dorothy Hamill[4] if you did this more often."

"Nobody's as sweet as Dorothy Hamill."

"I would be."

"Good night … Shannon!"

"Good night, Dean."

A New Identity

Shannon was at Dean's apartment the next day. "Come with me," he said.

"Where are we going?" she inquired.

"The Texas Department of Public Safety, Driver's License Bureau."

"How come?"

"You need a renewal."

"No I don't!"

"Trust me. It's time for a renewal."

"You're having an attack, Dean. Your mental illness is acting up!"

"Just hush your mouth and come with me." He led her to another apartment in the building.

"Who lives here?" she asked.

"The Texas Highway Department. It's a branch office the governor doesn't know about." She gave him a suspicious look.

A young man answered the door. "Is this her?" he asked.

"The very one," Dean replied.

"OK, come in."

He had a camera, lights and a paper backdrop set up in his living room. "Stand over here," he said.

"What is this, Steele?" Shannon asked.

"You're getting a new driver's license that misrepresents your age."

"A fake ID? Cool!"

"We need to practice dancing together, and the best places to do that require considerably more age than your real license affords you."

"Hey, I can get a lot more tickets with two driver's licenses!"

"Wrong, Speed Demon. If you ever show that phony license to a peace officer, you and I will both go to jail. It's strictly for the doorman. I'll keep it the rest of the time."

The young man took a few pictures of Shannon and promised the new license the following day.

---

1. Ekaterina Gordeeva and Sergei Grinkov, Russian four-time world champion and two-time Olympic gold medal pairs skaters.
2. A competition held at the Sugar Land Ice and Sports Center, located in Sugar Land, Texas, a suburb southwest of Houston.
3. See Book One, Chapter 5, page 68.
4. Dorothy Hamill, American figure skater, the 1976 Olympic champion in ladies' singles.

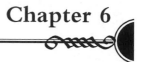

Chapter 6

The Queen's Return

Dean opened the door. Millie stood there in a short black spaghetti-strap cocktail dress and black patent leather pumps. "Hello, I'm Millie," she said, grinning coyly. "I'm here to work with Mr. Steele,"

"You must have caused a sensation at work today," he remarked, regarding her stunning appearance as she waltzed defiantly into his den.

"I stopped for gas and changed in the ladies room, Dear Boy," she said, as if letting him in on a closely guarded feminine secret.

Dean had hoped that she had made her point, and had her fun, last time, and would now be done with it, but that was obviously not the case. "Oh, shit!" he thought, "It looks like I'm in for another evening of teasing." He was concerned that Millie was bringing such an inappropriate aspect into their relationship, but at the same time thankful that he would have another opportunity to experience her beauty.

"Come in, dedicated co-worker," he said, pretending not to notice her sexy appearance. "I'd like to run some cool new dance steps by you."

They worked on dance diagrams for about an hour, pausing to listen to music that might work in the routines. At first Dean kept his mind on their work. But after a while he began to admire how wonderfully sexy Millie looked in her clingy thin black velvet spaghetti-strap dress and black heels. Every aspect of her appearance worked together to weave a tapestry of coordinated feminine beauty. He couldn't help but feel privileged to have such an esthetically pleasing image in his presence. He knew Millie had gone to a lot of trouble to present this vision to him, and he appreciated it, even if she had done so for her own selfish reasons.

Dean figured that Millie, now nearing her forties, had a need to demonstrate that she could still appeal to a young man, and he was the logical target. By responding to her sexuality, he verified unmistakably that she is still a beautiful and desirable woman. He was like a figure skating judge giving her performance high marks for technical merit and artistic interpretation. Despite the fact that she teased and taunted him unmercifully to obtain her marks, and she gloated insufferably over the effect she had on him, he still felt she deserved the win. He owed her the medal that her performance had earned.

He resigned himself to once again fall prey to her seductive appeal. Only this time he vowed to yield up his defeat verbally, rather than physically as before. He would acknowledge that she was sexy, rather than demonstrating it with an embarrassing physiological reaction.

Dean began to allow Millie to catch him gazing at her. He came to enjoy the almost imperceptible grin of satisfaction that would pass across her face when she realized he was admiring her. He became comfortable in the role of a captive of her beauty.

At first it was mainly an esthetic experience for him, admiring her carefully coordinated feminine beauty. The various components of her appearance fit together like the pieces of a jigsaw puzzle to present a complete picture of womanhood in full bloom. "This must have been what God had in mind when he created Eve," Dean thought.

In response to the attention Dean directed toward her, Millie began to place herself in poses that emphasized her voluptuous anatomy. She softened her voice, her movements became more serpentine, and she would return Dean's gaze as they worked on the diagrams.

In response to her revised attitude, Dean's thoughts of her moved from the esthetic toward the carnal. His attention would go to her bulging breasts or her shapely derriere. Before long his body began to respond as it had before. He felt a tenseness in his groin.

Knowing what he was in for, Dean considered his alternatives. He would not be able to keep his rebellious organ in check unless he stopped the game and made his guest leave the premises. The previous encounter had established a link between her and his organ that he could not control. The recalcitrant appendage would again embarrass him.

To send her away seemed a bit extreme. He could try not to look at her in the hope that his rowdy organ would settle down, but that was unappealing at best, and probably doomed to failure as well. He soon resigned himself to giving the woman another richly deserved demonstration of the physical effect she had on him.

Once he realized that was to be his destiny, he became comfortable with the scenario. His dick would grow, Millie would notice it, and she would tease him about it. He resolved to play the role for her benefit. If he couldn't prevent it, he could at least give the woman her money's worth. Her gloating, though irritating, was amusing as well.

Dean continued to admire his guest, and his dick continued to expand slowly. At one point he changed positions, Millie looked down, and a satisfied smile crossed her face. Dean knew she had discovered his secret.

Moments later Millie moved toward Dean to show him a dance diagram. As she passed by him, her left breast brushed his cheek. It was a poorly disguised teasing motion, and it had the intended effect on its intended victim. Either the soft touch of the thinly covered mammary flesh, the mere fact of her audacious flirtation, or perhaps both, opened the floodgates in his groin. His organ began to grow in time with his heartbeat. Within seconds his embarrassment was painfully noticeable.

Millie made no mention of Dean's newfound distress. Instead she suggested they dance to one of the songs to see if it fits into the program they were working on. She inserted the CD and selected the track. Then she held out her hand to Dean.

He took her in his arms and they began to dance. She melted into him as they swayed, and he lost all cognizance of the routine they were working on, concentrating instead only upon the sexy woman that he held in his arms. His right hand moved gently up and down her back and hips. His sex organ boldly attained its full stature and pressed itself firmly into her soft abdomen.

Finally Millie's hand slipped down from his back and then down inside his waistband. It closed around the rigid shaft, separated from the throbbing organ only by the thin cotton briefs he wore.

"You're thinking naughty thoughts again," she whispered.

"You're misbehaving again," he responded.

"What's the matter, Dean?" she asked. "You stood still for it before."

"I made allowances for your first offense," he said. "This time it isn't just 'slipsies'. You should know better."

"It's so big, Dean," she said. "I just can't believe it!"

Her praise stilled his objections for a time. He strongly suspected that she was about to make a move inside his briefs. He would need to eject her before she did so if he were to prevent that indiscretion. But if he did pull her away from him, he would never know if she had the audacity to try it. While he was evaluating the situation her soft hand deftly slipped into his shorts and closed in a velvety cocoon around his sensitive shaft.

The move surprised Dean, even though he expected it. Having her so intimately in contact with him made him feel quite vulnerable.

Millie quickly began amusing herself by caressing the rigid organ and examining it with her fingers. In response to her touch it attained its final state of total rigidity. Dean felt riveted to the spot as the woman explored his most private and intimate area. He couldn't bring himself to look at her face. Frozen, he merely endured the examination he was getting. Finally he awoke as if from a dream. "God, Millie!" he blurted, wide-eyed, pulling her hand out of his pants.

Millie gave him a soft smile. Then she pushed him gently toward the couch and they sat down. "Are you shocked, Dean? Are you surprised that I would touch you like that?" Her hand caressed his abdomen as her lips pressed against his. Some invisible force held him still as her hand slipped down and regained its grip on his vulnerable appendage.

After long moments, Dean broke off the kiss and again pulled her hand out of his pants. "This is crazy, Millie," he said. "We can't do this."

"I know," she said. "I was just playing with you. I took it too far. I'm sorry." She looked at him with sheepish eyes. "Can you forgive me?"

He sighed. "You're a tease, Millie. You should be ashamed."

"I know. I'm a bitch, and I sometimes misbehave. Don't let my tacky behavior bother you, Dean. OK? It's not your fault."

He exhaled his agreement. She smiled softly. "Are you mad at me, Dean? Are you mad because I made you flex your muscles for me? Are you mad because I touched you?" The sexy bitch was back.

"I'll live," he said, gradually recovering from his distress.

"I only did it because I like you," she said in a soft, little girl voice.

"Actually, I had no idea why you did it," he responded.

"So, now you know," she popped. Then her face took on a more ominous countenance. "The cold and powerful Ice Man gets excited by the Ice Queen," she said, "Doesn't he, Dean?"

"So it would seem," he admitted.

"And she's perfectly obnoxious about it, isn't she, Dean?"

"Perfectly."

Millie grinned. "So now the Ice Queen knows just how big and powerful the Ice Man really is, doesn't she Dean?"

"I expect she knows more about him than she has any right to," he replied, unable to avoid being amused by her audacious gloating.

"Poor Dean," she cooed, stroking his cheek. "The mean old Ice Queen found out all about him … and his secret desire for her." She was unable to suppress a grin of self-satisfaction.

"Millie," he said, "You are a beautiful and desirable woman. Of that there can be no doubt. No man, me included, is immune to your considerable charms. Now, can we get past that and just agree that you turn me on, and then get our relationship back on track?"

"As long as you understand it, Dean, I'm satisfied." She grinned.

"Good!" he exclaimed. Now, can we get back to life in the boring trek toward figure skating fame and fortune?"

"As you wish, Young Man." She gave him a knowing, and rather lusty look. Then she picked up her belongings and left.

Dean breathed a sigh of relief that the contest was finally over.

Chapter 7

Baton Rouge

After Dean and Shannon had been skating together a while, the word got out, and they began to get invitations to participate in events put on by skating clubs around the southwest. One was the Christmas pageant event organized by the Figure Skating Club of Texas (FSCT) and held at the Texas Ice Stadium in mid-December. As a senior pair, they received considerable attention, though they had not yet won any metal together.

An Invitation

"Did you hear?" Shannon asked excitedly. "They want us to skate an exhibition in Baton Rogue!"

"What is it?" Dean asked.

"The club over there is putting on a big event, and they're bringing in skaters from all over. They want us! They'll even pay for our flights."

"My goodness, it's almost a thirty-minute flight on Southwest Airlines!"

"Hey, somebody wants us to pay us to skate, Dean. Isn't it cool?"

"We don't have four and a half minutes of stuff ready to show. We'd fall on our butts."

"We could do that country song we been workin' on."

"You mean, hats and kicks? 'Who you gonna blame it on'?"

"Yeah. We could work that one up easy."

"It's under three minutes."

"Sylvia can stretch the audio. Besides, we can throw some other stuff in there, dance steps and stuff."

"I'd rather not skate a hodge-podge in front of paying customers. We're not ready for prime time."

"Come on, Elmer Fudd, we need to get some performing experience, and it'll be fun."

"We don't need 'falling on our butts in front of the locals' experience."

"It's all set! Mom is setting it up with 'em." Dean sighed.

Charity Ball

"Have you heard?" Shannon asked as they laced their boots.

"Heard what?"

"Mom said FSCT wants us to go down into the fifth ward and pick up some underprivileged kid and bring her down here to skate. It's a publicity stunt for the newspapers."

"I hadn't heard that. Who's running it, Sandy or Elise?"

"I don't know."

"Is our boy Walt Mason involved?"

"I don't know. Mom acted like it was a complete surprise. She was pissed that the club would set us up for something like that without asking her first."

"I'll talk to Sandy."

They skated their practice session, working on counter-rotating jumps and spins. As they finished up, Sandy Jenson, the new president of the Figure Skating Club of Texas, was bringing her daughter to skate. Dean approached her.

"Hi, Dean, she said, with a harried smile." How's your program coming?"

"It's coming," he replied, "Slowly but surely."

"That's good. I just know y'all will go to Nationals!"

Sandy was not a skater. She was an ice mom who ran a small air conditioning business with her husband. "Sandy," Dean said, "Is there some plan to have Shannon and me do some publicity thing?"

"Oh, my goodness. That's not supposed to be out yet! It's just an idea Elise and I have been kicking around."

"What's the idea?"

"Well, you know how hard it is to get the big corporations to sponsor our events. We're a new club, and they get tapped a lot. Basically, they say they don't want to donate money to help rich kids skate. They're only interested in charity events that create good publicity for them. You can understand that." She sighed, "Well, we were trying to figure out some way to get the kind of publicity for the club that'll make it easier to get corporations as sponsors."

"I see."

"So we had this idea, Elise really, that we could donate some lessons to a poor kid who can't afford to skate. Tina has agreed to give her some instruction, and the club can buy her some ice time. There's this little black girl who used to skate, but her parents split up, and now her mom can't afford it."

"OK. Where do we come in?"

"Well, we thought, and it's just an idea at this point, that you and Shannon could go down and pick her up and bring her here for her first lesson. Sheila could take pictures for the club newsletter, and we could use that next year when we're soliciting sponsors." She looked sheepish. "That's the idea, Dean, but it's not far enough along to even ask you yet."

"If you decide to do it, why don't you coordinate it with Walt Mason, our publicist. He has friends at the Chronicle, and he knows how to stage a media event. We'd all get more mileage out of it that way."

"Oh, that would be wonderful!" the woman said. "Thanks so much!"

Baton Rogue

Fred and Millie took an entourage to Baton Rouge in their van. At first it was assumed that just the skaters would go to the event, but as the time approached, more and more people decided to witness the new pair's first paid performance.

The ice arena in Baton Rouge was smaller than most, but modern and well appointed. Extra seating had been brought in to accommodate the annual ice show. Shannon and Dean took their skate bags inside and claimed their lockers. As they were preparing for the event, one of the local pairs girls approached Shannon. "Are you pairs," she asked, obviously marveling at Shannon's size, "Or freedance?"

"Pairs," Shannon replied, picking up the girl's thought with some irritation. "I'm Godzilla's partner."

"You're from that new club in Houston, aren't you?" the girl asked. "You're skating second on the program."

"That's right," Shannon replied in a "So what?" voice.

"Second - that's where they always put you when you're new," she explained with a condescending air. "One good performance to get the audience's attention, then they the run in the ... new ones." She took on a confident look. "We're skating next to last." She walked away.

"Bitch!" Shannon mumbled to herself.

The first act was a senior ladies silver medalist from Florida. She was very good, and the audience warmed up considerably to her.

"Our next pair is from the Figure Skating Club of Texas in Houston," a voice boomed over the PA system. "Shannon Foster and Dean Steele. They're a new team that skates USFSA senior pairs." There was a smattering of polite applause. This introduction was by far the briefest of the evening since they had no competition history to recite. Dean had insisted that his earlier singles history not be mentioned to their hosts, and Shannon followed suit, suppressing her Junior Nationals win as well. They were unsure enough of themselves that they wanted to be able to sneak out the back door if their program didn't go well.

Dean skated out to mid-ice and took up his starting pose. His right fist was on his right hip as his head reared back to look at an oversize watch on his left wrist. He wore an exasperated countenance.

The music blared from the PA system. It was a finger-picking guitar intro to a country music song. Dean snapped from one exasperated gesture to the next, in time with the music, as he skated around his little spot on the ice, alternately looking off-ice and at his watch.

Suddenly Shannon came racing out of the shadows. She was adjusting her outfit and excitedly explaining with her hands and arms waving. Her hair was up, and one large curler remained in place.

Then the voice of veteran country singer, Vern Gosden filled the arena. The first verse described a girl who is always late, but who always offers up a stream of excuses and alibis. Dean watched, exasperated, with hands on hips as Shannon skated in circles around him, animating her explanation with gestures of innocence and skillful skating moves. The song asked would be blamed for her tardiness this time.

After watching this display for a moment, Dean pushed off toward the rapidly moving young woman. Skating backward, she began to run from him, proclaiming her innocence with exaggerated gestures. "She's in trouble now!" the audience thought. Doggedly, he chased her in a large circle throughout the second verse. The song continued to query who would be blamed, and it commented on her past creativity at making up believable excuses.

Dean made a grab for the girl, but she eluded him. He continued to chase her around the rink. The singer's voice continued to ask expectantly what the current excuse would be and who would be blamed.

Dean finally grabbed the speeding girl's extended hand and jerked her forcefully into the Waltz position, with her skating backward, facing him. He pulled the oversize curler from her hair and tossed it causally into the stands, leaving a surprised young girl with a souvenir. Then he forcefully snapped her into the Kilian position, skating side by side, facing the same direction, with the tardy young woman on his right.

The chorus played as they skated together, bouncing to the strong, steady beat of the music. Shannon flopped like a rag doll as Dean forcefully snapped her from one position to the next. The chorus of the song pointed out that her creative excuse-making was the main basis of their relationship. Dean discretely pulled a plastic tie out of Shannon's long hair, causing it to fall free and begin flowing in the wind.

As the music went into an instrumental interlude, they dropped the exasperation theme and began to skate together with precision. Shannon now skated smoothly, in great contrast to her jerky performance when first she was apprehended by her partner.

This part of the program was more like ice dancing than a pairs program. They skated near the rail and picked up two white cowboy hats that Millie held out for them. They then circled the arena in the Killian position, alternately snapping their heads right and left on the first and third beats, and kicking right and left on the second and fourth beats of each measure. The kicks were high and snappy and executed in perfect unison. At one point they wagged their behinds in unison, to the beat of the music, and to the great delight of the audience.

Then they discarded the hats and punctuated the remainder of the program with a side-by-side double toe loop and a throw double Lutz. These moves brought "Oohs" from the crowd.

There was a noticeable awe in the arena when Dean lifted and threw Shannon since the audience had never seen such a big, muscular girl flying through the air. The contrast with the "big guy, little girl" routine was remarkable as Shannon's formidable body spun high above the ice.

Shannon and Dean, grinning at each other, bowed to a wildly cheering audience. "Oh, y'all were just magnificent!" Millie screamed as they approached the rail. "They loved it! Did you hear 'em?"

The program continued on an uneven keel. At one point, between skaters, a chant broke out from the audience, "Hats and kicks! Hats and kicks!" The chant died out when the announcer called out the next skater, but it picked up again when she was finished.

Walt rushed up to Shannon and Dean. "You gotta skate an encore!" he said excitedly. "Let me tell the emcee you'll do it!"

"We can't," Dean said, "We don't have another number ready."

"Then just do it again. I've got 'em screaming for you!"

Dean and Shannon looked at each other. "Do the same program?"

"They're screaming for you. Just say you'll skate again!"

The two skaters looked at each other and nodded. "Great!" Walt said.

"Ladies and gentlemen," the PA system blurted. "At the end of the program, Foster and Steele will skate again." A cheer went up.

The final performance of the program was by Lance Woodruff, a veteran professional figure skater from Las Vegas. "Shit," Dean said, "We're gonna look really bad, following this guy."

"No we won't," Shannon said. "We're gonna give 'em what they want. Lots of hats and kicks!" Dean shook his head and grinned.

They skated their program over again, but, inspired by the audience's enthusiasm, with more exaggerated movements. At Dean's call, they replaced the last part of the routine with another round of hats and kicks. The excited audience was standing, clapping to the beat and cheering.

On the way to the locker room Shannon passed the pairs girl she had encountered earlier. "Maybe next time you'll get to skate second."

"What was that all about?" Dean asked.

"Just being tacky," Shannon replied. "I couldn't help it."

Walt hastily arranged a private party room at a nearby Cajun restaurant. Millie invited so many people that it became rather crowded. She drank too much, and Fred had to walk her to the van.

Walt took Dean aside. "Dean," he confided, "You two don't need to win a medal. Judging from the way that audience responded, you could turn pro tonight. You don't need any gold medals, or triple loopers, or anything else. You've got some kind of magic. Just do what you did tonight, and I can sell you all over the damn world!"

"Thanks for the kind words, Walt, but I'd feel better if we get a second opinion from another audience before we call up Stars on Ice."

New Orleans

Fred suggested that the four of them go to New Orleans for a day on the way home. They took a boat tour of the Port of New Orleans on the Mississippi river and then ate diner at Alex Patout's restaurant. Then they went for a walk down Bourbon Street.

Shannon was excited by the party atmosphere, and she liked visiting the shops that sell T-shirts with obscene statements emblazoned on them.

"Oh, God, Dean!" she exclaimed, "You gotta buy me that one!" She pointed to a shirt that said,

I am not a bitch!

I am THE bitch!

And that's Ms. Bitch to you, Asshole!

Dean bought the shirt and had "Shannon" embroidered on it over her heart. He also secretly bought one for Millie. It was a thin, tight-fitting pink short-sleeve top that said

"I'm not as innocent as I look."

He had "The Ice Queen" embroidered on it. He later gave it to her privately. When she put it on her bosom bulged prodigiously, and the scoop neckline showed considerable cleavage.

"I don't look at all innocent in this," she said, looking in the mirror.

"I think that's the point," Dean said, grinning.

Chapter 8

Sexy Bitch

Shannon came bursting into the workout room. Her eyes flashed anger. "You bastard! How dare you refer to me as a spoiled brat in front of my friends? I want an apology right now!"

Dean looked up slowly from the bench where he was doing dumbbell rowing exercises. He finished his 12 reps and then studied her face for a while before answering. "And you shall have your apology, too … provided …," he paused for effect. "Provided I spoke in error."

"What's that supposed to mean?" she inquired with disgust.

"Well, first we have to determine if indeed I made a mistake. And if I was wrong, inaccurate, incorrect … well … I'll apologize profusely."

"Of course you made a mistake, you dumb shit! You called me a spoiled brat in front of my friends."

"Ah … but what if, in actual point of fact, you are, technically speaking, precisely that?"

"What? You're in enough trouble already, Buster!"

"Look. Here's the deal. Go get a dictionary and we'll look up the adjective 'spoiled' and the noun 'brat.' If none of the definitions fit you, then I'll apologize, both to you and to your giggly little friends. But if one of the definitions should fit like a sock, then no apology."

Dean's ploy distracted Shannon from her anger and piqued her interest. "Where am I going to get a dictionary?" she asked with disgust.

"There's probably one in the secretary's office," he replied. "Get it."

Shannon stood there fuming for a while, then sensing that nothing would happen otherwise, went to the secretary's office. In a few moments she returned to the weight room with a dictionary.

"Gimme that," Dean grabbed the book out of her hands. "Now let's see," he said, thumbing through to the S's.

"Ah, look at this … definition 2: 'Spoil - to injure the disposition of, especially by being too kind, generous, overindulgent, etc.'" He looked at her. "Well, you're the poster child for that one!"

"Bullshit!" Shannon responded. "Nobody is ever was kind or generous to me. I have to fight for everything I get!"

"Oh, I see. Then your disposition got that way without any help?"

"Asshole!" Shannon fought back a grin.

"Now, brat … brat … brat," Dean flipped the pages. "Ah, yes. 'A spoiled, unpleasant and annoying child.' Boy, Mr. Webster pegged your ass on that one!"

"You're crazy!" Shannon said. "That's not me at all!"

"OK, which one is not you, spoiled? unpleasant? annoying?"

"No! It's 'child' I'm not. I'm a woman, in case you didn't notice, Mr. Dumbbell." A victorious smirk crossed her face.

"Well, excuse me, Madam! Pardon my lack of perception. A woman you are, huh? I'll be damned! You grew up while my back was turned."

"You should take better notice, Mister!" She flashed a haughty grin.

"OK, I owe you an apology. I called you a 'spoiled brat' when you're really more along the lines of … 'selfish bitch.' How wrong I was!"

"Bastard!"

"Please let me make amends for my transgression. I'll tell all your friends I was wrong. You aren't merely a spoiled brat anymore. You've developed into a conceited, self-involved, selfish bitch! I'll even make an announcement on the PA system. Maybe I'll put it in the newspaper!"

"You like to live dangerously, don't you, Smartass?"

"Who can I tell first? What about the girls in the malt shop. Maybe we can have a sundae with them this afternoon."

"You're flirting with death and dismemberment, Cowboy."

"What a revelation! I see you in a whole different light now." He framed her face with his hands. "It seems the ugly duckling has matured into a buzzard. How charming!"

"I'm gonna stuff a dumbbell in your mouth!"

"OK, if you disagree, I'll compromise. I'll let you pick the first word, the adjective, and I'll pick the second word, the noun. Fair enough?"

Shannon looked at him quizzically. "OK, but you go first."

"Hmm, OK, let's see. 'Brat' doesn't work anymore. I'm afraid I'll just have to go with 'bitch.' It has the right texture to it, especially in view of your advanced age … and your recent behavior."

"OK, then. My word is … 'sexy!'"

"Sexy bitch? Hmm. That's got a ring to it. I think I like it. It could go over well with the fans."

Shannon grinned. She was happy with her new label. "So don't call me a spoiled brat anymore, OK?"

"Don't act like one anymore, OK?"

"OK. It's strictly 'sexy bitch' from now on." She curtsied and left the weight room grinning.

Know-it-all

"OK, I'll show you," Shannon said to Jenny as they approached Dean.

"Dean, I've got a question for you. Why does my hair dryer speed up when I cover up the hole with my hand?"

"What?"

"No, it really does. I put my hand over the end where the air comes out, and it runs faster. I can hear it. It goes whooo...ooo." Her voice raised in pitch.

"Oh, that's because the impeller stalls, and that unloads the motor."

"What?"

"OK, normally the motor is doing work. It's taking in slow-moving air and spitting out fast-moving air. That puts a load on the motor and slows it down. When you cover it up, the motor doesn't have to push any air anymore. It just spins the same air in a circle. So, with no work to do, it speeds up. The little fan blades stall out just like an airplane wing when it quits flying. It all adds up to no work being done by the motor."

"See?" Shannon said to her friend.

"OK," the girl replied. They walked away.

Later Dean was sitting next to Shannon. "What was that hair dryer thing with Jenny all about?"

"We were settling an argument."

"About hair dryers?"

"About you."

"What about me?"

"I told her you know everything, and she didn't believe me, so I showed her."

"Oh, so now I'm Mr. Wizard?"

"Yeah, I guess so," she replied flippantly.

"I am living in a zoo!" he mumbled to himself.

Name change

"Dean," Shannon said, "Do you think we'd get better marks if I changed my name to Katerina? A lot of the famous girl skaters are named Katerina."

"I think that's a great idea, Foster," Dean said. "If we were called Oxanna Foster and Alexi Steele, we couldn't lose!"

Shannon had to burst out giggling, despite being irritated by his sarcastic response to her idea. "You never take me seriously, Steele," she said, after the giggles finally stopped.

"Sorry, Precious," he said. "I'm just so caught off guard by your refreshing wit that I'm ill-prepared to respond, that's all."

"No, you're just a jerk, Steele, and proud of it!"

"But I'm the only skating partner you've got. You ever wake up in the middle of the night in a cold sweat, thinking about that one?"

"All the time," she said, matter-of-factly. "And I may dump you pretty soon, too, right after we win our first contest."

"I see," he grinned. "Just use me to get recognized as a pairs skater, then heave me over the gunnels with the rest of the jetsam, right?"

"Pretty much … yeah."

"Well, look, Princess" he said, rather insincerely, "I'll just be grateful for every second I spent as your partner." Then he got a sinister look on his face. "But if I'm to be sacrificed after our first win … then maybe we won't win anything for a while."

"Oh, no!" she said, "You can't just screw up in contests and make us lose, just so I'll keep you as my partner. That's no fair!"

"But ditching your hard-working partner as soon as he alerts the skating world to your radiance … that is fair?"

"Uh … yeah." She grinned. "That's the way it works. Umm, I find somebody better and drop you like a hot rock." She smiled triumphantly, pleased with her teasing response.

"I see," he mused. "And who's going to be better than me?"

"There's quite a list, Dean." she answered. "Let's see, Boitano, Browning, Eldredge, Hamilton, Wylie…, and don't even get me started on the Russians!"

"None of those guys can hoist you, Princess, unless you become anorexic overnight. You'd have to be 'Olive Oyle' on ice to skate with one of them."

"OK, Elvis Stojko's strong. He could lift me!"

"Elvis doesn't *want* to lift you, Sweetie. He doesn't have my patience. He'd drop *you* like a hot rock!"

"Lloyd Eisler, then!"

"Lloyd has a ninety-five-pound partner that he's won medals with for years. You think he'd dump Isabel for you?"

"OK, Dean, look. I know how much it means to you to skate with me, OK? And Mom would just die if I dumped you. So I guess I'll just keep you for a while, OK? Don't worry. I'll take care of you."

"Lucky me!" he mumbled audibly. Shannon grinned, and they hugged. "This is so cool!" Shannon said quietly. "I love teasing you."

Chapter 9

Muscle Girl

It was late morning at Bally's Gym in Clear Lake City. A brief rain had cooled the air and wetted the large plate glass windows that overlooked the parking lot. A few non-working housewives were using the treadmills and stair stepper machines in the front room. Dean walked up to the bench where Julie Harwood was preparing to do her incline bench presses. Her face was flushed, and her gray sweatshirt was damp from the walk in from her car.

"Hey, Muscle Girl," he said, grinning, "You need a spot'?"

The woman looked at him for a moment, recalling their date at the ballet. "Not from a wimp like you," she said, grinning victoriously.

"Yeah," he said, "Looks like you're up over eleven pounds there."

"So, how's the big ice skating deal going, Dean?"

"OK, I guess. No broken bones yet. No medals, either, though. Fame and fortune yet elude me."

"How are your bitches?"

"Oh, they're in rare form," he sighed.

The woman laughed. "Poor Dean. Got so many hooks in him he can't even wiggle."

"Speaking of hooks," he said, "I think a left hook to your jaw would be very appropriate."

"Not a chance, Wimp. You're too pussy-whipped to tangle with me."

"Remember the last time, Smartass?" he asked. "As I recall the events, you ended up on the bottom, and you liked it down there."

"I was drunk," she explained.

"On what, yogurt and apple juice?"

Unable to formulate an answer, she just gave him a disgusted look. "OK, Musclehead," she said, "Spot me ten." Dean assisted the woman as she pushed out ten repetitions of her exercise.

"Listen," he said when she finished, "My masochistic streak is acting up again. I wonder if you'd like to go out to a movie tonight and share some of your sarcastic, depreciating humor with me. I'm running a little low on brutal insults to my manhood lately."

"Gee, Dean, that's the nicest thing any guy ever said to me! You must be a charm school graduate."

"I just sweep you off your feet, don't I?"

"Are you serious about taking me out?"

"Deadly. I think the pleasure of your company this evening would be a very charming experience."

"What if I tell you to kiss off?"

"No problem. An old homeless woman with no teeth has been giving me the eye. I could hit on her. She was my second choice anyway."

Julie grinned. "OK, Dean. I'll go out with you. Just don't try any more of that male-dominant shit on me. You won't get away with it this time. Once was enough."

"For you, maybe, but not for me. I really like the part where you beg me to ream your tailpipe."

"I'm warning you, Weakling," she grinned. "Mess with this muscle girl and get hurt real bad!"

"Julie," he said, "Your wit and charming company are all I seek."

"Bullshit! You just want to wrestle me down and make me submit to your weird desires."

"You hope! Those are your weird desires you're talking about, not mine," he said.

The Date

Dean and Julie went to a Jean Claude Van Damme action movie at the 30-theater complex located at Beltway 8 and the Gulf Freeway.

"One of the guys at my apartment house is havin' a little get-together tonight," Dean said as they were walking out to his car. "You wanna drop by there and mingle with the lower class?"

"Sure." she grinned, taking his arm.

They spent about an hour at the party, drinking grape juice and chatting with the locals. The muscular couple attracted a lot of stares. Finally Julie looked at Dean. "Why don't we go up to your place?"

"I give up," he said, faking puzzlement, "Is that a trick question?"

"These guys aren't hittin' on me very hard since I'm with you," she complained. "I'm wastin' my time here."

"Sorry 'bout that," he said with a look of disdain.

"Come with me, Dickhead," she said, taking his arm. "I can see you need a workout." They walked over to his apartment, went inside and sat on the couch. "Poor Dean," Julie said. "Every time he gets too much abuse from the bitches that run his life, he has to come crawling back to Julie for a little TLC^2."

"You're so good to me!" Dean exclaimed, with an air of sarcasm. "What would I do without you?"

"Have they been mean to you, Poor Boy?" She caressed his forehead.

"Well, now that you mention it ..."

"Tell Mama Julie all about it. Have you fucked 'em yet?" He looked at her in silence. "Come on, Dean, pour out your little heart. Have you screwed the little one yet?"

"No, Julie. It's a felony in Texas, and Daddy has promised me a bullet and a jail term if I do – in that order."

"So, what have you done to her?" Dean was silent. "OK, then, what has she done to you?"

"She teases me."

"What?" Julie laughed. "You've got a sixteen-year-old prick teaser for a partner?"

"So it would seem. She's at the curious stage – curious about sex. She wants to be sexy, but she doesn't know how. She tries out all her ideas on me. She's got me set up as the yardstick."

"What does she do, Dean? Does she try to give you erections?" Dean's silence was his admission. "So, she just dangles her little nymphet ass in front of you and your dick pops up like a Jack-in-the-box!" Unable to deny her description, Dean simply gave her a disgusted look. She tried to stifle a giggle.

Dean couldn't help laughing. "It's ... embarrassing. I'm OK most of the time, but when she comes over here and starts teasing me, I can't help it. I get a rise in my Levis. It's ... automatic." Julie was laughing. "And, God forbid if she notices it! Then she starts giggling and teasing me about it. Then she's impossible to deal with."

"OK, what about Mama?"

"Oh, she teases me worse than the daughter does! She comes over here dressed like Miss July on her way to Hefner's birthday party, and starts purring like an alley cat in heat. Well, it doesn't take much of that to give me wood either. Then she gets this smug look on her face and just gets worse."

"Have you fucked her yet?"

"No, but she has hinted around at the possibility of a discreet affair," Dean said, avoiding a direct answer. "She quite possibly could be had."

"She wants you as a trophy, Dean. She wants your scalp on her belt."

"I thought it was just guys who did that."

"Don't kid yourself, Sonny," Julie replied. "That woman is every bit as predatory as any guy at that party tonight."

"So, what is your advice, Doctor?"

"I still say fuck her! But dominate the shit out of her when you do. Take her. Don't let her take you. Shit, you gotta be the boss, Dean!"

"And what about you? What should I do with you?"

"Do I ... give you wood?" she laughed.

"With that scrawny little bod?" he teased. "Not a chance! I can't even tell if you're a boy or a girl without a DNA test."

"Well, according to your research last time, I could pass for either."

"I remember. You are kind of a muscle-bound freak. What should I do with you?"

"I don't know, Dean," she said coyly. "What do you want to do?"

"Rape you," he said. The girl's face awoke with delight. "I want to hold you down, take off your clothes, and fuck your ears off!"

"Fat chance, Wimpo!" she said, trying unsuccessfully to hide her excitement. "It'll never happen to this muscle girl!"

"OK," Dean said, "It was just a thought."

Her face fell. "What? You're just gonna give up without trying?"

"Well, you said it won't work, so why bother?" he sighed.

"What a wimp!"

"Uh, don't look now, but our heroine is showing signs of submissiveness."

"Huh! No chance."

"Come on, Julie. It's nothing to be ashamed of. Admit that your fantasy is to be raped by a guy who's bigger and stronger than you are."

"Well, there's nobody like that around here. That's for sure!"

"Come on, Julie. Be honest. Open up your little heart."

"Go to Hell!"

"If you'll admit it, I'll do it." A grin slowly broke out on her face as she regarded him. "Come on, Freako. Just say you want it, and Old Uncle Dean will deliver the goods. And you *know* I'm packin' the gear!" She inhaled deeply and exhaled, but held her tongue. "You know, Julie, I'm a lot stronger than you are. I can pin you and hold you down with both hands while I take off your clothes with my teeth." His words were having an effect on her. "And when I get you naked," he paused, "I can turn you any way I want ... and poke anything I have ... in any hole you've got." He looked at her. "Just tell me you want it, and it's yours."

The girl inhaled. "OK, Dean. I guess you can try that if you want to."

"Oh, you'll have to do better than that," he said. "This is going to be forcible rape, and it's a first-degree felony if it's not consensual. You'll have to tell me in no uncertain terms you want it before I can do it. I wouldn't want you having second thoughts and filing charges on me."

She closed her eyes and sighed. She knew he was trying to force her to admit to her masochism. She tried to find a way out. "OK, Dean," she sighed at last. "I want it. I want you to try to rape me. I mean, really rape me. I want to be physically overpowered and forcibly fucked, not just play-like, if you're man enough to do it. Now, do you have a paper for me to sign, or what?" She faked disgust.

"No, my child," he said. "Your admission that you're a hopeless masochist freak will suffice." He removed his shoes, socks, and shirt. Then he glared at her. "Come here, you little bitch," he said. Her breathing was slow and deep. Her neck flushed red as she prepared to resist his advance. "Why don't you just make it easy on yourself?" he asked. "You know you can't fight me off. Just lay down and spread your legs for me."

The Fight

"Screw you, Wimpo!" she said. "This'll be the toughest piece of ass you ever got!"

"Just relax, Little Girl, and I won't hurt you."

"Don't ever call me 'little,' Shithead!" She swung, and he ducked.

"Don't piss me off, Tinker Belle," he said. "This is gonna be hard enough on you as it is." They began to wrestle. Dean allowed her to struggle until she was exhausted. Then he pinned her. She struggled until she realized she was helpless. "You've had it, Sweet Pea," he said. "You're down for the count." She struggled some more, but to no avail.

"If you lay real still while I undress you, I won't choke you out," he said, holding her throat. She began to struggle, and he cut off her air. She fought until she was almost unconscious, then she became suddenly still. He released his grip, and she gasped for air.

"Do you need any further demonstrations, or are you ready to submit to your master?" The girl again began fighting. Dean choked her until she became still. "If I choke you out, you'll miss the good part," he said. "I want you fully awake when I ream your tailpipe."

"Screw you!" she said, again fighting back. She had very little strength left, but she used it all.

Dean twisted her arms behind her, and she grimaced from the pain. "Give it up, Bitch!" he said. "Your tender hole belongs to me now." She became still. "Screw you," she said with the last of her strength.

He put one hand on her throat and began to undress her with the other. Every time she moved, he would cut off her air. After a few times, she finally became docile. "Tell me, Julie," he said as he slowly removed the last of her clothing, "I can have your ass." The girl looked at him in silence. "What about it, Sweetcakes? Am I going to ream your ass?"

"Yes," she whispered.

"I didn't get that," he said. "What did you say?"

"I said, yes," she replied softly. "You're going to fuck my ass."

"And are you going to suck my dick first?"

"Yes," she said. "I'll do anything you want."

"Are you my helpless victim?"

"Yes," she whispered.

"Are you my willing love slave?"

"Yes," she whispered, opening her thighs slightly as she writhed beneath him.

"Good girl," he said as he mounted her in the missionary position. They made love.

Round Two

A little over an hour later Julie woke up. A small table lamp beside the bed illuminated the bedroom softly. She studied Dean for a while, and then she began to drag her fingers gently across his cheek. "Did I wake you?" she asked when his eyes opened.

"I got my nap out," he replied.

"I've been thinking," she began, with a mischievous grin.

"About what?"

"About your situation – your ... bitches problem."

"Well, I've heard your thinking on that, and I'm unimpressed!"

She placed her face close to his. "Really, Dean. You ought to fuck that bitch. She really needs it."

"Oh, you want I should do her a favor?"

"No! I want you to dominate the Hell out of her! Punish her for making everybody miserable!"

"And a ... sexual encounter would accomplish that? Pray thee how?"

Julie's hand closed around his organ. "You have to take control of her, Stud. Show her who's boss." She paused to grin. "Kinda like you did me tonight. You have the knack for it, Hoss!"

"And what effect did it have on you, Fair Lady?"

"Well," Julie began with a knowing look on her face. "You had me completely under your control." Dean's organ was growing rapidly as a result of both Julie's manipulation, and her description. "I was a helpless love slave. I couldn't stop you from taking anything I had, and I loved it. I was strictly a passenger on your boat." She reached over and turned off the lamp, plunging the bedroom into darkness. "You controlled my passion, and it controlled me." She moved over on top of her bedmate and guided his appendage between her thighs. "That's what you need to do to that rich bitch from River Oaks." His tip pressed against her opening. "Just lay her down …" Julie increased the pressure. "Spread her legs …" The rigid shaft began to enter her. "And stick your dick in her till she gags!' As she delivered this admonition her velvety cocoon slowly engulfed Dean's erect shaft.

"You can fuck her, Dean," Julie said as she moved down until her pubis contacted his. "You can screw her 'til she screams!" Her abdomen was fully impaled on his rigid shaft. "You can control her." Julie's pelvis began to undulate in a slow serpentine dance. "You can conquer her." Sensation began to take its toll on Dean. "You can show her how weak she really is."

The Fantasy

In the darkness, Julie's words began to conjure images in Dean's mind. Julie spoke again, but this time in a lower, more self-assured voice that harbored a hint of cruelty. "I'm the Ice Queen," she said in a tone calculated to ring of Millie Foster. "I'm a bitch to the bone. I control people. I crush people. I live only for myself." The unyielding undulations of Julie's pelvis elicited sensations that clouded Dean's thinking. "I always win. I never lose. I never pay for my crimes, no matter how hideous." A weak moan escaped Dean's lips as Julie's hips continued to move upon him.

""I'm Millie Foster," Julie continued. "I tease you with my big boobs in a tiny, thousand-dollar dress. I mesmerize you with hundred-dollar-an-ounce perfume. I flirt and tease until you want me so bad you can't stand it. Then I laugh at you! I take immense delight in your suffering."

Julie's actions had brought Dean to a high state of arousal. His thinking was confused. In the darkness the identity of this woman became uncertain. Was it Julie, ribbing him about his relationship with his sponsor? Or was it the Ice Queen describing her hold on him?"

"I love the helpless look you get when I tease you," the woman, whoever she was, continued. "You're like a confused little boy. You go weak in the knees just looking at me."

By this time the only image in Dean's mind was of Millie Foster. He could see her lips moving in sync with Julie's words. Even Julie's voice sounded like the cruel monarch herself.

"You can look, but you can't touch," the Ice Queen mocked in the darkness. "I make you want me, but I won't let you have me." The incessant grinding of Julie's groin against his had brought Dean to the point of impending release. His breathing was shallow and desperate.

"I can't let you have me," the Ice Queen continued, "Because I'd lose my power over you. Then I'd become your slave."

Dean was breathing in helpless gasps as Julie brought him to the threshold of explosion. "Don't fuck me, Dean. Please! I don't want to lose control of you."

With a groan that resembled a growl, Dean rolled the woman over forcefully until he was lying firmly between her legs. "Don't fuck me," she admonished. "You don't have permission, Dean." He began to thrust against the woman's body with slow, powerful strokes. "Don't fuck me, Dean," the Ice Queen continued to say. "I won't let you. You can't do it to me." The pace of Dean's thrusting began to increase. "I can tease you, but you can't fuck me," The woman said. "I won't let you!"

Finally Julie Harwood's much softer voice returned. "Fuck the Ice Queen!" it said. "Screw her eyeballs out!' Dean was thrusting like a madman, without control over his body. "Punish her! Make her pay!"

Soon passion overcame Julie, and the two muscular bodies thrashed about in a tumultuous program of unbridled lust, until, at last, heaving and moaning and gasping for breath, they collapsed into a tangle of entwined body parts. It took considerable time for the two to recover from the exertion of the lovemaking session. They lay in the darkness for long moments, entangled, breathing, and sweating.

Julie's Point

Finally Dean's head slowly began to clear. "What in the Hell was that?" he inquired.

Julie moved her nose against his neck. "I think somebody just … dominated the Ice Queen," she said, grinning in the darkness.

"What are you, Harwood? Some kind of freak? Pretending to be another woman when we have sex?"

"No, just making a point," she said nonchalantly.

"Making a point?"

"Yes. My words weren't getting through your muscle-bound skull, so I gave you a demonstration."

"A demonstration of what?"

"Of what it's like to dominate Millie Foster! Now that you've seen it first hand, you're bound to agree with me."

"You're seriously ill, Harwood! That didn't make any sense!"

"Calm down! After you think about it a while, you'll be glad I gave you a chance to punish her! Without my help, you'd probably just go through life letting her screw you around."

"Oh, you just did that … whatever it was … for my benefit?"

"Well, I got my just reward too. You gave me a pretty wild ride!"

"My God, Julie! You had my head so messed up, I actually thought you were her!'

"Uh, that was the point of the exercise, Dean. And don't be so surprised about your … temporary insanity. It happens to guys all the time. You're wired for it."

"It was a shitty thing to do!"

"Oh, and raping me was … polite?"

"You asked for that one, Julie. I never asked you to pull a … Millie Foster on me."

"I judged that it was what you needed, just like you figured out I needed to be raped."

"It's not the same!"

"Lighten up, Dean! That woman has you totally enslaved. Tonight we made some progress on breaking you free."

"You're a very sick woman, Harwood. You need years of therapy."

Julie laughed. "Well, let's make a deal. You treat me, and I'll treat you. It may not cure anything, but it sure will be fun!"

Dean exhaled a sigh that indicated he had relaxed. "I still say it was a shitty thing to do."

"Hey, when you get this girl in your bed, you never know what you're in for. If missionary position sex is all you want, go find a preacher's daughter somewhere!"

Dean sighed. "OK, Harwood, I'll accept the risks of the battlefield when we bunk in together, but just as soon as my dick wakes up, I'm gonna fuck your ears off!"

"Now, that's what I like to hear from a bed partner!"

They relaxed in each other's arms.

---

1. Spotting – when one's weightlifting partner steadies the barbell and assists with the last few reps.
2. TLC – tender, loving care

Chapter 10

Lolita

Teasing Shannon

"You know, I suppose," Shannon said, "That all my girlfriends are really teasing me about you now."

Dean raised his eyebrows in mock surprise. "And why, pray tell, do they do that?"

"Because!" Shannon responded. "You know… you're a hunk! They think there's something between us."

"What kind of something?"

"Don't be naïve, Dean. You know … something… romantic!"

"Gimme a break. I'm old enough to be your …"

"Lover," Shannon finished his sentence for him.

"You're going through puberty, and I'm going through male pattern baldness!"

"I am not going through puberty! I'm almost seventeen. I'm a full grown woman!" She inhaled and thrust out her bosom.

Dean frowned disgustedly. "I'm almost ten years older than you are. Guys like me go to jail for messing around with nymphets like you."

Shannon donned a haughty look. "Wouldn't it be worth the risk?" She drew both hands behind her neck, arched her back and spread her long blond hair out over the couch in a slow sexy movement, staring seductively at Dean the whole time.

"OK, Cleopatra. Sure, it's fun chasing teeny boppers, but it's not worth the trouble it causes. Girls your age aren't ready for that."

Shannon closed her eyes below raised eyebrows. "Have it your way, then. But you don't know what you're missing!"

"What do they say … your girlfriends?" Dean became interested.

"It's mostly how they look at each other and giggle. They tease me about how strong and muscular you are. They like to look at your butt."

"My butt?"

"Yeah, they think your butt is awesome!"

"You mean, I'm out there skating my little heart out, and your giggly girlfriends are watching my butt?" He feigned disgust.

"It's their favorite pastime. They gossip about it all the time."

"I can't believe this!" He pretended to be repulsed by the idea.

"And they say things to me like, 'Dean really puts his hands all over you during practice, doesn't he?' They'll say, 'What's it like when Dean holds you close to him like that. Does it make your panties wet?'"

"No shit? They really ask you that?"

"Oh yeah. Beverly even accused me of sneaking off and spending the night with you."

"What a bunch of little bitches! We've never done anything to create suspicion. I've been a perfect gentleman. Even your Daddy thinks so."

"Well, it's just the situation, I guess. You know, a strong and virile older man and a sexy, innocent young girl. It gives them strange ideas."

Virgin

"Are you a virgin?" The words surprised Dean more than Shannon.

Shannon tightened her lips and exhaled before answering. "Yes," she said, in an "if you must know" voice.

"Hey, I had no right to ask that," Dean said. "You don't have to tell me the truth. Just say whatever you want to. It's not a fair question."

"No, I answered it. I have no secrets from you. My cherry has survived all my dating so far, but not by a whole lot. Battered but unbroken, you might say."

Dean felt himself getting excited hearing Shannon talk about her sexual experiences. "How close did you get?" he heard himself ask.

"Well," Shannon began, apparently without reservation, "Two..., no, three boys have played with my tits, I mean with their hand actually inside my bra. And a couple have slid their hand up under my skirt."

"Inside your panties?"

"No, but one of them rubbed my box through my panties."

The Crush

"Are you embarrassed telling me about this?"

"Wake up, Dean!" Everybody at the rink knows I have a thing for you. I've been dreaming about you for weeks."

"Oh, Bullshit!" Dean suspected she was messing with him.

"No, Meathead, I've got a crush on my skating partner, and he doesn't even know it!"

Shannon's exploits

Dean didn't know what use to make of this information, or even whether to take it seriously. He decided to change the subject and sort it out later. For now he had a strong desire to hear more about Shannon's exploits with boys. "OK, then, did anybody ever get your bra off?"

"Tommy ... I mean, one boy got it unhooked so he could reach my tits better, but nobody ever took it all the way off."

"What about your panties?"

Shannon smiled and flicked her eyebrows up and down seductively. "What about 'em?"

"Did anybody ever get 'em off?" he asked, pointedly.

Shannon was pleased with Dean's sudden interest in her. "Well, I don't know ... wanna try?"

"C'mon," he scolded.

"Nope. Nobody even got his hand inside my panties. That's where I always drew the line. Hey! Why are you so interested in my bra and panties, anyway? What does this have to do with our skating, partner?"

"Nothing," Dean retorted, "I'm just a sociology professor doing research for a book on virgins."

Shannon laughed. "Professor, huh? Dirty old man is more like it. Now it's my turn. Are you a virgin?"

"Shannon, don't be nosey."

"Hey, I told you! Now you tell me. It's only fair."

"Well, OK, what are the chances that I would survive 27 years of life in the jungle without porking some young lady?"

"Porking?" Shannon roared with laughter. "You call it Porking?"

"The sex act goes under many names, and that is but one."

"Well how many 'young ladies' have you 'porked'?" She was laughing.

"I don't have an exact count."

"Well, is it ... over a million?" Shannon asked mockingly, "Or is it just 'one true love?'"

"Somewhere in between, I think."

"Lots of cheap sluts and whores in there, I guess?"

"Actually, no. I prefer the more expensive sluts and whores. I've always tried to be a bit discriminating."

"Oh, good for you! Mr. Discipline, already!"

"Now it's my turn again. I have some more questions."

"Shoot, Mr. Dirty Old Man," she grinned.

"Has anyone ever sucked your nipples 'til they stand up and point at the stars?"

"No, but here they are."

"Has anyone ever held you down and removed your panties with his teeth?"

"No, wanna try?"

"Anyone ever French kiss your navel 'til you moaned with delight?"

"Not yet, but there's always a first time."

Dean looked embarrassed. "I probably shouldn't be talking to you that way," he said. "I guess I got a little carried away."

"I'll tell you one thing, Steele, if you fuck as good as you talk about it, you are one hot lover!"

Their Image

"You know," Dean said, changing the subject, "Our skating doesn't have a theme yet. I think that's why it isn't coming together too well. It's just two people skating around out there. It doesn't tell a story."

"Yeah, but two great skaters skating around," Shannon added in jest.

"Granted," Dean acknowledged, "But it needs a story line ... a plot."

"How about a murder mystery?"

"No," Dean teased, "If I killed you, there would be no mystery at all why I did it." Shannon stuck out her tongue.

There was a pause, then Shannon spoke. "What kind of image do you think we could have as a pairs team?"

"Well, I think Mr. and Mrs. Skatefan will naturally look at us like this. He'll say, 'He's screwin' her Maude! You mark my words.' And she'll say, 'Oh, no, Claude! She's a sweet and innocent child. See how he takes care of her?' And he'll say, 'Wrong, Maude! He's bangin' her like a drum! I can tell by lookin' at 'em.' And she'll say, 'Oh, that's just an act they do out there on the ice. She's so innocent, and he's such a nice boy.' And then they'll decide they better come back tomorrow night and watch us again, so maybe they can figure it out. A mystery like that will make fans stick like glue."

"So, are you gonna 'bang' me?"

"Uh ... I don't know. You think I should?"

"Well, you are Dean Steele. You seem to have the habit!"

"Actually, no Ma'am. It's a felony in this state to bang a sixteen-year-old, punishable by twenty years in prison. So, if you don't mind, I'll pass on the bangin'. I'll just skate like I might be bangin' ya. It'll add that air of mystery to our act."

"Ohoo, that sounds like fun!" she said. "And I can act all innocent and vulnerable, right?"

"Actually, that gives me an idea," Dean said. "This could be the theme our skating needs."

Shannon perked up. "What is it?"

"Well, it goes like this. Innocent but sexy young girl places herself in the hands of powerful older guy. At first we, the audience, think maybe it's OK - that she's safe - like he's her protector, or something. But then we see maybe he's a dark force. As the routine develops, we begin to see that she may be in danger from him. Her innocently playful antics excite him, and this leaves her vulnerable to being seduced, abused, degraded, and debased by his evil dark side. She frolics with abandon in front of him, never realizing that she could, at any minute, become the helpless victim of his evil lust. The danger would build suspense into the act."

"Holy shit, Shakespeare. That's pretty … uh, complicated. But it's good. It's kinda like what's really happening between us!" she laughed.

"Get serious, kid. But we could develop the whole routine around this theme. It fits our skating style, and it even fits the rumors about us. It may be a little heavy for the skating crowd, but we can tone it down to where it's just a subtle undercurrent."

"I think I like it. Run it by me again."

"OK, here's you. First, you're the perfectly sweet little angel that any Maude and Claude would just love to have as their granddaughter. Second, you're an innocent child whose body has recently developed into flowering womanhood. You're budding sexiness shows up in the way you look and the way you move. You're on the brink of adulthood, but you don't realize it yet. You haven't noticed you're getting sexy."

"OK."

"Third, you're energetic and playful. This forms the basis for your teasing me, see?"

"Yeah."

"Forth, you're also curious. Curious about adult type things. This is what puts you in danger around me. Can you dig it?"

"Well, duh! You just described me, Dean."

"Good," he replied sarcastically. "Then you won't have any trouble skating the part."

"What about you? Let me do you. You're arrogant. A real macho asshole, and you've really got the hots for me. You want to just throw me down and screw me on the ice."

"Whoa, let's back up a little. First, I'm smug. Smug to the point of arrogance, as you pointed out. I'm having fun out there, and the audience is having fun watching me, and I know it. Hence the smugness."

"OK."

"Second. I'm your loyal protector. I take care of you, kinda like a daddy. No, more like a big brother. I lift you, and show you off, and keep you from bumping your pretty little head on that hard old ice."

"Yeah."

"Now third. We occasionally see evidence of a hidden agenda. I may have a darker, unwholesome interest in you. There's just a hint of it, but it could be really bad. Your innocence could be in serious danger."

"Yeah!"

"But you're so innocent and playful you don't realize the danger."

"Ooh! Sounds like I'm in a lot to trouble!"

"Fourth," he continued. "My desire for you becomes an obsession, a weakness that you can use to control me. Then I become your plaything. You have fun manipulating me, using my desire as a means of control."

"Cool!"

"Number five. After a while, my lust turns to love, as does your playful manipulation. If the process goes all the way to completion, then we're finally united in love. I'm redeemed by your innocence, or some such bullshit, and you're fulfilled as a woman. That would be the whole cycle. I guess most routines wouldn't go that far, but some could."

"OK, summarize it for me."

Dean inhaled. "I am the sinister and powerful man in the shadows of the domain where you frolic. At first I merely observe you while you play. I'm like a father figure, looking out for you as I do for all the gentle creatures of the forest. As the dance develops, though, I begin to notice you as a woman, not as a child, and I develop dark and evil intentions toward you as you frolic with innocent abandon. The audience will begin to wonder if you'll escape with your virtue intact, or fall victim to my evil desires."

"Great, only what if we add this? Eventually I notice that you get turned on, and it amuses me, see? Then I begin to tease you, subtly but deliberately, just to see the effect. The audience will then be wondering if I can get away with it, flirting with danger like that, or if you'll just throw me down and screw my brains out right there on the ice."

"That's good," Dean said, "Although I would state it more delicately."

"To Hell with delicately! We'll have the hottest act at the competition," Shannon blurted confidently.

"That's actually consistent with a lot of nineteenth century literature, and a bunch of movies from the twenties and thirties that had the nymphet theme. It's kind of the Lolita thing. It breeds mystery on two counts. Does he love her like a daughter and only want to protect her from the dangers of the world, or … is he a deadly stalker, harboring an evil desire to degrade and debase her? And what about her? Is she really the innocent child, oblivious to the ways of the adult world? Or is she a scheming Lolita, relishing the things she can make him do with only a simple girlish movement? Who is really the victim here, her or him?"

"Yeah, so they'll argue about it. Maude will say I'm an innocent child, and you're a dirty old man, but Claude will say you're just a guy, and I'm a teasing little slut!"

"Something like that. Anyway. it'll keep 'em coming back for more, as long as we keep the mystery going."

"Cool!"

"But we'll have to work that theme into the routine very, very subtly, though," Dean added. "Otherwise we'd be drummed out of the Corps by the judges. Figure skating is a refined family sport. We have to pretend we're only in it for the art."

Shannon grinned. "I can do the Lolita thing. Just watch me!"

"I'm sure you can," he grinned. "I've seen your work."

Nymphets

Shannon took on a puzzled frown. "What exactly is a nymphet anyway, Dean? I mean, I looked it up and all, but it only says is 'a sexually desirable young woman. There's got to be more to it than that."

"Well," he began. "According to the experts, there are two types of nymphets. First we have the woman-child, the young girl with pretty face and as yet undeveloped body who has become aware of the effect she can have on the opposite sex. And since boys her age aren't interested in girls, that means older men. She uses coquettish facial expressions and girlish movements to attract the interest of older men."

"You mean, she teases old guys?"

"Not exactly. Her actions are not overtly sexy. She is innocence personified. She just knows which girlish moves produce which reactions in men. She's basically into attracting attention to herself, both for the sheer satisfaction of it, and for the rewards it brings. You see this in the young girl who sings and dances for her grandfather, and he rewards her with a stick of gum. She doesn't know about sex yet, although she senses that the old gentlemen might like to do something truly naughty to her if he thought he could get away with it.

"OK, so what's the other kind?"

"That's the girl whose body has matured faster than her mind. She's a child in the body of a woman. She doesn't realize she's walking around in something that a whole lot of dirty old men would just love to get their hands on. She has 'em drooling over her, but she hasn't a clue."

"'The body of a woman and the mind of a child.' You said that about me once."

"These nymphets are exactly the opposite of the other kind. They have the sexy body, at least the beginnings of one, but they don't have a clue about what effect they have on men."

"Which type am I?" Shannon asked, grinning.

"Actually, you're a third type. The body of a child and the mind of a child. This group is commonly called ... 'children'."

"That's bullshit, Dean! This is not the body of a child!" She thrust out her hip defiantly.

"OK," he admitted. "You're in the early stages of flowering womanhood. Maybe you're a type two nymphet."

"Yeah, but I don't have the mind of a child. I'm way too mature. What does that make me?"

"It would make you a sexy young woman ... if it were true."

"Sexy bitch, Dean! That's me."

"Whatever. But I've seen you come on as both types of nymphet."

"When?" she demanded indignantly.

"Well, you work your dear ole dad pretty well when you want something from him. I think these chicks usually cut their teeth on Daddy, and then they find out it works on most older men as well."

Shannon pondered what he had said. "So, when am I the other one?"

"When you pull your 'poor little waif' act on me, for instance. You pout and whine and bat your eyelashes. It's classic. My heart would just overflow with pity and sympathy if I didn't know it was pure bullshit."

She gave him a pouty look. "Check the mirror, Kid," he said. "There it is, right there."

"OK, but now I'm confused. How am I gonna use all this nymphet business in my skating?"

"Well, start with 'sexy bitch' as your basic persona. Then, if you drop the flirtatious behavior and substitute wide-eyed innocence, then you're the voluptuous child. On the other hand, if you downplay your physical maturity and emphasize your youth, but you still tease, then you're the saucy woman-child. And you can move back and forth from one to the other at will."

"OK, so in one program, I might start out as, you know, innocent and stuff, and then get really sexy by the end, right?"

"If that's what the story and the music call for, yeah."

"Cool! Or maybe I can start out teasing you, like, accidentally, and then, when I see what it does to you, I can do it on purpose."

"I can hardly wait to see the video tape."

She grinned.

Evolution

"So, where do dirty old men come from, Dean? I mean, why do you hear so much about it? Are all men really like that?"

"Well, let's look at the survival value of being a dirty old man. Remember evolutionary biology? I'll have the traits of my ancestors, and they're the ones who had grandkids, right?"

"Yeah. I remember."

"OK, let's say there are two young men in a primitive village a million years ago. One is attracted to older women, and the other one likes young girls."

"OK."

"How many kids is each one gonna have?"

"OK, so older women make better mothers, and their kids will survive better. And a girl can't get pregnant if she's too young. So that guy who likes old broads is your grandfather, right?"

"There is truth in what you say. But older women were wiser and less likely to find themselves pregnant if they didn't want to be. They were just generally harder to get than an innocent, vulnerable girl who doesn't know any better. And women had a rather brief span of fertility back then, so a lot of his reproductive effort would be wasted on older women who can no longer conceive. So, he's probably not in my family tree."

"OK, so what about the other one, then?"

"As he gets older he'll find it easier to take advantage of young girls. He will accumulate knowledge, power and possessions. He can bribe them with food from the hunt and other trinkets, for example. If he focuses his attentions on young girls he can sire a whole bunch of offspring over time."

"So, he's your great granddaddy?"

"More than likely."

"I can't believe you're such a beast!" she teased. "You just prey on innocent young girls like me!"

"It's a heavy burden, to be sure."

"So, you are a dirty old man! You've got the gene for it! You're just lurking around, waiting to grab me and throw me down on the ground!"

"It kinda makes you think, don't it?"

She grinned. "OK, Dean. So, how long are you going to be able to resist this urge? How much time do I have?"

"It could happen at any time." He looked at his watch and took on a sinister look. "When you least expect it."

"Oh, my God! I'm in constant danger!"

"Forewarned is forearmed."

"This is too cool! You're like a ticking time bomb, waiting to pop!"

"Can you skate that? Can you show it to an audience?"

"Sure, Dean! I can frolic and light your fuse. Then I can run away from you in terror. But I won't actually get away. By the end of the program I'll give in, and you'll get me."

"I think we have a theme!" he announced, "And it just might get us thrown out of the sport."

Lolita

Shannon laughed. Then she took on a quizzical look. "OK, so how do I do the Lolita thing? I mean, what's she really like?"

"Maybe you should do some research. Read the book, or watch the movie."

"Oh, my God, Dean!" she erupted, "Let's rent the movie and watch it together!"

"OK. I'll get it tomorrow. We can watch it tomorrow night."

The following day they went to Dean's apartment after their last practice. "Did you rent that movie?" she asked excitedly.

"I certainly did," he responded. "I had to go to three Blockbusters to find it, though. It's gettin' kinda obscure."

"OK, Dean," she said. "I'll make the popcorn while you get it ready." She soon emerged from his kitchen with a bowl of popcorn.

"This is a Stanley Kubrick movie," he explained, "So it has Kubrick characters in it. They kinda wear their weaknesses on their sleeve. And he put the ending first and then flashed back for the rest of the story."

"Why'd he do that?"

"I think he wanted to capture our attention before we lost interest. The story starts off kinda slow. Also, it was 1962, and films like that had big problems with censors. This kinda made it into a murder story ... instead of a sex film. However, for your convenience, I copied it to a blank tape and put it in chronological sequence for you."

"Cool! Let's see it."

They munched the popcorn and watched the movie.

"That was kinda sad," Shannon observed when it ended. "Nobody lived happily ever after."

"Yeah, most of 'em didn't live at all. All four main characters died. It's kind of a tragedy, I guess."

"How old was she?"

"Lolita was only twelve in the book, but Kubrick made her fourteen, initially, in the film. Sue Lyon was sixteen when she played the role, but with makeup she looked about eighteen on camera. That took some of the heat off of Kubrick. He'd have been crucified if he had put up James Mason goin' at it with a twelve-year-old. But it also changed the nature of the story. The movie was kind of a tragic May-December romance, but the book was presented as the diary of a pervert. Humbert wrote his memoirs in jail, awaiting trial for killing Quilty."

"So did Lolita ever love Humbert? Even a little?"

"No. The book made that very clear. She just tolerated him, and used him, kinda like he had used her mother. He gave her stuff and took care of her. She mainly didn't want to go to an orphanage after her mom died, so she played along with his fantasy. Her two years with Humbert were just a bad dream she endured. Besides, she said Quilty was the only man she was ever crazy about."

"The guy Humbert killed, right? He was a pedophile too."

"Yeah. Peter Sellers' character. Lolita was carrying on with him the whole time too. She was a busy girl. She eventually ran away with Quilty, but when she refused to star in his porno flick, he threw her out."

"So, Humbert was just a dirty old man?"

"Definitely. He would bribe her with gifts and, later, with money to have sex with him, then he'd search her room and steal the money back. She was trying to save up enough cash to run away from him. Even though she didn't get along with her mother, playing Humbert's game was even worse." He paused. "But, after she did run away, he kinda seemed to fall in love with her. Obsession turned to love, I guess. At the end he wanted her to come live with him, even though she was old and ugly and married and pregnant. In fact, he loved her so much he wrote his memoirs just to immortalize her, or so he said."

"What do you mean by that?"

"My English prof at UT said the book was really Humbert's dishonest apology, written simply to beg the jury for pity. He thinks Hum was lying about Lolita's complicity, and how she abused him, and even how he loved her in the end. He pointed out that she once referred to their first hotel as 'that place where you raped me.' He thinks she was a totally innocent victim of

Humbert's perverted lust, and Hum was just trying to save his skin with his memoirs."

"So, why did he kill Quilty? Because of what he did to Lolita?"

"No, because of what Quilty did to him. Humbert bore a terrible guilt burden because he knew he had denied Lolita a normal childhood, and ruined her life, basically. But he planned to atone for his sins by marrying her and raising a litter of little Lolitas. In his mind this would have made up the damage. By taking her away, Quilty denied him that opportunity for atonement."

"Kinda like you, Dean! You're denying me a normal childhood."

"You're the one denying you a normal childhood," he responded. "I'm a minor actor in your movie."

"So, Humbert said he did love Lolita? At the end, I mean."

"Yeah, but it would have to be a very compulsive, possessive kind of love. I think he misjudged her badly. He didn't actually know her at all. He had some fantasy that made him see her as a woman in a child's body, but she was really just a little girl. He would read her poetry and then not notice that she was simply bored by it. She said Edgar Allen Poe was 'corny.' He wanted a mature woman in a little girl's body, but such things don't exist. Hummer was pretty well blinded by his image of her."

"So, was it really bad – what Humbert did to her?"

"Well, society frowned on it severely, as you saw, and his 'victim' didn't come out of it in very good condition either. But he's the one who suffered the most from the relationship. First, he was tormented by the guilty secret he carried, and constantly afraid he'd be found out, and Quilty tormented him all throughout the story. And as Lolita began to realize the power she had over him, she made it pretty rough on him too. All the while, he kept expecting her to act responsibly, like his image of her, and she never would, because she was just a self-centered little kid."

"Kinda like you and me, huh?" She grinned.

"Hey! There is an analogy there," he teased.

"So, she was really a bitch, huh?"

"Well, it wasn't her fault he was obsessed. She just took advantage of it when she realized it was so easy to jerk him around. And she had very little regard for his feelings. But neither did he for her mom, and he really abused Lo for selfish purposes, so I guess he kinda deserved it."

"Yeah, like she didn't even care when he was having a heart attack!"

"Right. He was hopelessly obsessed with her, but she didn't have any fondness for him. She just made the best of the situation she found herself in. It was survival for her. That was clear at the end. She considered her two years with him just a bad dream that she finally woke up from. And I think she even enjoyed seeing him get upset. It amused her that she had such control over him. She could turn a dignified professor into a child's plaything with a word or a glance. Of course, his affection kinda smothered her, too. That was the downside."

"So, she wasn't a bitch, then?"

"Well, she can be criticized for a lack of respect for her step-dad, and she was selfish and irresponsible. But she was just a kid who had been put in a very bad situation, and she mainly just took advantage of Humbert's obsession. That's what made the whole thing work. He had this weakness for her, and she learned to use it against him."

"How was the book different from the movie?"

"Well, in Nabokov's novel, Humbert just simply liked nymphets. The only thing special about Lolita, at first, was that she belonged to him. He felt very fortunate about that. He had married her mother in order to hang around and look at her, and when Mom conveniently died, he became her only living relative. Then he just made screwing her his life's work."

"Really?"

"Yeah. He said he enjoyed sex with a mature woman as much as any man, but that having sex with a nymphet was ten times better, the pinnacle of existence – as good as it gets. He tolerated her insults and fits of temper because she gave him access to her little pre-pubescent bod. He would buy her whatever she wanted, but it was always a bribe. He would make coffee for her in the morning and then not give her any until she had sex with him. If she got too uncooperative, he would threaten to send her to an orphanage, or a reform school. It was all bullshit, though, 'cause he'd never willingly let her go. He kept her enslaved, actually."

"Shit!"

"Yeah. He took her on a year-long 'vacation,' all over the country, from one motel to the next, just so he could have sex with her several times a day. And it wasn't love then. He just wanted to exert his power over her and use her nymphet body for his bizarre gratification."

"Wow!"

"You see," Dean said, waxing philosophical, "When a guy wants to have sex, he needs access to a female body. So he has to deal with the woman who owns it. Some guys send flowers. Others get 'em drunk ..."

"Some guys skate with 'em!" Shannon interjected.

"I wouldn't know about that."

"Ha! That's what you're using on me, you cad! You brute!" She giggled.

"Don't flatter yourself, Kid" he frowned at her from underneath his eyebrows. "Anyway, a pedophile considers a child easy to deal with. He can use a combination of bribes and intimidation to get her cooperation, and a true nymphet has that combination of curiosity and naughtiness that lets him get her once. From then on, it's all downhill. His main problem then is keeping the big secret. He has to be really careful."

"So, who's using who then?"

"Both, actually. He's using threats and bribes to get sex from a child, but she's using his obsession to get him to act like an idiot. In the end, though, he's the villain because he should know better. She's just a kid. She can't be expected to have the knowledge and integrity to resist him." Shannon paused to contemplate that. "Humbert had a eye for other nymphets too," Dean continued. "And he even spotted a couple who were maybe better than Lolita. But she belonged to him, so he just kept what he had. The point is, he was into nymphets, and he was lucky enough to get one as his step-daughter. He didn't want to lose her, or even let her grow up. He wanted the fantasy to go on forever."

"He didn't like grown-up girls?"

"No. He thought college-age girls were disgusting. He said their lumpy bodies were caskets inside which a nymphet was buried alive. He figured that when Lolita grew up he'd get her pregnant so she could make him a new nymphet. He would have loved to have sex with his own nine-year-old daughter."

"Ick!"

"Humbert said it takes a true pervert to spot the nymphet in a group of girl children. They have a special look, he said. A certain combination of innocence and eerie vulgarity."

"You could do it, Dean. You could spot 'em. You da man! You da man!" she cheered him.

"I don't share Humbert's particular form of mental disease," Shannon.

"Well, maybe you're not a real prevert, but you've got an eye for Lolitas. I just know it."

"I don't think so."

"Sure you do. Come on, Dean. We'll give you a test." She grinned mischievously. "Am I a nymphet?"

"Uh, that's an easy one. You are not."

"What?" She was wide-eyed with shock and disappointment.

"Sorry kid. You're too old. Too many curves and bulges. Humbert says a girl's nymphet years are age nine through fourteen. He'd puke if he had to touch you now."

She took on a puzzled frown. "OK, was I a nymphet when I was younger?"

"I didn't know you when you were younger."

"Come on, Dean. You've seen lots of pictures and videos of me when I was young. Was I a nymphet?"

"I hope not."

"Why?" She was puzzled.

"Because nymphets, according to Humbert, are not very bright, but they are curious and cunningly naughty. They have a sleaziness about them. They give off a sense of low morals, like they would be willing to do something naughty, even if they didn't understand or enjoy it, as long as they got something in return."

"Huh. I thought they were just sexy."

"Well, there is such a thing as a sexy little girl. You may well have been that. But a true Humbertian nymphet is probably not something you would aspire to."

"Do you think I was sexy when I was little?"

"I refuse to answer." He gave her a "So there!" look.

"What! You can't refuse to answer! You have to tell me!"

"Says whom?" He regarded her smugly.

"Says me! Don't be a jerk, Dean, for Pete's sake! This is important!"

Dean sighed, as if relenting reluctantly. "OK, Foster," he began, "If I had any interest in preteen pulchritude, which I don't, and if I had known you when you were twelve or thirteen, which I didn't, I might have thought, 'Boy, I'd sure like to have that little Foster girl sit in my lap for a minute! I could run my hands up and down those spindly little legs and squeeze that narrow little butt, and maybe even kiss those thin little lips before she either says something totally irritating or does something completely repulsive.' Something like that."

Shannon gave him a disgusted glare. "No, Dean. I'd sit in your lap and giggle and be cute, and your heart would start pounding and you'd start sweating, and you'd get this huge desire to touch me all over and kiss me and stuff."

"Stuff?" He raised his eyebrows.

"Yeah. You know … stuff."

"Well, have fun with your fantasy, Shannon."

She made a face at him. "What a jerk old Humbert was!" she said.

"Yeah. You can see why Kubrick had to soften the story a bit in 1962. His version was almost just an off-beat love story between a teenager and an older man. Humbert's bizarre perversion didn't come out so strong, even though it was the central theme of the book."

"But, did Lolita like it? In the book, I mean."

"Not much. I think she just tolerated it. She cried herself to sleep every night. At twelve, a girl's estrogen hasn't had time to turn her body in to a sex machine yet, and having a grunting, groaning adult on top of her isn't very appealing. Lolita would only do kissing mouth-to-mouth, and straight intercourse. No licking and sucking and stuff. Except Humbert would sometimes caress her naked bod while she read movie magazines and popped her gum."

"Humm." Shannon was deep in thought.

"Eventually she began to realize the power she had over him. Not only did she supply the only thing in life that mattered to him, but she knew his horribly guilty secret as well. She could get pretty rough on him at times. Life with Humbert was no picnic, but it was better than an orphanage, so she didn't ever blow the whistle on him. But she would threaten him with it."

"Maybe I should read the book."

"Probably not."

"Why not, Dean? Too hot for me? Is that what you think?"

"No. It was published in 1955. The prose is tame by today's standards. It's just that Nabokov was an English prof, and those guys are as obsessed with words and Humbert was with nymphets. I had to read it with a dictionary in the other hand. I had to look up at least a couple of words on every page. He would include whole sentences in French, with no translation. Reading it was very hard work."

"That's OK. I know lots of words. Try one on me."

"OK, 'parsimonious.' What's it mean?"

"Uh, it means it sounds good."

"Oh, like harmonious?"

"Yeah, kinda."

"Wrong, Mini-brain. It means miserly, tightwad, stingy with a buck."

"Yeah, that's what I meant."

"I'm sure it was," he grinned.

"So, are you obsessed with me, Dean?" She grinned mischievously.

"Completely," he grinned. "I'm a victim of your childlike charm. Why else would I put up with your cheap bullshit?"

"That's bullshit! I can't make you do anything. You're a monster!"

"Well, that too, I suppose." They laughed.

"OK, Dean, I think you oughta be obsessed with me. Like Humbert. It'd be good for our skating."

"That's your assessment, Professor?"

"Yeah. It'd be cool. Can you do it?"

83

"I can act it if necessary, but a true obsession like that is pathological. I wouldn't want to really have one."

"Oh, come on, Dean! Be obsessed with me!"

"OK, maybe you're right. Sometimes, like right now, I have this intense urge to just throw you down, peel the soft silk panties off your tender young buns, and …,"

He paused. Shannon was wide-eyed.

"… paddle your little bottom for all the tacky things you do!"

"Not cool, Dean. What we want is sexual obsession here. You need to crave me in a carnal way. Like Humbert craved Lolita."

"Well, I think I'll pass on the craving for now," he said. "Paddling you would do us both a lot more good."

"No fun, Steele! You are no fun!"

"No felon, Foster. I am no felon. Doesn't that count for something? Humbert would have been tarred and feathered by an angry mob if anybody had found out what he did to that little girl."

"OK, Dean. I just think it'd be fun to have you mooning over me like that. You wanna paint my toenails?"

"You'd lose respect for me, Shannon. Lolita didn't respect Humbert. She considered him a clown … disgusting even."

"No problem, Dean. I already think you're a clown!"

Shannon shrieked when he grabbed her, and she giggled uncontrollably as he tickled her ribs.

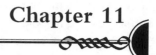

Chapter 11

Trashy Women

"Did you hear?" the girl said. "Dean's skating to 'Trashy Women' tonight at Club Ice!"

"Oh, my God! I can't believe it," the other girl squealed.

"Yeah, Darlene saw his tape. It said on the label, 'Trashy Women.'"

"Oh, my God! That has got to be too cool!"

Shannon

"Hey, Dean," Shannon said, "The chatter in the caf is, you're skating to 'Trashy Women' tonight."

"Just kinda proves you can hear anything in 'the caf' doesn't it?"

"Why won't you tell me what your routine is, you shit? I'm your partner, for Pete's sake!"

"The need to know, Sweetcakes. You ain't got it!"

"That's bullshit. You're just an asshole, and proud of it."

"Everybody needs a hobby," he said.

"With you it's a profession, you shithook!" He blew her a kiss.

The Performance

As 7:30 approached the anticipation of Dean's routine filled the chilly air at the Texas Ice Stadium. Girls and women began to gravitate toward the ice. All they had been told was that Dean would premier a new singles number at Club Ice at 7:30. With the stir his dogtag dance had created, there was considerable interest and speculation.

"Skaters, please clear the ice," the announcer said. There was a moderate scramble for good viewing position along the rail as the last few stragglers vacated the sheet.

Dean skated out to center ice in an elegant business suit. A murmur went through the crowd. The music started with a heavy beat. A scream erupted when several of the girls recognized the introduction to the song "Trashy Women" by Confederate Railroad. Dean danced in an animated style to the heavy beat during the instrumental intro. Then he skated the first verse in a snooty, arrogant style.

At the end of the first verse he ripped off the tearaway suit, revealing a much louder, but considerably less classy outfit underneath. He skated the first chorus in a much more flamboyant style.

Dean skated to the rail and picked up a plastic mannequin wearing a white waitress dress, overstuffed boobs and a large platinum-blonde wig. It had working joints at its hips, knees, shoulders, and elbows. He skated the next verse with his new partner. With his right hand behind her back, he operated a handle that made her head turn in unison with his in the dance steps. The mannequin had Velcro on her feet that he attached to Velcro on the toes of his boots. He held her right hand in his left, and her left arm curled around his back. This way she followed his lead perfectly as he waltzed around the arena.

He put the doll away and skated the second chorus, last verse and third chorus with classic moves, jumps and spins.

The conclusion of the number was met by cheers and wild applause. Many of the girls and women were throwing him hugs and kisses. Some threw flowers onto the ice.

Millie

Millie caught Dean as he was packing his skate bag. "Trashy women, Dean?" she said from beneath raised eyebrows.

"Hello, Millie."

"That was cute, Dean, The only problem is, all the little girls around here will be soon be wearing, 'too much lipstick and too much rouge.'"

"Sorry about that, Millie." he replied.

"No, you aren't! You love being the fantasy heartthrob of a hundred pubescent girls, not to mention a couple of dozen ice moms."

"I just skate the program," he said, "I don't write the songs."

"Oh, you're too modest, Dean." she replied in a catty voice. "You seduce those females every time you take to the ice. You could father a whole generation of new skaters."

"Thank you, Millie, for your kind words. Now get out of my face."

"No, Dean, wait! I'm sorry. I wasn't …"

"Wasn't what?"

"I wasn't… very nice. You did a great job developing and presenting that program. I'm terribly proud of you. It's just …"

"Just what?"

"Damn it, Dean. I get extremely jealous when I see you do that. I don't like sharing you with those bitches, especially the ice moms. I'm sorry, but I'm not completely rational where you're concerned."

"OK, Millie. Thanks for the complement on my routine."

"Am I forgiven?"

"Completely. Now … get out of my face." They laughed.

Chapter 12

The Queen's Closet

Dean didn't quite know what to expect when he answered the door. He had once again agreed to meet with Millie to work on competition programs. Millie stood there in what was, for her, a rather conservative business suit. She carried a small black leather bag.

"Why, Millie," he said, smiling, "You look positively … decent." He assumed that the adventure of her previous visits was now over.

"Would you be a dear and let me freshen up a bit?" she asked. "I spent most of the day in a stuffy meeting, and I smell like a horse that's been rode hard and put up wet."

"You pay the rent now, Ma'am. Use whatever facilities you desire."

"No, Dean. It's still your home," she lectured, "Despite whatever financial arrangements we've made. I'm here as your guest, and strictly by your invitation."

"Then, may I invite you to use the local accommodations to your heart's content?"

"You may. Damn, I hate those marathon boredom-fests!"

She disappeared into his bathroom for about ten minutes. Dean, though relieved that her prick-teasing phase had finally passed, nonetheless felt a twinge of disappointment. Spending an hour with Millie, when she was in her sexy mode, was a thoroughly enjoyable experience, even if it did tend to brutalize his ego.

Millie emerged in a daring cocktail dress that could only have come from Frederick's of Hollywood. Her hair and makeup had been completely redone, and she looked immaculate. She also looked even sexier even than on her previous visits.

"Damn, Millie!" Dean exclaimed. Then he sighed.

"What is it Dean? I was miserable in that stuffy suit."

"Millie," he said in a pained voice, "Haven't we established that you are the most beautiful, and sexiest woman on the planet, and that I'm helpless to resist your overwhelming appeal and irresistible charm? Hasn't that been in all the papers and on the evening news? Can't we just get on with the skating?"

"I don't know what you're talking about," she said, flashing him a deliberately blank look.

"That outfit, Millie. You look way too good to work on skating routines."

"Nonsense, Dean. I picked this little thing up because it was cool and comfortable. And it was on sale too."

Dean signed as he realized that Millie was still playing her game. This was merely round three. "What do you want from me, Millie?" he asked. "What do you want me to say that I haven't already said?"

"It's simple, Dear Boy. I want you to win a medal skating with my darling daughter."

Dean groaned. He realized he was in for another of her teasing sessions. She would again flaunt her voluptuous body in front of him, he would again display his involuntary response to her, and she would once more gloat unmercifully about his arousal. He paused to collect his thoughts. It irritated him that she would continue to use him in this way to gratify her ego once her point had been made. He looked at her and took a few deep breaths.

His frustration subsided as he gazed at her. She was indeed beautiful, and amazingly sexy. He marveled at how appealing she was, standing in his den, radiating sex appeal. "OK," he thought, "What's so bad about having such a specimen to ogle for a while?" He decided to enjoy her to the fullest, and if he must endure her gloating over his lack of self-control, it was a small price to pay for an afternoon's entertainment.

"Well, let's get to it," he said.

Millie began to describe her ideas for costumes and music for a program that complied with the requirements for a novice-level short program. It was well-conceived, and she described it in animated tones.

After a time Dean's attention began to drift from the oration to the speaker. Soon he was more watching her than listening to what she had to say. The intoxication began to take effect, and his thoughts began to focus on her body parts. He felt a tension in his groin, followed by an expansion.

"Are you listening to me, Dean? I swear you have this glazed over look that says you're a million miles away."

"I'm right here, Millie," he responded, matter-of-factly. He made no effort to hide his budding arousal, and she noticed it at that point.

"I'm sorry, Dean," she said, moving over to him. "I didn't mean to be short with you." her voice was soft and tender. "I just thought you had drifted away from me."

"I drifted away, all right," he said, "But it wasn't from you." She raised her eyebrows in puzzlement. "Millie," he asked, "Why do you do this? Why do you come over here looking so damn gorgeous?"

"Dean," she explained. "I'm the morale officer in this group, among many other roles that I play. My job is to keep everybody happy. Shannon, Fred ... you. And if I can show you a pretty face while you work endlessly on this skating project, then you'll be happier, and you'll do better at it. That's all."

"This goes way beyond a pretty face, Millie."

She grinned. "You're a strong, healthy ... and virile young man, Dean. And as such, you can appreciate more than a woman's face. So I have the ability to ... entertain you, shall we say. It's just another way to keep you happy and in top form."

"But there's a problem, Millie," he offered. "You're a married woman; my partner's mother; my sponsor's wife. When you tease me like this, it's ... bizarre, that's all. And grabbing my dick, as you have done in the past? Now, that's totally out of bounds."

"Dean," she began softly, "What we do over here is nobody's business. Nobody will ever know. If it doesn't hurt you or me, it can't possibly harm anybody at all. Besides, we haven't done anything wrong. Just a couple of little things we need to keep to ourselves, that's all."

Dean sighed. "OK, Millie. I enjoy working with you, and I appreciate the trouble you take to ... 'entertain' me. And you are knockout gorgeous to be sure. Let's just color inside the lines, shall we? It just gets too bizarre if we don't keep it under control."

"Why, Dean Steele, I'm shocked!" she responded. "Surely you don't think I'd even consider doing anything tacky over here!"

Dean grinned at the woman who only two days before was fondling his private parts. "Of course not, Millie," he replied. "You're a choir angel, and I'm an altar boy."

Laughter erupted from the woman. "OK, Dean," she said. "We're consenting adults, here. We won't do anything tacky. But we deserve a little bit of leeway because we work so hard, that's all."

"OK," Dean said. "A little leeway, then." They grinned at each other.

"Now that we've got that all settled," she grinned mischievously, "Why don't you show me what you've got for me?"

"You're incorrigible, Millie," Dean chuckled.

"Only where you're concerned, Young Man," she replied.

They resumed their work on the skating program. Millie teased, Dean responded, and Millie gleefully noticed the outward manifestation of his desire for her.

"OK, she said at last. I think we just about have it." She looked at him. "I think I need a hug before I go."

"Is it one of 'those' hugs?" he inquired.

"A hug is just a hug, Dean," she lectured. "What are you afraid of?"

He sighed at the challenge she had issued to him. She was implying he was afraid to hug her. He now had to do it to save his honor.

"Am I going to do this?" he asked himself. "Am I going to let the Ice Queen grab me again and then gloat about it?" He sighed. "Come here, Millie," he said. "Give me a big ole hug!"

A smile broke out on her face at his submission. She moved slowly into his arms. "You like me, don't you, Dean?" she whispered.

"I'm your biggest fan," he chuckled.

"You think I'm pretty, don't you?"

"No, I think you're drop dead gorgeous."

"You think I'm sexy, don't you?"

"I'm thoroughly convinced of it," he said. "I could write a book."

"You get a physical reaction to me, don't you?"

"I get a rack of hardwood, Millie," he explained dryly. "Are you satisfied?"

"No, Dean, I'm merely complimented. I'm glad you respond to me."

"You're a tease, Millie. and a very talented one. You can get me going with almost no effort at all."

Dean had finally become comfortable with admitting that she turned him on. It was undeniable physiological fact, and nothing to be ashamed of. Besides, it seemed to do her so much good. He considered it a harmless way to gratify the woman and keep her happy. Even her merciless gloating was somewhat amusing, though irritating as well.

Millie's hand deftly slipped under his waistband and inside his shorts and closed softly around his enlarged, if not totally rigid shaft. "My goodness, Dean," she cooed, "You've been thinking naughty thoughts about the Ice Queen again."

"Fancy that!" he mumbled sarcastically. The organ immediately began to expand further under her gentle touch, aided by the sheer eroticism of the situation.

"Oh, Dean, Look what you're doing!" she exclaimed. "You're making it bigger!"

"Uh, you're driving that train, Madam," he replied. "I'm just a passenger here."

"I can't believe how it just keeps getting bigger," she cooed. "I hope it doesn't burst!"

Dean stood still, enduring her chiding as she amused herself at his expense. He might have called a halt to the proceedings, except she seemed to be enjoying it too much, and he didn't want to be teased about being afraid to let her do it. He also took satisfaction in the steady flow of compliments on his manhood, even if they were punctuated by her insufferable gloating, and the strong implication that he had no self-control where she was concerned.

"I have to see it, Dean," she said. "Just stand real still."

She slipped her other hand under his waistband in preparation to slide his pants down. Dean was shocked. Would she really expose him like this? Would he actually allow her to drop his pants? While he was pondering those mysteries, his pants began to slip smoothly down his thigh.

"Oh, My God!" she swooned before he could respond, "It's huge!" She looked at him. "This is amazing, Dean. I can't wait to tell all my girlfriends." Perhaps it was shock at her audacity that held the young man suspended. Or maybe it was simply the determined woman's intense intention, but some unseen force kept him frozen in position as he stood for his examination. Millie dropped slowly to a squatting position, bringing her face-to-face with the object of her interest. "It's beautiful," she mused.

Suddenly Dean snapped out of the trance. He pulled up his pants, and Millie stood up to face him. "Party pooper!" she said.

"Now, that was tacky," he scolded her.

"Come on, Dean," he pleaded in a pouty voice, "It wasn't so bad, now was it? You could just let the Ice Queen see what you brought out for her, can't you? You can be forgiven for that. Besides, you've already let me feel it several times."

Dean chuckled in amazement. The woman who had teased an erection out of him, and then fondled it for her amusement, was now offering him forgiveness for his misbehavior. "Millie," he said sternly, "Do not pull my pants down, OK? It's a tacky thing to do!"

"You have nothing to be ashamed of, Dean" she said. "It's a beautiful thing. You should be proud to be such a stud."

"Whether or not I'm a stud is not a matter of your concern."

She put on a mildly hurt look. "But, Dean. We're friends. We appreciate each other. You appreciate my beauty, and I appreciate your … manly charm."

"So, what is it you really want, Millie?" What's the bottom line?"

"OK, Dean," she began, "Two things. First, I want you to be happy. And I want you to understand the awesome power you have so you can use it in your skating." She paused.

Dean stopped to think. Maybe she was doing to him what he was doing to Shannon … bringing out his sexuality for the benefit of his skating. Or maybe she was just a psychotic housewife dramatizing her sexual hang-ups. He couldn't decide.

"And second," she continued, "I'd like to borrow a little bit of closet space. I have to change clothes twice at a gas station in Clear Lake City every time

I come over here. If I could keep a few things in one of your closets, it would save me an awful lot of hassle."

One thing was sure. If he allowed her to keep her sexy dresses and shoes at his apartment, he would be in for many more of these teasing incidents. "Do you think it's worth the trouble?" he asked. "I mean, will we be working on these routines much longer?"

"Oh, I don't know. But I can't work in those stuffy business suits, and if I have to change clothes one more time in that filthy rest room, with those dirty old men leering at me when I go in and come out, I think I'll just scream!"

A grin came across Dean's face as he pondered the idea of Millie being disgusted by having men 'leer' at her, no matter how dirty and old. He didn't know what he would be getting himself into by letting her maintain a sexy wardrobe in his apartment, but he was fresh out of valid objections to her proposal. "OK," he said. "I'll clean out a spot in … that small closet in the hall."

"Thanks, Sweetie," she said. "You're a dear. Make some room in there while I go out and get the rest of my things."

Dean grinned to himself when he realized she had come over fully equipped with her wardrobe, knowing that she would leave it there. He moved some items to another closet, and Millie returned with an armload of apparel. "I would have offered to help if I'd known it was such a load," he said, grinning. "It looks like you'll be staying a while."

"Oh, nonsense," she fluttered. "It's just a couple of comfortable old things I had lying around. Rather than throw them away, I might as well just leave them over here, in case I ever need them." She hung the garments on the pole and put a bag of shoes and a makeup kit on the floor. "Thanks, Sweetie," she said, giving him a peck on the cheek.

"My pleasure," he said, wondering what she would look like in those "comfortable old things" she had just deposited, one of which still sported a price tag.

Millie went into his bathroom and changed back into her business suit. When she emerged, she added the cocktail dress to her wardrobe in Dean's closet. "Dean," she said, "I don't want you to worry about anything that happened today, OK? You did nothing wrong. We did nothing wrong. It's just our private time, understand?"

Dean grinned. "Yes, Mom," he said.

Her eyebrows raised as she grinned at his joke. "I just want to take good care of you, that's all," she said. "I just want you to be happy and well-adjusted, OK?"

"With you around to 'adjust' me, how can I miss?"

She grinned. "'Bye, Sweetie." She left.

Dean went back and examined the sexy female wardrobe now residing in his closet. Millie's perfume hung in the air. He wondered what he was in for, now that he hosted the paraphernalia of her sexiness. He wondered if Millie would act differently toward him, now that she had viewed his organ in a fully aroused state. She clearly considered that a victory in their ongoing game of one-upmanship. Even if she never verbalized it, she could give him a self-satisfied grin that overflowed with gloating about her victory.

Chapter 13

The Walk

Dean was sitting on the white velvet sofa in the Foster's spacious living room in River Oaks. The expensive oil paintings on the walls were complemented by the mounted head of a deer that Fred had shot a few years before. "How's it going with your dance lessons?" Dean asked Shannon. "Do you like Celie?"

"Oh, yeah," Shannon replied while leafing through a magazine. "She's cool. You were right about her. She has serious moves."

"What's she got you doin'?"

"Oh, lots of stuff. She's mainly workin' on my moves."

"Moves?"

"Yeah, like walking, and stuff."

"She's teaching you how to walk?"

"No, Dum-dum. Not just walkin'. I call it prancing. It's way cool." Dean gave her a skeptical look. "No, really. It's too cool. I just strut around and look cool, like I'm a bitch, or something."

"That must be difficult," Dean said wryly.

"No, Dean. Lookin' cool is what I do!" Her nose wrinkled as her tongue protruded from between her lips.

"I see," was the skeptical reply.

"No, I'll show you. It's too cool! But I can't do it in jeans. I have to be standin' up on really tall heels." The girl retired to her bedroom for a few moments, emerging in a short dress and high heels. She loaded a CD and selected a track. "Now watch this, Punk!" she admonished.

The music erupted with a slow, heavy drum beat. Shannon tossed her head and gave Dean a hard sexy stare. Then she turned quickly away and began to cross the room in long strides. After a few steps she stopped and again looked at Dean. Her chin was down as she peered at him from beneath lowered eyebrows. It was an extremely condescending stare that harbored considerable disdain. Then suddenly she tossed her yellow mane, turned up her nose, and began to stride back across the room in step with the percussion coming from the speakers. At the end of this trek she again regarded Dean, this time with hands on hips and an extremely bored countenance.

Dean watched intently as the young woman's shapely calves, thighs and hips carried her gracefully back and forth across the room. He felt the vision of that movement gripping him. The sight was mesmerizing, and the message unmistakable. She was beautiful, she was sexy, she knew it, and she wanted absolutely nothing to do with him.

Shannon continued to prance back and forth across the room. Each stop was punctuated by a sexy pose, a disgusted stare, and a toss of her hair as she resumed her travels. Finally she curtailed the performance and stopped the music. "So, what did you think, Dean?" Cool, huh?"

"Mighty cool!" he replied. "Who was that babe, anyway. Is she new around here? What a fox! Kinda stuck up, though."

"She's a bitch, Dean. Real choosy about guys. Wouldn't give you the time of day, that's for sure!"

"I think I'll ask her out."

"Forget about it, Dean," Shannon laughed. "She's too stuck up. She wouldn't even say 'Hello' to ya!"

"No, really. Maybe if I put some really smooth moves on her ..."

"Ha! She'd break your heart, Dean. She's untouchable. She'd chew you up and spit you out!"

"I think I know how to get her."

"No way, Dean! Nobody gets her. She's a rock. She hates men. She gets off on how bad you want her, and she revels in your pain!"

"I gotta try!"

"She'll kill you, Dean! She'll rip your heart out and laugh in your face. She'll tease you 'till you're salivating, then she'll call you a clown! She'll stomp on your feelings, Cowboy."

"OK, Shannon. I'm impressed. I really like that look ... those moves. It's ... how shall I say it? ... Way cool!"

"Really? You really like it?"

"Yeah. It's real good to put in one of our programs. But, can you do it on the ice?"

"Umm, I don't know. I'm supposed to have high heels on."

"OK, that's the challenge, then. We gotta figure a way to get that same look in skating boots."

"How do I do that?"

"OK, OK, look," Dean said, becoming more excited. "Let's see ... stroking backward, uh, the face thing and the hair thing ... that's no problem. And your calves. You need to point your toe. Let's see, uh, alternating blades, leaving the other foot out in front of you, toe pointed. Maybe that'll work. We'll see what Celie thinks."

"You're really getin' into this, aren't you, Dean?"

"I think we can use it Shannon. It's good stuff. Actually you should be able to do it going forward or backward. Your hair will blow better skating forward. But if you're going backward, I can chase you."

"Dean! I can't believe this! You're actually going to make a routine around this?"

"We'll use it in our skating, Shannon. Some of the time, at least. It's a theme. It's good because it can be so … overdone. We can milk the Hell out of it. We can jam it in their faces. It can be made extremely intense. We can ham it up 'till the cows come home!"

"I'm not believin' this! I've never seen you get so worked up about something I do!"

"About our program, Shannon. About our act. We have to entertain an audience. And it's an audience that has seen a lot of skating, most of it by people better than us. We need to hit 'em with a sledge hammer to be noticed, and something like this could do it."

The girl looked at him in awe. "I've never seen you like this before," she said cautiously.

"I might say the same," he replied grinning.

"Yeah, but I was just actin'. You're serious!"

"Deadly serious, Kid. We're gonna show 'em something they've never seen before!"

"Mom!" Shannon yelled in the direction of the kitchen, "My partner's gone all weird on me!"

"No, Shannon," came the reply. "He's always been weird." They laughed.

Chapter 14

Bluebonnet Open

Dean and Shannon made the 160 mile drive to Austin in the Mustang. Fred and Millie went in the Cadillac. They checked into their rooms at the Doubletree Inn on the Interregional Expressway, a few miles north of the University of Texas Campus.

The Contest

The Bluebonnet Open, named for the state flower of Texas, was held at the Chaparral Ice Center on the north side of Austin. It was hosted by the Austin Figure Skating Club. Adult pairs skated at 4:40 PM on Saturday. Dean and Shannon arrived about 1:30 PM and walked around the well-appointed new facility. They watched some of the singles events. There was only one other pairs event at the contest, Beginners Pairs, and it had gone off on Friday morning. There were three couples registered for Event 75, Adult pairs.

There was an ice cut at 4:25, and their group got a five-minute warm-up skating period at 4:35. They were the last of the three adult pairs to skate. Four teams had registered for the contest, but one had dropped out.

The first pair was an older couple, a man and wife from Austin who had won gold there the previous several years. They were active in the local club, and they rarely skated competitively anymore, but they were quite competent. Their program was technically well-skated, but with little emotion. Dean figured they would most likely place first, due to their maturity and poise on the ice.

The second couple was younger than Dean, but older than Shannon, and from another Houston club. They had less experience than the first pair, and their program was good, but imperfect. Dean figured he and Shannon might have a chance at silver if they skated their best. Any bobbles would send them home with bronze.

The Program

Foster and Steele sat on a cold aluminum bench waiting for their turn to skate. The bleachers were less sparsely populated than during the earlier

98

events. Many of the local skating fans had dropped by for the Adult Ladies, Men's and Pairs competitions that took place that afternoon. It was a rare chance to see such performances, even though they were not of Olympic quality. Millie and Fred were getting anxious, and had moved up into the stands. Shannon was tense and silent.

"One thing's for sure," Dean said. "You're the sexiest pairs girl at *this* contest."

"Shannon looked at him as if waking up from a dream. "What?"

"You'll take the fox prize, no matter how we skate. You look good enough to eat!"

"Who are you, and what have they done with my skating partner?" she asked with mouth agape.

"I'm afraid," he said with a concerned look on his face, "That I may get distracted, just looking at you, and fall down." She raised her eyebrows and gaped at him. "If your skirt comes up when you spin, I'm a goner."

"And why is that?" she asked, suspiciously.

"Because of your sexy ass! I've got this intense urge to grab it."

"Oh, so competitions make you horny, right?"

"No, sexy bitch. You make me horny!"

"My God, Dean, I can't believe you're saying this!"

"I'm sorry to break it to you now, but I had to get it off my chest. I've been having naughty thoughts about you lately, and I wanted to clear the air before we go out there."

"You're shittin' me, of course, you old turd!" she replied.

"Actually not. I've been acting like you don't turn me on for a long time. I just can't live the lie anymore."

"Our final adult pair," the announcer said, "Is Shannon Foster and Dean Steele, representing the Figure Skating Club of Texas." There was a smattering of applause, and isolated cheers from the few FSCT members present.

Shannon and Dean skated to center ice and took up their opening pose. Their music started, and they skated into their routine. The brief program was gracefully done, but Shannon two-footed a side-by-side double toe loop, and Dean lost his edge briefly in a camel spin. Their lifts were smoothly done, and their synchronized spins were close but not quite perfect.

Throughout their performance, Shannon skated with an idyllic smile on her face. She looked at Dean with the soft glowing face normally seen only on a woman in love. Her moves were graceful and fluid. Dean grinned when he saw the magic appear about twenty seconds into the routine. It remained almost throughout.

Their final pose brought a surprisingly enthusiastic round of applause in the sparsely-populated ice arena. They skated back to their bench to wait while the judges worked out the standings. Millie and Fred met them at the boards.

"Y'all did great!" Millie said, "Just great!"

"Real good," Fred said, "Real good." Shannon gave her parents a brief, tense smile.

"You did good, Kid," Dean said softly when they got back to the bench. "I saw the magic."

"I busted that double toe," she said. "Damn!"

"I know. I damn near fell out of a camel! But we did OK," Dean said. "The audience liked us, and we have a shot at the silver."

Fred and Millie kept their seats in the bleachers, allowing Shannon and Dean to be alone together while they waited for the tabulation of results. "In the adult pairs competition," the announcer said, "Bert and Partridge, third; Arello and Arello second; Foster and Steele first."

The two skaters looked at each other wide-eyed. "Oh, my God!" Shannon gasped. Millie broke into a run to get to them.

"What the Hell happened?" Dean asked nobody.

Shannon's parents rained praise and congratulations on the two skaters. Shannon's eyes went moist. Dean was flabbergasted. "I've got to see the score sheet," he said, making his way upstairs to the bulletin board where the results were being posted. "We won by a tenth!" he reported when he returned to the gathering. "A tenth of a point!"

"Uh-oh!" Shannon said, looking down the aisle. Madge and David Arello were making their way toward them, walking on sheathed blades.

"You two were wonderful!" the woman said, smiling warmly. "Just great. That's the best pairs skating we've ever seen at this arena."

"Did you see the scores?" Dean asked. "It was only by a tenth."

"They were just padding us because we've been around so long," David said. "It wasn't anywhere near that close."

"I thought you'd beat us," Dean said.

"No, Young man," Madge said. "We aren't even in your league. I saw that as soon as your music started. Y'all are in a class by yourselves. You can win at Nationals."

"You're very gracious," Dean said. "I really enjoyed your program. It was expertly skated."

"Well, we've done it enough," David said. "You know what they say about old dogs and new tricks."

"I certainly hope y'all go to Nationals," Madge said. "You really belong up there."

"Thank you," Shannon said. The older couple smiled and left. "That's sad," Shannon said when they were out of earshot.

"What?"

"Them. They're never going to win again."

"They seem happy, Shannon. I expect they've had their fun at this game. They don't need any more medals. They have each other."

"I guess," she said. "But still...."

Millie and Fred, who had remained silent while the other pair was present, resumed their congratulatory exuberance. There was some picture taking, and more congratulations from some of the Houston people, and then they left the arena. Winning a gold medal at the Bluebonnet Open is not a life-changing event.

Togs

"We need neat matching workout clothes and practice suits," Shannon said. "If we're gonna be a spectacle, we gotta look spectacular."

"OK," Dean said, "You wanna go shopping when we get home?"

"Not in Houston, Dean. We can get what we need at the University Co-Op while we're in Austin!"

"Why here?"

"Because, that orange and white stuff with longhorns on it is way cool! And besides, we'll both be going to school at UT some day."

Shannon and Dean went shopping at the University Co-Op bookstore, had dinner with Fred and Millie and then went back to the ice arena. The final two events on Saturday were two groups of six Adult Artistic Interpretation contests. It these events the emphasis is on how the skating and costumes express the music. The skating is not always expert, but they have a lot of fun. One woman, for example, skated to Tiny Tim's "Tiptoe Through the Tulips," dressed as a tulip.

In the Adult Artistic, Group A event, Shannon skated "Fancy," and, due to deductions because Dean joined her on the ice, took sixth place. In the Adult Artistic, Group B event, Dean skated "Trashy Women," and, because Shannon joined him on the ice, took sixth place. The audience, however, warmly awarded them the gold in both cases.

The next day they competed in six dance events, taking two gold and three silver medals. That evening Millie and Fred drove back to Houston, leaving Shannon and Dean to spend an extra day for sightseeing in Austin. They visited the State Capitol, the Texas History Museum, and the University of Texas campus, where Shannon made Dean show her all the places where he had lived and hung out when he was a student.

Disney on Ice

"I can't believe we're doing this," Shannon said as they stood in the will-call line at the Frank Erwin Center on the University of Texas campus. "Snow White, for Pete's sake!"

"Hey," Dean said, "This is where you'll end up if we don't win anything at Nationals."

"Ha!" Shannon responded. "Disney on Ice? I don't think so!"

"Hey, it's not so bad. You get to skate in front of paying customers twice a day."

"Yeah, in a dwarf costume! Nobody can even see your face!"

"Well, if you don't want to spend your career skating in a dwarf suit, maybe you better practice your spins!"

"Is that why you dragged me here, Dean? You think it'll make me practice harder after I see this?"

"I'm still groping for something that might work, where your practice is concerned." The girl grinned as she swatted his shoulder.

They went inside and took their seats. A huge curtain cut the arena in half, leaving only the south end with audience seating. The north end was reserved for props and costume changes. "Can you believe this?" Shannon remarked. "There's nobody here!"

"It'll fill up some by showtime," Dean said.

"This is so sad," Shannon mused. "This big empty arena and nobody to watch the skaters."

"They make up for the small crowds by not paying the skaters very much," Dean submitted, grinning. "And, of course, there are fines for the girls if they gain any weight. It's quite a revenue booster."

"You're threatening me, aren't you, Dean? You're holding this Disney thing over my head so I won't eat junk food, and I'll practice."

"Why no," he replied, suppressing a grin. "I'm just showing you the consolation prize if ten years go by and we never medal at Nationals."

"Well, you'd have to do it too! Don't be so high and mighty, Mr. Big Shot! You'll be skating in a Goofy costume!"

"Ah, but don't forget … I'm a computer programmer. I have a marketable job skill. For you, on the other hand, it's skate or starve."

"Kiss this, Dean," she laughed, deliberately not revealing what anatomical component she was offering up. "And if you think I'd have to skate in a Mickey Mouse suit just to stay alive, you're crazy, too."

"I doubt if you could get the part."

"Are you kidding? I'll bet there's not a double jump in the whole cast. I could have any part I wanted in this thing!"

"Well, play your cards wrong, and we'll get to test that theory."

The performance was entertaining, but not from the aspect of spectacular skating. "Did you see that, Dean?" Shannon asked toward the end of the show. "Prince Charming did a single Axel. That's the high point of the show!"

"Aladdin and Jasmine did some pretty good lifts."

"Ha! Nothing we can't already do."

"There was a hip star[1] with one hand."

"Yeah, he eventually got his other hand off her ass! And they held it for almost a second!"

"Are you saying we could skate Aladdin and Jasmine?"

"In our sleep! I've seen better skating in novice classes."

The final number was skated by Snow White and Prince Charming. The cast members who had finished their skating lined up at the edge of the arena. They watched the final performance in a state of awe. "Look at 'em, Dean. They think this is just so great. I can't believe it!"

"It's all relative, Shannon. To these kids, Snow White and the Prince are heroes."

"Hey, let's go talk to the cast!" Shannon blurted when the performance was finished.

"You want to … hang out with the skaters?" He was grinning.

"Sure, Dean. It'll be fun." She grinned. "If I'm gonna be one of 'em, I need to know what it's like!" She playfully elbowed him in the ribs.

Dean approached a woman wearing a headset and a radio. "Excuse me," he said. "My daughter is a skater. She's thinking about trying out for the Disney troupe when she grows up. Can we go backstage and take a look at the costumes and stuff? She'd just be so excited!"

The woman looked at Shannon and groaned audibly. "OK," she said in a bored voice. "We're not supposed to, but … follow me." She led them backstage and approached one of the junior cast members. "This girl wants to be a skater," she said. "Show her around."

The young cast member was named Stephanie, and she explained how she had joined the troupe in Iowa, and what a great opportunity it was to travel and meet people. Shannon stepped into the role of wide-eyed skating hopeful and asked the girl a number of questions. "Do you have to practice a lot?"

"Oh, yes. At least an hour every day. Well, most days, that is."

"Is it hard skating in those heavy costumes?"

"You get used to it."

"Do you travel a lot?"

"Oh, yes. We go to a new town every week."

"Is there a lot of sex on the road?"

"What?"

"You know. Do the cast members screw around a lot?"

"Uh, no. We don't … do that. Well, some of the skaters are dating, but, you know, they don't …"

"I see," Shannon said. "I just wondered." The girl gave up an embarrassed smile. "OK, Daddy," she said to Dean, "I really think this is what I want to do. I'm going to practice my skating for a whole hour every day, and then, when I graduate, I'm gonna try out for Disney on Ice!"

"Mom and I will support you all the way, Sugar," Dean replied. They thanked their hostess and left the arena snickering.

"I thought she was gonna shit when I asked her about the sex," Shannon laughed.

"You are a cruel little bitch, aren't you?"

"No, I'm a sexy bitch, if you don't mind!"

"Well, I do mind."

"Well, screw you, then!" They laughed.

The Return

That evening the two skaters drove back to Houston in the Mustang. "Why did you do it, Dean?" Shannon asked as they rode through the gently rolling green Central Texas countryside.

"Do what?"

"Tell me I'm sexy just before we skated our program."

"I don't know. Nerves, I guess."

"Bullshit. You weren't nervous … I was."

"Well, maybe I just didn't want to go out with a barrier between us."

"More bullshit!" Shannon said. "You just did it to distract me and make me mess up!"

"Now that's clever!" he said sarcastically.

"Yeah, you figured we'd lose anyway, so you wanted to make sure it would be my fault, right?"

"There's just no foolin' you, is there?"

She looked at him softly. "I know you did it to put me in the right mood," she said. "And it worked. I really felt good out there after you said what you did."

He smiled. "You looked good out there. I saw the magic."

"But did you really mean it, Dean? Or just say it?"

He put his arm around her and grinned. "Truer words were never spoken," he said. "You are the fox!"

She snuggled quietly against him as the car purred down the highway. "It's cool that we won the Bluebonnet Open."

---

1. Hip Star – a lift where the man holds the lady above his head with only one hand on her hip, The lady's head, arms, and legs are extended in different directions, like the points of a star.

Chapter 15

Janine

Millie showed up at Dean's apartment conservatively dressed. "Don't look at me," she said as she waltzed inside. "I look awful. Just give me a minute." She took some of her garments out of his closet and disappeared into the bathroom. Ten minutes later she emerged in a vision of femininity that took Dean's breath.

"Oh, this feels much better," she said. "Ready to work, compadre?"

"No," he said. "I'd much rather just sit here and look at you."

The woman softened visibly. "And why would you want to do that?" she asked coyly.

"Oh, I don't know," he said. "Maybe it's because you're the most gorgeous creature I've even seen in my whole life. Or maybe it's because you capture the entire essence of femininity in one incredibly lovely package. Or maybe it's just because you're so damn sexy, and you know it." Everything Dean said was true. He just no longer saw any reason to deny the woman the compliments she deserved. He was willing to give this devil her due.

"My goodness, Dean," she said, "What's gotten into you lately? Too much growth hormone?"

"Too much Millie Foster," he said. "I've ODed on 'Ice Queen'."

"Well, I have a cure for that," she said, moving slowly toward him. She struck a couple of sexy poses in front of him, then pressed herself against him and sighed in his ear.

"Uh, I think this 'miracle cure' of yours is only making the disease worse," he advised her.

"It's not a disease," she whispered. "It's an addiction." She paused to regard his face. "It's not so bad, is it? To be addicted to the Ice Queen?"

"She can be a cruel mistress," He pointed out.

"But she can be so ... very ... gentle," she whispered hoarsely as her body melted against his. She delivered another soft sigh into his ear. He took her in his arms and began to run his hands rather liberally over her scantily clad body. "Are your muscles getting hard, Mr. Ice Man?" She inquired softly.

"What do you think, Madam Ice Queen?"

"I believe you're thinking the most scandalous thoughts about me right now. And I think that pesky thing of yours is trying to bust out of your britches. I think you're about to show me how much you like me."

"Are you flirting with me, Madam?"

"Heavens no!" she said. "I just came over there to work on skating." Her grin was positively evil.

"Then why is my dick about ten times normal size?"

"It must be because you're a naughty boy, and you ogle the Ice Queen too much." She grinned. "You give yourself away, Mr. Steele." Dean didn't flinch when her hand slipped inside his shorts. "Oh, my God!" she said. "It's even bigger than last time!" She gave him a knowing look. "It doesn't take you long to get hot for the Ice Queen, does it, Stud?"

"Given what I'm up against, mere seconds are required," he admitted. Dean allowed the woman to amuse herself at his expense. "By the way," he said as she fondled him, "When do I get to see the royal tits?"

"Nobody sees those," she said. "They're sacred."

Dean had been caressing her ass and concentrating on their verbal exchange. He didn't notice that she had pulled out a small bottle and squeezed a puddle of massage oil into her palm. "Fred?" he asked.

"Occasionally, but it's very expensive."

Dean chuckled at the situation. This woman was digging around in his pants while telling him that her breasts were off limits, even to her husband. "I think turn about is fair play," he said. "You've seen … most of me. Maybe it's time I saw more of you."

"No, Dean. It doesn't work that way."

Dean suddenly became aware of intense sensation coming from his groin. What Millie was doing down there was feeling extremely good. He felt the urge to tense his thighs and buttocks and thrust his throbbing organ outward, offering it up to her touch. He noticed she was studying his face. Each gentle stroke of her oily fingers along his sensitive organ sent shivers of sensation shooting through his nervous system. He heard himself gasp. A wave of panic sobered him up as he realized he was losing control. He was well on his way to a sexual release. "That's enough, Millie," he said, pulling her arms away from him.

"Jesus, Dean!" she said, appearing shocked by his suddenly gruff manner. She stared at him, blinking in wonder.

"That's enough," he repeated, "Play time's over."

"Sorry, Dean!" She appeared hurt. "I didn't mean to annoy you."

"It's OK," he said. "Sorry if I was brusque."

"Are you all right?"

"Yeah. I'm fine," he said. "No problem."

"OK, do you want to work on the program now?"

"Yeah," he replied. "That'll be fine."

They worked together on the skating program. Again Dean cast the occasional admiring glance at Millie's formidable feminine anatomy, but this time it was different. Previously he had admired her aesthetically, and even though it caused a physical arousal, it was primarily an artistic appreciation that he felt. This time it was different. She had 'raised his sap.' She had stimulated him well toward a sexual release. He no longer watched admiringly as her boobies bounced, bobbled, and struggled to escape their fragile bonds. He craved to rip off that scant covering and take them firmly in his mouth. He no longer gazed at her well-rounded bottom with artistic admiration. He now longed to lay her down and take her forcefully. He desperately desired to have sex with this unattainable woman, and he hated her for doing that to him.

Dean endured the torture of sitting beside the body he longed to ravage for another half hour. The urge did not subside. Craving her and not having her was not nearly as enjoyable as merely admiring her beauty had been. Perhaps most distressing, Dean was almost certain that she knew exactly what he was going through. Her flirtatious tack didn't change, but he sensed that his newfound desire for her had been detected. Finally he suggested they end off. After Millie changed back into her business suit, he spoke. "Let's not work over here anymore," he said. "Let's just work at the rink if we need to do anything else."

Millie was shocked. "What's the matter, Dean?" She asked, with a worried look on her face.

"Nothing," he said. "I just don't want us to work over here any more"

"But it's so convenient," she protested. "We get so much done. I even have a change of clothes here." Her voice was pleading, almost to the point of a whine.

"Bad idea," he said. "I'll see you at the rink tomorrow." Thus dismissed, Millie left with a dazed and confused look on her face.

After Millie left, Dean pondered what had happened. She had deliberately teased him up to a high state of arousal. She had even amused herself by fondling his private parts. If he had not stopped her, how far would she have taken this little game of hers? Would she actually get him off? She had shown no signs of stopping. Would she actually have sex with him? He admitted he didn't know what she was up to, except that she was having great fun at his expense. He also knew she had awakened in him a strong desire for her. She had aroused an intense urge to have sex with her. He didn't know exactly what that meant, but he considered it an unfortunate turn of events.

Normally he could go for several days without much thought of sex. But that afternoon's activities had left him with unfinished business. A physiological process had been set in motion and left incomplete. His body had been sent well down the path toward sexual release. Powerful hormones had been released into his bloodstream, leaving him in an altered mental state. He found it difficult to concentrate. Millie's face kept showing up in his thoughts, taunting and teasing him.

Janine

After a while Dean realized he needed something to distract him. He needed to relieve the pressure. He needed a short-notice solution to his problem. He picked up the phone and the Piccadilly Apartments directory. He dialed a number. Another phone rang several units away in the same building.

"Hello," Janine Wilson's voice said.

"Janine?"

"This is Janine."

"Hi, Janine. This is Dean Steele in 201."

"Dean Steele? Oh, hi. How are you?" She seemed surprised.

"I'm fine, how are you?"

"I'm OK. What's … uhmm … going on, Dean?"

"I was wondering if you might like to come over tonight and watch a movie with me."

There was a long pause. "Uh … sure Dean. You really want me to?"

"Yeah, I think it might be fun. Nothing fancy. Just a decent film we both might like."

"OK," she said. "Sure. When do you want me?"

"What about 8:30? Most of the pay channel movies start at nine."

"OK. Is there anything special you want? What should I wear?"

"Just something cute and charming, Janine. I know you'll be radiant."

"OK, Dean. I'll be there at 8:30."

About 8:20 his doorbell rang. When he opened the door, Janine stood there with an embarrassed smile on her face. "Here I am … Janine," she explained, as if to remind him who she was and that she had been invited.

"You look lovely," he said. "Come in."

She walked in the door and began to take in the surroundings. She had never been inside his apartment before.

"Did you have any trouble finding the place?" Dean joked.

"Oh, no," she replied. "Everybody knows where Dean Steele lives."

Janine Wilson was a tallish girl of rather slight build. She had long straight "dishwater blonde" hair with somewhat darker roots showing. Her makeup was almost correctly applied, and the colors only slightly missed working together. She wore a thin gray plaid sundress that had been washed too many times, obviously without bra, and scuffed red flats. A high school dropout, about five years his junior, she worked as a secretary at a local insurance office. Her meager wage went mostly for the rent on her apartment, which she shared with another single woman.

"Would you like something to drink?" Dean asked his guest.

"Oh, just make me one of whatever you're drinking," she responded.

"Better be careful, Janine," he warned. "I'm a certified health nut. You risk an overdose of nutrition by saying that."

The girl laughed self-consciously. He made up two purple frozen grape juice drinks in the blender and joined her on the couch. "Can I … just ask a question?" she inquired over her embarrassment.

"Janine, you can do anything you want," he replied, smiling warmly.

"Well … why did you invite me over? I mean, you never hardly spoke to me before today. I didn't mean you were rude or anything," she said, flustered. "It's just that, you … never seemed to notice me. It's like, I'm not … your type. And when you called me, I just … I don't know."

Dean recognized that the girl felt socially inferior to him. She was probably right about him ignoring her. Before tonight he had classed her with all the other non-descript kids who dropped out of high school in a small Texas town and moved to the big city in search of adventure. They hung out all over the Piccadilly Apartment complex, and he summarily ignored them all.

"Well," he said, smiling slyly, "I'm a very tricky guy. I don't like to let on when I notice a girl." He was lying. He had never paid any attention to this one before.

"Really? You noticed me? When?"

Dean was in trouble He had to scan his memory banks to recall a time he had been in the vicinity of this girl. "Well," he said running the clock while he searched for an answer, "There was that party…," He was flying blind. He assumed there must have been some party at which they were both present. "Or out by the pool." He assumed she must have been among the girls who sunbathed occasionally.

"Was it the time you pulled that kid out after he hit his head? You saved his life!" The incident she referred to had happened the previous summer. The timing was right, so he seized it.

"I guess that was the first time I really noticed you," he offered. "But I was very cool about it."

"Boy, you didn't let on at all!" she said.

"Well, I'm kinda busy, and ... a slow mover, and I'm kinda shy."

"Oh, sure!" she giggled. "You can have any girl you want."

He smiled at her warmly. "Now it's my turn," he said. "Why did you accept my invitation?"

"Are you kidding? I never dreamed I'd get the chance to come over here. This is the coolest place in the whole complex!"

He chuckled. "Is it the zebra skin wallpaper or the floccati rug?"

"No, it's you!" she replied excitedly. "This is Dean Steele's pad!"

He smiled. "I didn't realize I was living in Disneyland. I thought it was just another tacky apartment."

"Oh, you know what I mean," she said, somewhat embarrassed. "You're a celebrity." By that she meant he was a bit older and more responsible, held a steady job, didn't party every night, and seldom got drunk and threw up. His relatively civilized lifestyle set him apart.

"So, where did you come from?" he asked, changing the subject.

"Borger," she replied. But I grew up in Marfa."

"Why did you leave?"

"Couldn't stand it anymore. I thought Houston would be better."

"Is it?"

"Yeah." She grinned.

"What does your dad do?"

"I don't know. He left when I was little." She paused. "He used to send me cards on my birthday, but he stopped years ago."

"Why do you think he left?"

"My fault, I guess. He didn't like being tied down that much."

A twinge of pain shot through Dean as he realized this girl blamed herself for being fatherless. Some irresponsible asshole had abandoned his family, and his daughter took the rap for it. "What about your mom?"

"She's a waitress."

"Does she have a boyfriend?"

"Yeah," she sighed. "A different one very night."

"Does she drink?"

"Yeah. I used to send her a little money off and on, but she just drank it up, so I stopped. Her boyfriends buy her plenty of booze."

Dean detected that Janine also felt guilty about not taking better care of her mom. She most likely equated herself with her father in the abandonment of her mother. "OK, Kiddo," he said, finally changing the subject. "What do you want to watch? We have here the best senseless violence and perverse human carnage that Hollywood can offer up."

"You pick it, Dean. I want to watch what you want to watch."

"You could be in for some serious boredom, there, Young Lady."

"Is that what you think I am, Dean?" she blushed. "A 'young lady'?"

Dean surmised that she had not been thusly labeled for a long time. "Unless you tell me otherwise. I'm just going by outward appearances, here." He grinned. "Is there something you need to tell me?"

"No," she grinned self-consciously. "You can call me a 'young lady' if you want to." She seemed pleased.

There was an action movie that Dean had wanted to see on one of the digital satellite pay channels. It was about a team of half-human, half-robot soldiers with laser weapons who had rebelled against the army and had to be annihilated. He keyed in the code to authorize the purchase.

Dean and Janine watched the movie in silence for about ten minutes. Then Dean put his arm around the girl's shoulders. She slipped her shoes off and cuddled softly against his chest, somewhat like a contented kitten. She was warm and shy, and it was pleasant to have her there. They watched some of the thin plot unfold, until Dean turned to the girl and tilted her face up to his. He kissed her softly on the lips. The second kiss was more intense. A third kiss held passion.

The young woman took this as her cue to go to work. She slipped off her thin sundress, leaving herself clad only in white bikini panties. She positioned herself in front of him and began kissing his neck and caressing his chest and abdomen. Dean's hands slipped up and down her slight frame as she worked on him. She unbuttoned his shirt and pulled it out of his pants, and she unhitched his belt. Dean would pull her up for the occasional kiss, after which she would go back to her business.

Soon her hand closed softly around his shaft, which had been erected by her activities. Then her mouth took over that duty, and Dean settled back on the couch to let her proceed with practicing her skill. As he lay there he saw explosions and splattering body parts on the wide screen TV, he saw Janine's slender body working diligently upon his, and, in his mind, he saw Millie Foster's face laughing at him.

It was she who had orchestrated this little drama. She had ignited the fire that drove him to summon this slender minion to complete the act. The face that refused to leave his thoughts grinned victoriously. "I got you," it seemed to say. "That little slut is just doing my dirty work."

Dean looked at Janine. He realized he never would have invited her to share an evening with him under ordinary circumstances. The Ice Queen had given him a problem, and he had recruited this naïve waif to solve it for him. He knew there was no future for him and Janine - that this was a one-night stand. This unsophisticated young woman had been called in to pinch-hit for the Ice Queen, after which she would be unceremoniously relegated to Millie Foster's scrap pile.

The taunting face invading Dean's thoughts smiled smugly. "You can't win, Dean," it said. "I'll get you, one way or another. You'll spill your seed for me, even if I have to call in a ignorant misfit to take it."

Janine was working skillfully and diligently, and Dean felt himself beginning to lose control of his body. Millie's face looked positively evil as she watched the proceedings from inside his mind. As desperation began to engulf him, Dean began to think of Janine as Millie, working by remote control to complete the job he had not let her finish earlier. Was Janine real, or was she just a puppet on the Ice Queen's hand? Had he really refused to let Millie have his innocence, or had he merely delayed the inevitable? One way or the other, Millie had won. She already owned the fluid he was about to unload.

Dean felt his hips and thighs tensing up, raising upward in an unconditional offering to this woman, whoever she was, who held his very existence in her mouth. His thoughts blurred as sensation became overwhelming. The roar in his ears seemed to be coming from the Ice Queens' mouth. He held on to the couch with both hands as he began to slip off into an uncontrolled slide through time and space.

He heard a gasp, and then a groan. Was it his? His heartbeat was deafening as waves of intense sensation swept over him. He felt himself at the center of the explosions on the TV screen. He was the bomb. His fuse was armed. His clock was counting down. There was no way to disarm him. Millie Foster was watching and laughing as Janine Wilson from Borger, Texas pushed his countdown clock, second by second, toward zero. He was helpless. He had no choice but to cling to the sofa and try to survive until it was over.

After long agonizing seconds, the explosion came. Dean jerked and gasped and moaned under the skillful manipulation of the two women who controlled him. Like a psychiatric patient strapped to an electroshock table, he writhed and convulsed for the duration of the treatment. When the current was finally turned off, he collapsed in a wasted heap, gasping for air.

When his eyes opened, he saw Janine, watching his face as she continued to work on him. He felt naked, vulnerable and embarrassed in front of her. She continued to work on him, forcing involuntary jerks and twitches out of his tortured body. He wanted to make her stop, but he had neither strength nor will to do so. He merely lay there, enduring the embarrassment as she pulled the last pitiful jerk and gasp out of him.

Finally, satisfied that he was totally spent, the girl released him and dumped a mouthful of semen and saliva into the glass that still contained about half of her frozen grape juice drink. The creamy discharge floated like a cloud above the purple liquid.

Shame and embarrassment flooded Dean's being. Janine's face, gazing at him softly, only made it worse. He wanted to hitch up his pants and tuck in his shirt, but he had no strength. He lay there helpless and exposed as she kissed his face tenderly.

"Was it good, Dean?" she whispered in his ear. He couldn't decide if it was the fragile girl from down the hall asking, or the evil Ice Queen. He didn't answer. Janine wasn't offended. She had her answer. She had sucked him off within an inch of his life, and they both knew it.

Finally Dean summoned his strength, got up and went into the bathroom. He wiped himself off with a damp washrag and repositioned his clothing. He tossed the purple and white contents of the glass into the toilet and flushed it. Then he went back out to join his guest.

Janine had slipped her dress back on. She was curled up demurely on the sofa when he returned. "I think this is the good part," she offered. "They have the cyborgs trapped in the old mine." Sensing that he was embarrassed by what had happened, she was trying to ease the pressure on him. Silently, he took her in an embrace. She cuddled warmly into his arms, savoring a feeling she knew was not likely to recur. Several minutes later Janine turned her face up to Dean.

"I guess I blew it, didn't I?" she observed. "You don't usually get that on the first date. I hadn't even been here an hour before I went down on you. You must think I'm a slut."

"I think that was something we both wanted, Janine. It was OK."

"I guess I'm not nice like the girls you're used to. Are you shocked by my ..." She left her utterance unfinished.

"No, Janine," he said. "I've dated all kinds of women, and there are no two alike. There's only one Janine Wilson from Borger, Texas ... and you're her." He smiled at her. "And that's exactly who you need to be."

"I wasn't always like this," she said. "Back home ... in Borger ... I was a nice girl. I mean, I wasn't a virgin or anything, but I wouldn't do anything with a boy unless we were going steady." She paused. "That all changed when I moved to Houston."

"How come?" Dean inquired, gently.

She inhaled and gazed off into space. "Well, for one thing, there was nobody here tellin' me I shouldn't. All the other girls here just brag about who all they've been with. Sometimes they even sleep together, and it's no secret. Back home that would be the scandal of the century." She paused. "And guys seem to like a girl a lot more if she … 'knows how to party.' I don't think a good girl would do very well around here."

"Is that why you picked the Piccadilly?" Dean asked.

"No," she said, "I met this girl who needed a roommate, and …" A look of sad resignation slowly took over her face. "I guess I wanted to see what it was like. She talked about the wild parties and the interesting people. She didn't tell me I'd turn into a slut if I moved in with her."

Dean put his index finger to his pursed lips. "Don't call yourself that, Janine," he coaxed her. "You're only a slut if you decide you are."

She sighed and continued her confession. "There's also the booze. I kinda lose my willpower when I drink. If a guy starts comin' on to me when I've been drinkin', I get this idea that I have to give him whatever he wants. It's crazy, I know, but it happens every time I get wasted."

She looked at him. "My God! I did it with you, and I only had grape juice! You must be appalled."

"No, young lady. I'm actually very happy."

"But still, it must have been a shock for you … me comin' on to you like that, right after I got here."

"When I saw you tonight," he said, "How good you looked … I was hoping we could do something together. I just wasn't expecting to get so carried away, that's all."

"That embarrassed you, didn't it?" she asked softly. "I mean, you coming so hard, and all."

Dean was stunned by her inquiry. She was right, of course, but he had hoped she didn't know, or, at least wouldn't mention it. "You really got to me, Janine," he admitted, quietly. "I never expected such a wild ride. I'm sorry if I seemed a little stunned when it was over. I was just … kinda … knocked out by it all."

"You shouldn't be embarrassed by that, you know," she explained. "It's good when a guy comes real big like that. It means he's real … macho, I guess. It makes me feel really good when you do that for me." Her face pleaded for understanding.

Dean looked at her tenderly. She was trying to cheer him up. He sensed that giving sexual pleasure to a man was perhaps her only real area of competence in life. If she failed in that, she failed utterly. "OK," he said, smiling. "I won't worry about it."

The girl smiled and cuddled up under his arm. He sensed that giving Dean Steele an intense sexual experience was a high point in her life, not a conquest so much as an honorable accomplishment. By the end of the movie, Dean had recovered from the physical and emotional thrashing he had received. He turned to Janine and kissed her again.

"Back for more so soon, Big Guy?" she asked, grinning coyly. She was now more comfortable in her newfound role and obviously prepared to replay their earlier adventure.

"No, it's your turn," he said. "You worked me over pretty good. Now I get to do you."

"Dean," she said, frowning self-consciously, "You don't have to do that. I mean, you can fuck me if you want to, but I ... I don't ... get off." A puzzled look voiced his question silently. "I don't know why, but I don't ... orgasm. I mean, it feels good, and all ... but I don't come."

"Not ever?"

"Almost never. I don't know why."

He inhaled. "Were you molested as a child?" he asked gently.

"No," she said, unconvincingly. "No more than I deserved, I guess."

Dean knew that it would take someone more skilled than he to sort out the emotional scars that held this unfortunate girl down. He slipped her dress off, kissed her all over and mounted her. As a result of his previous adventure, he was able to make love to the young woman for an extended period before again discharging his fluid. She displayed signs of enjoyment, more emotional than physical, but she did not have an orgasm. Finally they got dressed.

"This was wonderful tonight," she said. "I know you don't like me, or anything, but if you ever want me again ... just call me."

"Janine, I do like you."

"You know what I mean. I'm not ... your kind of girl."

He wanted to say something. He wanted to boost her flagging self-esteem. He wanted to drain that ocean of sadness that lay just below her surface. But anything he could say would be a lie that would either be transparent or simply build false hope in her mind. He groped for some way to compliment the girl without making her out to be a slut. He couldn't find one. She was a sex machine, and he had used her for exactly that purpose.

"Are you OK, Sweetheart?" he asked. "Do you need anything?"

"You don't have to pay me, Dean," she said, with a note of sadness.

"No ... that's not what I meant." He was flustered. "Friends help each other out. Are you facing any problems where I might help out?"

"No, Dean. I'm OK. And I'm a lot better now." She grinned and touched his cheek. "And I won't tell anybody about this."

As he watched her walk away, he realized she would suppress the urge to brag to her friends about her "date" with Dean Steele in order to save him the embarrassment. In her own way, she was much more moral than Millie, and a lot less selfish.

Dean sat on the edge of his bed, trying to understand what had happened. Millie had gotten him severely aroused, and he had called in an emotional cripple to relieve the pressure. He couldn't offer the unfortunate young woman anything except to be used to relieve the strain Millie had put him under. Janine was of so little self-esteem that she was content merely to serve the sexual needs of a man. It was her purpose in life. It was also a road to self-destruction, and he had merely led her one more step down the stairway to oblivion.

He tried to console himself. Janine had considered his invitation an honor. Like a groupie with a rock star. It was a new feather in her cap. It was also no excuse for him. He had no interest in this unsophisticated girl from the outset. He had called on her because he knew of her reputation as an easy lay. He had taken advantage of someone caught in a trap not of her own making, and he hated himself for it.

"I shoulda took a cold shower," he mumbled to nobody.

Chapter 16

The Slap

Surprise

Dean and Shannon were reviewing tapes of their practice sessions. "Wait!" Dean exclaimed. "Look at that!" He took the remote control from Shannon's hand and backed up the tape.

"OK, Dean, what did I do?" Shannon braced herself for a lecture.

"Watch," he said. "Look at your face."

"What's wrong with my face?"

"OK, look at the entry into this lift. You bend your knee, preparing to jump, but ... here ... you get this wide-eyed, 'Oh my God, he's gonna lift me!' look on your face."

"That's bad?"

"No, that's great. That's wonderful, don't you see?" He paused to inhale. "The guys in the WWF[1] couldn't do it any better. You jump into that lift just like always, but you get this look of total surprise on your face, like this big guy just ran up and grabbed you and threw you up in the air. It's very cool. It's ... totally awesome!"

"You ... want me to do that?"

"It will work in a lot of our routines, like 'Indian Outlaw' for example. After the chase, when I finally catch you, you can act like you're being forcibly lifted and thrown. You can even shriek and squeal when this big Indian guy grabs you up and has his way with you, like you're not expecting it, see? It fits with the program. Nobody else does it. They all look very deliberate going into the lifts. We can make it look like you were caught by surprise. Can you work on that?"

"Yeah," the girl mused. "I can act surprised when you lift me. No problemo!"

"I think we can use that little trick a lot. It'll fit real good in those numbers where I chase you for a while and then finally catch you."

"Yeah, like 'Hats and kicks,' right?

"Yeah. It'll be cool. Work on looking surprised, even though you're preparing to jump into the lift."

"Got it," she said, nodding her head up and down.

The Encounter

Dean and Shannon were walking by the pool on their way from the parking lot to his apartment. They heard loud voices and rounded a corner just in time to see a young man give Janine Wilson a hard slap across the face, knocking her down on one knee. Dean bolted to the scene and grabbed the boy. "Don't ever do that, Asshole!" he yelled in his face as he slammed him against the wall of the building. "Either treat her nice, or leave her the Hell alone! You hear me, Punk?"

The boy looked at him in wide-eyed fear for long moments. Finally the other boy spoke. "Hey, Man," he said. "He didn't mean nothin'. It was just ... a mistake, that's all." Dean turned to look at the second boy. "It's cool," the boy said. "We're all friends here, right?"

Dean inhaled. "Yeah," he said, releasing the boy from his grip. He walked over to Janine, who had since stood up. "You OK, Honey?" he inquired. She nodded her head up and down. "OK, guys," he said. "That's cool. Sorry I blew up. Let's just take care of the women, OK?"

"Yeah, Dude," the second boy said. "It's cool. We're all friends here."

Dean walked away, and Shannon followed him. "You know that girl?" she asked with a puzzled look.

"Uh, she just lives here, I think," he replied.

"Boy, you sure rode to her rescue! You do that for all the Piccadilly trailer trash?"

Dean glared at her from underneath raised eyebrows. "No, he said, "Just the skinny ones that can't defend themselves. If it was you, I'd stand by gleefully watching you kick his ass, Muscle Girl."

"Some partner I've got!" she mused. They continued walking in silence. "You know," Shannon said as they reached his apartment, "You overdid it back there. You coulda come on a little less Rambo, and still saved the poor little damsel in distress."

"So I get 'Gene and Roger[2]' from my partner now?" he asked. "You give advice on the care and feeding of redneck punks?"

"Ooh, sensitive, Dean," she said. Then she looked at him. "You have some history with that girl, Dean?"

"I don't know her," he lied.

"I've just never seen you fly off the handle like that before. You sure you never dragged her home from some wild party? Think hard, Dean. I saw the love-light in her eyes."

"I believe I would remember if I'd had prior social interaction with the young woman," he said.

"Forget social," Shannon laughed. "With you, the intercourse would be purely sexual!"

"Are you finished, Foster? Or do you have more of this cheap, insufferable bullshit to slosh all over my boots?"

"Why, I've never seen you like this, Steele. First you leap to the aid of a poor little waif, scaring the shit outta some pimply-face cowboy. Then you pretend you don't know her. Who is she, Dean? Your illegitimate daughter?"

"I didn't want to tell you about it," he said, "But if you must know, I knocked up my kindergarten teacher when I was five, and she's the result."

"Have you dated that girl, Dean?"

"Not since our divorce went final."

"Come on, Dean. What is it with that little tramp?"

"What is it with you, Foster? Inquiring minds want to know!"

"OK, if you won't tell me, then I'll ask her. What's her name?"

"Penelope Pigpimple."

"Get real, Steele. You know I can find out who she is. Are you gonna tell me, or what?"

"I've talked to her at parties, Shannon. Maybe she came over here once. Can we get on to the next topic, please?"

"Did you have sex with her?"

"Say, what?"

"Read my lips. Did ... you ... screw ... her?"

"We had one date, Shannon. One date!"

"Where did you go?"

"To a movie."

"Where?"

"Here."

"Oh, you didn't even take her out anywhere on your first date, Dean? Mucho tacky!"

"She didn't seem to mind."

"I guess not. So how many times did you bang her before the first commercial?"

"It was pay-per-view. Commercial-free."

"OK, then, how many times before the opening credits finished rolling?"

"I recall a tender good-night kiss. That's all."

"Bullshit, Steele!"

"That's my story, and I'm stickin' to it."

"You expect me to believe you held hands for two hours, and then she went home? I don't think so!"

"I give not the slightest shit what you think, Princess."

"I can get the truth out of her."

"If she tells you anything, then *I'll* slap the shit out of her."

"So you admit it!"

"I don't admit Jack Shit!"

"No fun, Dean. You are no ... fun!"

"You think I'm no fun? I've got a nosey skating partner who won't get off my ass about something she knows absolutely nothing about."

"Really, Dean. That girl's hardly any older than I am. She's cheap and trashy. Why her and not me?"

"You've just listed three of the reasons why I didn't sleep with her. There are hundreds of reasons why you never made the team!"

"But you did screw her, Dean. You can't help it."

"I think I'll use that as my excuse for caving in your face. 'Sorry Fred, I just couldn't help it!'"

"No need to be defensive, Dean. I don't care if you banged that little tramp. I just think we should maintain some degree of honesty in our partnership, that's all."

"OK, fine. I honestly think I'll punch your lights out! How's that?"

"You're tense, Dean. You need to just relax and tell your partner all about your wild affair with Penelope Pigface. You'll feel a lot better."

"How do you do it, Foster? How do you raise being irritating to such a high art form?"

"These skating partnerships require a lot of effort to hold 'em together. I'm just doin' my part."

"If you're working so hard to keep this act together, then why do I have this overwhelming urge to cram you snippy little ass in that dumpster out back?"

"Guilty conscience, I suppose," she replied. "You've banged too many tacky girls and haven't confessed it to your partner. It creates stress in the relationship."

"You create stress, Foster! Now get outta my face."

They worked on dance steps for a while, and Shannon left.

---

1. World Wrestling Federation
2. Gene and Roger – criticism (after movie critics Gene Siskel and Roger Ebert).

Chapter 17

The Spanking

Trashy Two

Dean was scheduled to perform his "Trashy Women" routine again at club ice that evening. When he approached his mannequin it turned around and looked at him. He was shocked to see that it was Shannon, wearing a short, tight white dress, platinum blonde wig and overstuffed boobs. He doubled up with laughter, skated past her and ran into the rail. She skated up to where he stood, laughing uncontrollably.

"You're on, Dean," she said cooly.

Still laughing convulsively, he took her in the Killian position and they skated away. They skated quietly together until he regained his composure, then Shannon began to dramatize "trashy" with hip-swinging, head-tossing, and other suggestive moves. Dean mainly tried to keep up with her. Toward the end of the song he took her in dance positions and called out compulsory dance steps that they could do together.

When they finished, the applause was boisterous. The audience knew that Dean had been caught by surprise by the cast substitution in his act.

"That was a shitty thing to do," Dean said.

"I know," Shannon replied. "Mom put me up to it. We shopped all afternoon for my 'trashy' outfit. How did you like skating 'Trashy' with a real girl?"

"The other dummy followed better."

"No, really. How did I do?"

"Well, you did very well, actually. I should have substituted you for that rag doll a long time ago. I guess I just haven't gotten used to having a live girl for a partner."

"Better get on the program, Dean. You've got more partner than you know what to do with!"

He grinned at her. "I guess I do!"

Shannon's Spanking

About midway through their practice session, two days later, Dean said, "Let's do some synchronized camel spins."

"I don't want to do camels today," Shannon replied.

"Why not?"

"Because I know how to do a camel. It's my best spin."

"Well, good. If we get our camels really well synchronized, it'll be our best spin too."

"No."

"No, what?"

"No camels. Practice them by yourself if you want to. I'm going to work on my spread eagle."

"It's a waste of our ice time to practice separately, Shannon. We have tests to pass here. We need to work together."

"I'm not your slave, Dean Steele. I'll do what I damn well please. So get out of my face!"

"Technically, you're right. I haven't finished making the payments on you yet, so your parents still hold title to you. But you are my skating partner, and I expect cooperation in practice."

"Expect whatever you like, but I don't have to do every little thing you say. I'm tired of you always bossing me around. It just sucks."

"Why do you say I boss you around?"

"Because. You tell me what to eat, how to exercise, which vitamins to take, what to practice, and all I get back from you is a large dose of Gene and Roger[1]. Well, I'm not gonna put up with it any more!"

"All right, emancipated one, what would you like to practice?"

"I guess we could do some lateral lifts or maybe a throw Salchow."

"Fine. We'll do that."

The two skaters practiced the moves with very little conversation. Finally their practice period was just about over.

"I want to go to IHOP after practice," Shannon said.

"We can entertain that as a possibility," Dean replied.

"Dean," she responded sharply, "Why do you do that?"

"Do what?"

"Talk like that. Why can't you just say 'OK,' or 'cool,' or something a normal person might say. You sound like some kind of English teacher, for Pete's sake, and I'm getting really sick of it."

"Doth my speech offend thee, Fair Lady?"

"Oh, shit! Now you sound like Shakespeare already! What's the matter with you, Steele? Are you just simple in the head, or are you seriously mentally ill?"

"Do you have your cell phone with you?"

"Uh, yeah."

"May I borrow it, please?

Shannon took the instrument from her jacket and handed it to him.

"Which button is the Ice Queen?"

"Star six," she replied, puzzled.

Dean entered that and Millie answered. He turned on the speaker.

"Madam," he began, "Your daughter has been acting the perfect bitch all afternoon. She is in dire need of corporal punishment. It is my policy never to discipline a child without parental consent. Do I have your permission to beat the shit out of this snotty little brat?"

"Sure, Dean. Just give her a couple of swats for me," Millie said.

"Thank you Madam." He slipped the phone in his pocket.

"I can't believe this!" Shannon said. You borrow my phone to ask my Mom if you can spank me? As if, Shithead!" She glared at him. "You and the US Marines, maybe!"

"Shannon," he said, "If you submit to this spanking without making a scene, I'll use my hand, and I'll be as gentle as I can, under the circumstances. Like my dad always told me, it'll hurt me more than it hurts you … just not in the same place."

"If you think you are going to lay a hand on me, you musclebound retard, you're living in Looney-Land."

"But if you don't," he continued, "I'll use my belt, and I'll enjoy the Hell out of it." He stared at her, awaiting an answer.

"Forget it, Dean. Not in this lifetime. No spanking is in my movie!"

"Au contraire, oh venom-tongued one. It is your very next scene, and you shall play it with grace and style, I'm sure." He unbuckled his belt and slipped it out of its loops. "We can go to a more private venue if you'd like to minimize the embarrassment factor."

"Put your belt back on before your pants fall down," she said defiantly. "And don't even consider hitting me with that thing." He began to skate around her in circles. Finally he popped the inside of her left thigh with the belt. "Ouch! Damn you, Dean! That hurt!"

"The pain is the point," he said. "After all, this is a spanking we're doing here. Would you like to retire to the locker room for the remainder of the program?"

The girl's eyes began to widen as she realized he was serious. She skated away. Dean followed her, swinging his belt and singing, "Yippie ki yi yea, git along little doggie. It's your misfortune and none of my own." He followed her closely behind, pressuring her to skate faster and faster. Once she reached full speed, he popped her on the back of the right thigh. She let out a shriek of pain and almost stumbled. He popped her again.

"It's a kick to spank a moving target," he said, popping her on the right buttock. "More fun than a video game. We oughta do this every day." He popped her other bun with deadly accuracy. A collection of young hockey players, standing outside the rink, watching the clock and awaiting their turn on the ice, took an interest in the proceedings.

"Dammit, Dean, stop this!" she screamed. "It hurts!"

"Shannon, the spankee is not the one who decides when the spanking is over. And I'm having way too much fun to even consider curtailing it so soon." He popped her left thigh again.

The girl skidded to a stop. "Stop it, Dean! Stop it, stop it, stop it!" Tears of anger and pain filled her eyes. "You can't do this to me! You can't just keep hitting me!"

"Follow me down to the end of the rink so we can finish up the spanking," he said.

"No!" She stomped the ice with her blade.

He popped her butt again. She shrieked. "Follow me!" he ordered. With tears streaming down her face she complied. He knelt on his right knee, with his left knee extended. "Bend over," he said.

"No," she pleaded. "Please stop this!"

He motioned for her to lay across his knee. Sobbing softly, she slowly complied. He pulled her short skirt up and her leotard down, exposing a pair of white silk bikini panties covering two pink buns. The hockey players began to drift toward the end of the arena for a better look. "Ooh," he said. "This is the cutest little butt I've spanked all day!" He struck her with his open palm.

The girl lay across his knee, sobbing quietly, while the man administered a painful lesson. The hockey players pressed against the Plexiglas. Finally he pulled up her leotard and helped her stand up. "It's been a pleasure doing pain with you," he said. "If I can ever be of service again, just start acting like a bitch. I'm on call 24/7."

The girl looked at him with an extremely sad face. Then she grabbed him in a hug and sobbed violently. When that subsided, she looked in his eyes. "Do you still like me, Dean" she pleaded.

"Yes, Shannon," he replied, "I like you a lot."

She grabbed him and resumed sobbing.

Millie

"How was your spanking?" Millie asked when Shannon got home.

"What spanking?" Shannon responded innocently.

"The spanking Dean gave you all over the ice this afternoon. It's the talk of the town. I fully expect to see it on the ten o'clock news."

"Oh, we just did that for the benefit of the puckheads. They're always saying how dull and boring figure skating is. We were just messin' with 'em."

"A little 'Marquis de Sade on Ice' for the pairs program, huh?"

"Yeah, I guess, but I don't know if we'll actually use it in our program."

"I see," Millie grinned. "Well, I hope it did you some good."

The Rink

The next day, as Shannon was walking toward the lockers, she passed a young hockey player.

"Hi, Shannon," he said.

"Hi," she responded, blandly.

"Cute butt," he said. She swung at him, but he dodged and she missed. "Asshole!" she sneered.

A few minutes later another boy passed her. "Hi, Shannon," he said.

"Hi," she responded, in a bored voice.

"Nice ass!" he added.

"Kiss my ass, Shithead!" she shouted.

"OK," he said. "How about right now?" He made a puckering face.

"Screw you!" she said, angrily showing him her middle finger.

"We can do that too!" he replied. "Over behind the Zamboni machine." He laughed at his joke.

"Listen, you little bastard!" she said. "I don't want to hear any more shit from you or your puckface friends about my butt, do you hear me?"

"Gee, Shannon, since you flashed it all over the arena, everybody's saying how cute it is."

"I did not flash it, you prick! Now crawl back in your hole." She stomped away.

Dean

"I guess you know you've made me a total joke at the Texas Ice Stadium," Shannon said.

"How's that?" Dean asked.

"All the hockey players are telling me how cute my butt is and asking me out. They're being total turds about it."

"You're upset because you're getting complements and date invitations?"

"Dean! They're all saying, 'Hi, Shannon, cute butt. Hi, Shannon, nice ass.' They only want to go out with me because of my butt. It's insulting and degrading."

"What would you do if one of the boys said, 'Hi, Shannon, your hair looks really nice.'?"

"I don't know, say 'Thanks,' I guess."

"What if one of 'em said, 'That was a really good looking Axel you did.'?"

"I'd say thanks. But it's not the same, Dean. They're teasing me, giving me a hard time about that ridiculous spanking you gave me."

"When they ask you out?"

"Sure! Ever since you showed everybody my ass, I'm real popular with the peach fuzz crowd. They don't want to date me. They just want to see my butt and tell their friends about it! I hear they're even taking up a collection to pay me to show my butt to the ones who missed the show yesterday. I'm ruined, Dean!"

"It's an insult because you take it as an insult. What if you took it as a compliment?"

"I can't do that!"

"Why not?"

"You mean, just say, 'Glad you like it. Maybe I'll let you touch it sometime'?"

"Well, just assume they meant it as a sincere compliment."

"But they don't. They're just making fun of me."

"Because they know you're embarrassed about it. If you stop reacting so wildly, they'll stop doing it. You can turn this thing around."

"What are you talking about?" She was exasperated.

"This incident has made you a local celebrity of sorts. You went from being 'just some girl who skates here' to "Shannon with the cute butt.' You need to know how to handle notoriety. If we ever win anything metallic at Nationals, you'll get plenty of it. Now is a good time to learn."

"Oh, right, Dean! Like flashing my ass to the Junior NHL is the same as winning a medal!"

"It *is* the same. You've attracted the attention of the crowd. Handle it in a cool, professional manner. Turn notoriety into a good thing."

"And how do I do that, Professor? My partner pulled down my pants and spanked my butt in front of God and the Bay Area Hockey League!"

"They're not teasing you about getting a spanking. They're teasing you because they got to see your butt. What they're saying is, 'I saw your butt, Shannon, and I liked it.'"

"It's the same thing."

"No it's not. They're teasing you because they know you would never let them see it voluntarily. So it's like they got a sneak peek at you. But they're also saying they like what they saw. They're even putting their money where their mouth is by asking you out."

"Yeah, they're saying, 'Let's go out, Shannon, and maybe I'll get another look at your ass.'"

"Shannon, you've been noticed. You've attracted the interest of those boys. That's all. You now have a unique identity. Instead of being anonymous, you're now 'that figure skater with the cute butt.' It's a new public image for you."

The girl was pensive. "So, maybe I could go, like, 'Sure I have a cute butt. Eat your heart out, asshole!'"

"Yeah, something like that. Only you wouldn't have to be quite so unfriendly to your fans."

"Fans? That's what you call those smart-alec little twerps?"

"They are fans, Shannon. They admire something about you."

"Yeah, my big butt!"

"It's a big, muscular, shapely ... dare I say it ... sexy butt, Shannon. I'm sure you'd rather be admired for your skating, your charm, or your intellect, but with teenage boys ... having your ass admired is about as good as it's gonna get."

"So I could treat them like my fan club, right? I could be their pin-up girl, huh? Cool!"

"I think you're beginning to see it my way."

"Oh, God, Dean! Those boys think I'm sexy! The whole hockey team thinks I'm sexy!"

"Well, I couldn't say it's unanimous, but you do have a substantial majority on your side."

"This is so cool! I'm the sex object of the hockey team!"

"Maybe they'll elect you as their mascot."

She frowned at his joke. "Maybe I'll have pictures made with my butt showing so they can stick 'em up in their lockers."

"We can make Shannon Foster trading cards," he added. "Collect the whole set!"

"Come on, Dean. You're just jealous 'cause I'm so popular with the hockey boys."

"That must be it!" he replied sarcastically.

The next day a young boy approached Shannon. "Uh, Hi, Shannon," he stammered.

The girl glared at him. "What's on your mind, twerp?" she asked coldly. "You got some smartass crack to make?"

"Uh, I just ..." he swallowed, "Think you're cool."

Shannon suddenly realized that the boy had spent most of the morning raking up the courage to approach her. She smiled coyly and said, "Thanks, Sweetie." The boy smiled meekly. "Hey," she said, reaching into her bag. "I've got something for you." She pulled out an eight by ten publicity photo of herself. "Your name's Billy, right?"

"Billy Ray," he said.

"OK," she said, signing her name to the photograph. She started to hand the picture to him, then pulled it back. She added a line of x's and o's to the bottom. "There," she said, giving him the photo.

"Gee, thanks!" he beamed as he saw what he had received. Shannon gave him a wink.

The Next Day

"How's it going with your fan club?" Dean asked.

"OK, I guess. I'm getting more compliments than ever from the puberty puck-suckers."

"Yeah? What do you do in the face of such admiration?"

"I just give 'em a little grin and say 'Thanks.' I try to act a little embarrassed. They like that. And sometimes I give 'em a wiggle."

"A wiggle?"

"You know. I just kinda shake it a little."

"An impromptu performance for your admiring audience?"

"Just a little wiggle. They get this real funny look on their faces."

"Believe me when I say I know the look!"

"So, what do you think, Dean? Is it OK that I'm the sex queen of the fifteen-year-old hockey players? Or is it sick and perverted?"

"That depends on your viewpoint. I'm just glad you're learning how to handle fame."

"Yeah, right! Like this is being famous!"

"You have a group of admirers, Shannon. It's a place to start. It's better you learn the ropes now, with the local hockey team, than when the TV cameras are pointed at you."

"TV cameras? Are we going to be famous?"

"We're not going to all this trouble to be anonymous."

"Cool!"

"Dean," Shannon said as they were putting on their skates.

"What?"

"Did it really hurt you more than it did me? That spanking, I mean."

Dean grinned. "Why, sure, Princess," he said, insincerely. "It was sheer torture for me, having to discipline my wayward partner in front of the hockey league."

"No, it wasn't, you pervert! You loved it!"

"And I thought I was being so cool about it!"

A grin broke out on her face. "You really enjoyed that, didn't you? You got to bend me over your knee. You got to pull my pants down, and you got to see my sexy ass. And you got to make it turn all pink."

"It was already pink. I turned it a bright red."

"OK, red then."

"And besides, I didn't actually pull your panties down, in deference to your modesty."

"Oh, like I had any shred of modesty left!"

"I just did what I had to do." He effected a dutiful air.

"But you liked it, didn't you, Dean?"

He looked at the girl. She was relentlessly pushing him to admit he found her sexy, and she seemed confident that the answer would be "yes." He saw a spark of the persona he wanted her to express on the ice - that cool, confident, sexy young girl image. He decided to play along to develop this image in her mind.

"Now what makes you think I would derive any pleasure whatsoever out of bending you over my knee and lighting up your buns?"

"Because you're a pervert, and I have a sexy ass!"

"Oh, you do, do you? I ... hadn't noticed."

"Bullshit, Dean! You can't keep your eyes off of it, or your hands either. It drives you crazy with desire. You dream about it at night. You wouldn't be able to get up in the mornings, except you know you might get a glimpse of my sexy ass. It's the only thing that keeps you going."

"Damn, I didn't know it showed!" he said sarcastically.

"It's written all over you, Dean," she chided him. "I've known it for ages. So just admit it!"

He liked what he saw developing in the girl. It was the right attitude for several of their exhibition numbers. He looked at her as if he were suppressing a confession.

"Come on, Steele, admit it! You're crazy about my sexy ass."

Dean inhaled to speak, than stopped, hoping she would push harder.

"You're totally transparent, Dean," she said. "You're hopelessly in love with my sexy ass and you can't help it, so just say so!" Her tone was demanding.

"OK, let's just say that I have come to appreciate your anatomical structure to a limited extent."

"Bullshit! You love my ass. Say it!"

Dean squirmed as if he were weakening under her relentless pressure. "Well, uh … I do like the way your little skirt hangs over the back of your rump. And I think your hips and thighs tie together very nicely."

"Not good enough, Dean! You love my ass. Admit it!"

He inhaled deeply. "All right, damn it!" he blurted. "I love to look at your big sexy ass. And turning you over my knee and pulling down your leotard and paddling your succulent young butt was a life-changing religious experience for me. Are you happy now?"

A confident grin slowly took her face as she regarded him. "I knew it!" she said. "Dean Steele likes my butt!"

"Now," he said. "Lace up those boots and let's go skate that. I want to see you tease me with your sexy ass."

Her eyes widened, and she started hastily pulling at her laces. Then she ran for the opening in the boards. "Come on, Dean," she yelled back at him. "I've got something here you're dying to see!"

As he skated around the rink behind her, she would wiggle her derriere and look at him as if to say, "You want it, but you can't have it!" Dean was very pleased with her skating that day.

Dean and Shannon stopped by his apartment briefly after practice.

"I think that spanking did you some good. Young lady," Dean said.

"Oh, right! Like getting beat half to death was therapeutic!"

"No, really. I sense that you're more reliable, dependable and mature since your close encounter with my right hand."

"I'm living in fear, that's all! I never know when this madman I skate with will thrash the living daylights out of me!"

"Well, if that's it, I think you skate better scared."

"No, I skate my best when I'm petted, pampered and praised."

"I see. Well, I guess I'll just have to settle for the fear reaction then."

"Come on, Dean. What would it hurt for you to treat me like a lady?"

"What would it hurt for you to act like a lady?"

"Maybe if you treated me like a lady I would!"

"Maybe we could get the horse in front of the cart, here. You need to act like a lady first."

"If I did, would you pamper and pet me?"

"Uh…, probably not."

"Why not?"

131

"Because your parents do plenty of that."

"No, they don't! I never get any tender love and affection."

"Poor baby!"

"No, really. I get ignored by my parents and ordered around by my partner, that is, when he's not beating me!"

"My goodness!" Dean said, "I didn't realize what a poor mistreated little waif you really are."

"So, what are you gonna do about it?"

"What could I possibly do about such a modern American tragedy?"

"You could give me a hug."

"Would that fix it?"

"It would help."

"OK," he said, "One hug for the poor mistreated little waif."

He embraced the girl. "And a smoochie would help too," she added.

"I can't do that," he responded."

"Why not?"

"Your giggly girlfriends might tease you about it."

"Oh, as if, Dean! Like they don't already tease me worse than that."

"We wouldn't want to make it any worse. It embarrasses you."

"Is that what you think, Dean? That it embarrasses me?"

"Well, you bitch about it all the time."

"That doesn't mean I don't like it."

"What, them teasing you?"

"Yeah. They're just jealous 'cause they don't have a big hunkin' guy to skate with all the time."

"OK, then I won't lose any more sleep over you being teased by your girlfriends."

"Yeah, like you ever lost any sleep over me at all!"

"I've lost sleep over you."

"When?" she demanded incredulously.

"Well, like the time you called me at midnight to talk about 'Fancy.'"

She gave him a disgusted look. "No, I mean lying awake worrying about me. That kind of losing sleep."

"I do that," he said.

"When? What did you worry about?"

"I worry about whether you're going to land your double jumps on one foot or not."

She gave him another disgusted look. "No, I mean lying awake worrying about, you know, like whether I'm happy or not." She paused. "Or whether I like you or not."

"Well, you keep skating with me. That must mean something."

"Yes it does," she said. "It means I'm a masochist. I just love skating with someone who takes me for granted and ignores me, and bosses me around … oh, and occasionally beats my butt with his belt!"

"Once doesn't make 'occasionally,' I'm afraid," he said.

"But you'll probably do it again."

"Not if you learned your lesson." She pouted. "OK, Kid," he said, deciding she had endured enough. "I really liked that hug you gave me. I think I need another one. And could I trouble you for a smoochie too?"

A grin broke out on her face. "Well," she said, "It you really need it, I guess so."

"Oh, thank goodness," he grinned as he grabbed the girl.

---

1. Gene and Roger – criticism (after movie critics Gene Siskel and Roger Ebert).

Chapter 18

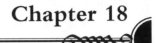

Janine's Problem

The Call

"Hello," Dean said into the cordless phone in his apartment. It was about 10:30 PM on a cool, clear night in Clear Lake City.

"I saw your light on," a soft female voice said. This is Janine. Is it OK to call you?"

"Sure, Sweetheart," he said. "How are you?"

"Oh, I'm OK. I just wanted to thank you."

"For what?"

"For sticking up for me the other day. You made me real proud."

"You mean over by the pool? I guess I kinda blew it."

"No, you were wonderful! You made me feel like a million dollars."

"I was kinda rough on your boyfriend."

"He's not my boyfriend. Not really. But he's sure been nice to me since then. Everybody has."

"You think it did some good?"

"Oh, sure. I'm the talk of the complex now. Everybody treats me like royalty, now that Dean Steel takes care of me."

"You make me sound like … The Godfather."

"No, it's just that you're a celebrity, and if you think I'm worth taking care of, everybody else figures I must be something special."

Thoughts of Janine had been lurking around in Dean's mind ever since their first encounter. The sexual experience she had given him haunted his thoughts. With Millie, the theme of the encounter was always desire. She would tease him into a high level of arousal and then delight in his lust. With Janine it was pleasure. She made him feel good from the start, and she made it last a long time. It was completely different. The shy, slender girl only tried to give him something. Millie was consistently a taker.

"Hey," he said. "Can you save Thursday night for me?"

"Sure, Dean. You want me to come over?"

"I want to take you out. We'll need to be a bit discreet about it, though. I'll let you know more after I get it all set up, OK?"

"Heck, I don't mind keeping it a secret, Dean. I know you have …"

"Bitches." Dean said. "Too many bitches in my life."

"Yeah," she said. "I know."

The Date

Dean met Janine after work, and they left her car at a shopping center. They went to Pasadena since the Fosters would never go there. They had portraits made at the Glamour Shots studio in the mall and ate Mexican food at a local restaurant. Then they went back to pick up her pictures.

"Is that me?" Janine marveled as she saw how her portrait turned out. It was strikingly beautiful.

Dean held it up beside her face and furrowed his brow as if executing a detailed comparison. "Looks just like you, Kid." he said.

"My God, I look like a cover girl!" she exclaimed. With blow-dried hair and professionally applied makeup, her facial features gave her the look of a fashion model.

"I knew that," Dean said, "Before they ever took your picture."

"It's just the makeup," she said. "Or maybe they use trick photography or something. They process it in the computer."

"Yeah, they tricked you into being yourself," he said. The girl laughed self-consciously. "Hey," he said, "I know a guy who supplies models for catalogues and stuff. I'll send him one of these and see if he thinks he can use you sometime."

"You've got to be kidding!"

"No, you look as good as any of those underfed, overpaid bitches that model all that merchandise. He'll know if you have the look they want."

"Don't waste a stamp! Nobody'll take my picture unless I pay 'em."

Piccadilly

They picked up her car and drove separately back to Clear Lake City. She followed Dean to his door and came inside. He mixed up a strawberry drink in the blender and they sat on the sofa and talked.

Janine was gazing at Dean and grinning. "What is it?" he asked.

"I … got invited back," she said with an air of significance.

"You're surprised?"

"Well, after last time, when I … came on so strong, I … couldn't be sure what you thought of me. I mean, I wasn't a very nice girl."

"Janine," he said, grinning at her, "We clicked. We hit it off. There was some pretty strong chemistry between us from the beginning. And you gave me something very special. I was totally knocked out by it." He paused.

"When I opened the door and saw you standing there, I thought, whoa, is this Janine? You just seemed to glow."

"I was so excited when you called and asked me over. I kept thinking maybe you had me mixed up with one of the other girls and you'd say, 'Hey, you're not who I wanted!' I couldn't eat anything I was so excited. And when I got here, all I could think about was making you happy." She paused. "I guess I kinda overdid it."

"Well, you sure did make me happy." He gave her a tender hug.

Sam's Pictures

"Do you know who Sam Alexander is?" Dean asked after they had sat and relaxed for a while. "He lives here at the Piccadilly."

"Yes," she replied, looking at him sheepishly.

"Did you know … he has pictures of you on his computer?"

"Yes," she said. A hint of sadness tinged her voice.

"Have you seen them?" He asked.

"Yes," she replied, with big sad eyes. "Did he show them to you?"

"Not exactly," Dean replied.

"But you've seen them?"

"Yes."

The girl looked away and shook her head sadly. "I really messed up, didn't I?" She was clearly embarrassed that Dean had seen these pictures. "You must think I'm a terrible tramp."

"What happened?" he asked, avoiding an answer to her question.

Janine's Confession

She was silent for a moment. Then she sighed and looked at him. She was near tears. "There was this party," she began, "Here at the Piccadilly. I … drank too much, and one of the guys started hittin' on me. He took me into the bedroom, and started making out with me. I wasn't thinking very clearly, and he … got me out of my clothes. Sam was hiding in there with his camera. The guy must have been in on it, 'cause he didn't turn off the lights."

She paused to inhale. "He started fucking me, and Sam just walked up and started taking pictures. I couldn't believe it! And this guy was turning me around so Sam could see it all, and I was trying to make him stop. But I didn't have much strength, and my head was pretty messed up, so they just made these porno pictures with me. Pretty soon I got sick and went in the bathroom and threw up, and then I passed out. They just left me lying on the bed, naked. I guess everybody saw me when they came in to get their coats. I was so embarrassed when I woke up."

"What happened then?"

"I got dressed, and Sam showed me the pictures. I got real upset and called him a lot of names. I was so pissed that he would do that. I told him he'd better erase all those pictures right then or I'd call the cops. He said he'd print 'em out and go to Kinko's and make a hundred copies and pin 'em up all over the complex, with my apartment number on 'em, if I didn't calm down and stay over with him that night."

"What did you do?"

"He said he'd erase the pictures if I'd just stay with him, so I … spent the night with him." She paused. "He … fucked me a few times, and the next morning he was in a better mood. He said he was real sorry he had done that, and he'd get rid of the pictures if I'd just pose for some bikini shots. He said that was really all he wanted."

"What did you do?"

The Photoshoot

"A couple of days later I went over to his place in my bikini. He had his camera and some big lights set up in the bedroom. He gave me this drink. I knew he must have put drugs in it. Everybody knows he runs a pharmacy in 117. I said I wasn't thirsty, but he said I had to drink it before we could start shooting. He said it would put me in the right mood – make a model out of me."

"What did you do?"

"I drank it. I figured I had to. I wanted to make sure he erased those awful pictures."

"What happened?"

"I was OK at first, and he took some pictures of me in my swimsuit. But pretty soon I got kinda crazy. He asked me to take off my top, and I did. And then he asked me to take off my bottom, and I did. I was so light-headed and giddy I just didn't care. Finally I was showing him everything I had, and he was taking pictures of it. I was laughing, and I just didn't care. It got real pornographic, what he was askin' me to do, and I was doin' it all and laughing like an idiot."

"Then this other guy comes in. I'd never seen him before. He was just wearing a robe, with nothing under it. He was kinda good looking … muscular and all, and he had this really big dick. So Sam starts telling him what to do, and pretty soon I figure out it's gonna be a porno shoot, as if it wasn't already, except now there was this guy in it with me."

"So, how did it go?"

"Well, this guy, Brad I think Sam called him, just kept lookin' at me, until his dick got hard. Then he came over and put it in my face and Sam took some pictures. Then he made me suck it, and Sam took more pictures. And it was weird, because, every few minutes, Sam's camera would get full, and he'd have to go copy the pictures into his computer to make room to take some more. And Brad would just get up and put his robe on and sit down. I mean, even if he was screwing me, he'd just stop. And he wouldn't even look at me, the whole time, like I didn't exist. Then when Sam came back, he'd look at me till his dick was hard again, and he'd start screwin' me some more, or whatever Sam told him to do. I couldn't believe it."

"What else happened?"

"Well, one time Sam told him to fuck me in the ass. I didn't want that, 'cause it would hurt, his dick bein' so big and all. But Brad said Sam wasn't payin' him enough, and it would be fifty dollars extra, and Sam said twenty-five, and Brad said, 'No deal.' So Sam told him to just do it doggie style, and he did."

She paused to gaze into space. "He never said one word to me. Brad, I mean. He fucked me at least six different ways, and he never said one word to me, the whole time."

"What else happened?" Dean asked softly.

"Well, I was laying there while this guy I didn't even know was humpin' me like a madman, and Sam was walkin' all around takin' pictures of it from every possible angle, and I started thinking, 'Boy, Janine, you really are a slut!' And I started to feel real sad about how I had turned out since I moved to Houston. I had such high hopes when I left Borger, and here I was in a guy's apartment, having sex for the camera with some guy I didn't even know. So I just began to feel really terrible, And then Sam started saying, 'Show us how much you like it, you little bitch,' and 'Suck it, you little slut' and things like that. And … I did. I just started acting like a whore. I made faces and acted like it was the greatest thing I had ever done. It wasn't, but I showed him, and his camera, just what a slut I had become. Little Janine Wilson from Borger, Texas moved to the big city and became a whore."

She fell silent, and Dean left her in her reverie for a time. Then he spoke. "What happened next?"

"Well, Sam finally got all the pictures he wanted, and Brad put on his robe and left. He never did come. He fucked me for almost an hour and never once came. But Sam was horny by that time, and he sure as Hell came. I got sick by that time, and I was throwing up while he was humpin' me from behind, but he didn't care. And then I wiped my face off and took a nap, or maybe I just passed out."

"When I finally woke up, he showed me he now had two sets of pictures. I asked him to at least erase the first set, like he promised, but he said he had changed his mind. He said if I kicked up a fuss about it he'd put them all over the Internet with my name and address on 'em. But he said if I came to his party that weekend he'd give me all the pictures back, even the bikini ones."

"What did you do?"

Second Party

"I worried about it a lot, but I showed up at his party that weekend. He met me at the door with a drink. I knew it was more drugs, and I said I didn't want it, but he said if I didn't drink it he'd fax some of the pictures to the office where I work."

"What did you do?"

"I drank it. He stood there and watched me 'till I drank every drop."

"Then what happened?"

"I don't remember it very well. It was kind of a blur. I know I took off my clothes and had sex with two guys while he took more pictures. I think it was in the living room, with everybody watching. Maybe most of the people had left by then and it was just a few of his buddies left. I think several of 'em fucked me. I don't know how many."

"Anyway, now he has three sets of pictures of me, and the last ones are really awful, I mean, with several guys. So he said that anytime he called me, I had to come spend the night with him, or come to his party, or do whatever he wanted. He said if I didn't, he'd mail the pictures to my mom and the Borger newspaper and everybody I know."

"How often does he call on you?"

"Not so much anymore. It was, like, twice a week at first. He'd invite me to a party and make me stay over with him afterward, like I was his date or something. After that it was maybe once a week, or less, and usually just a quickie or a blow job. He hasn't called me in a while. I guess he got tired of me."

Release

"What if I told you that you don't have to do that anymore?"

"What?"

"What if I told you he doesn't have any pictures of you anymore?"

"I can't believe it! How could you do that?"

"I'm a computer geek, remember? I can do anything."

"You can really get those pictures off of his computer?"

"I already have."

"Sam let you work on his computer, or something?"

"Not exactly."

"You hacked him?"

"I just ... performed some ... remote maintenance."

"Does he know they're gone?"

"No. But the next time he goes looking for 'em, he'll just think he had a disk crash and the files got trashed."

"Are there any other copies somewhere else?"

"Possibly, but I checked his backup log, and he hasn't backed up his hard drive since well before the date on those files, so I doubt that he has 'em saved anywhere. He might have E-mailed a few of 'em to his friends, but I scanned his outgoing message log, and I didn't see any E-mail that went out with picture files attached. I also saw that he's been taking other pictures with his digital camera since then, so there won't be any of them left in there. I expect they're all gone, Sweetie."

"Did you keep copies?" she asked sheepishly.

"Maybe just a few of the more tasteful ones," he replied. "Do you mind? I'll erase them if you say so."

"None of 'em are tasteful, Dean, but you can keep any of 'em that are just me by myself." She paused. "I'm such a stupid little shit! I'm just so embarrassed I did that. You must think I'm terrible."

"You kinda got ganged up on, Sweetie. Ole Sam is pretty slimy."

"Well, yeah, but if I had any sense I wouldn't get myself into those messes in the first place."

Dean grinned. "Outta the frying pan, into the fire," he said mischievously.

"What do you mean?" An inquisitive grin took her face.

"Well, maybe now you'll just have to come over here whenever I call." He grinned. "I have pictures of you in a bikini! If you don't do everything I say, I'll put you in the Sports Illustrated swimsuit issue."

"Oh, Dean," she sighed, "You don't need pictures to get me to come see you." She moved her face close to his. "Just ask me. Anytime." She paused. "I'll be your midnight girl," she whispered in his ear.

He gave her a hug. "Let's go back to that story for a minute," he said. "I want to mention something that I thought of while you were talking."

"What's that?"

"Go back to the part where you decided you're just a slut, and you convinced yourself of it by acting like one. Remember?"

"Yeah."

"Well, I just want to mention that you should be a little suspicious of any life-changing realizations you have while under the influence of psychotropic drugs. They usually aren't very accurate."

"What kind of drugs?"

"From the sound of it, I think old Sam has gotten hold of some of the really nasty chemistry that psychiatrists use on their patients. It's a lot more damaging than anything you can get on the street."

"So, you think I might be wrong about that? Maybe I'm not a slut?"

"You're the one who has to decide, Sweetheart, 'cause whichever way you decide, that's the way it is."

"What do you mean?"

"I mean, if you decide you're a whore, then you'll act like one, and, bingo! You'll be one. If you decide you aren't, then you won't, and you won't be. So you need to make sure you get it right."

"You make it sound like I can … just decide."

"Of course you can … 'just decide!' That's the only thing that determines what you really are."

"Well, I can see that if I decide I am, like I did that day, then it becomes true, kind of … automatically."

"Right."

"But if I decide I'm not, it doesn't work, 'cause I've already done all those terrible things, and I can't change that."

"Hey, I'm not saying you should decide that stuff didn't happen. It did, and that's a fact. But the future is what counts. What you do today and tomorrow, not what you did yesterday."

"So, even though I did all that bad stuff, I can go ahead with my life, just like it didn't happen?"

"Maybe. But it's for sure that you can go forward either being a slut or not being a slut if you want to. That one is completely in your hands."

She pondered what he had said, and she brightened up. "Oh, Dean!" she said. "I can't believe it. You got rid of those awful pictures. You are so wonderful!" She heaved a huge sigh of relief. "I can tell Sam to kiss off!" Then she started kissing him, but she paused. "I'll bet you don't want me anymore, now that you've seen all the bad stuff I've done." Dean just looked at her, grinning softly. Janine wanted to give him another experience that evening, and he allowed the girl to show her gratitude in the way she knew best.

Chapter 19

Seventeen

Stages

It was late morning practice at the Texas Ice Stadium. Shannon skated over to where Dean was standing. "I don't need to practice that Lutz anymore, Dean. I can do it in my sleep."

You're only at stage three," he replied.

"What are you talking about … stage three?" She was irritated.

Dean inhaled. "When you're learning to do a jump, there are four stages you go through. First you can't do it. Then you get to where you can do it sometimes. That's stage one. Then, if you practice a lot, you can do it most of the time. That's stage two. Most skaters go to contests basically in stage two." He paused. "But if you practice more, you get to stage three. That's where you can do it all the time."

"That's where I am on this jump."

"Well, that's not good enough. We need to be at stage four on everything."

"OK, Mr. Know-it-all, what's stage four?"

"That's where you can do it without thinking about it. It's automatic. It just happens."

"We'll never get there, Dean."

"Sure we will, Precious. It just takes a lot of practice,"

Precious

"Precious?" Shannon said, visibly irritated. "You called me, 'Precious?'"

"Well, aren't you?"

"'Precious,' is what proud parents call their little baby," she lectured, "Not what an athlete calls his partner. And you say it with that smart-ass sarcastic-looking smirk! You don't mean it, Dean. You only say it when you're mad at me." She was angry. "You're making fun of me. You always make fun of me. Why do you do that?" She stomped her foot.

"Perhaps, Young Lady, it's because I harbor a deep-rooted resentment for what you represent. Nothing personal, but you've had everything you ever wanted handed to you on a silver platter. Your life centers around the shopping mall. You and your cell phone clog up the airwaves with mindless chatter about nail polish colors." He inhaled. "I know kids, sweet little kids, who don't have any hair because they're on chemotherapy. I know kids, good kids, who don't get any Christmas presents because their parents are poor. So excuse me if I can't get very upset when you have a bad hair day!"

"What does it take, Dean?" the girl responded angrily. "What do I have to do to make you like me? I work my butt off practicing with you. I do everything you tell me to do, and still you hate me because I don't have cancer? Because my parents give me stuff? It just sucks!" She began to cry. "Would you like me better if I was sick? If I had some hideous disease, would that do it? Should I just give all my clothes to Goodwill and wear rags everyday? What do I have to do, Dean?" Her face was twisted with anger and frustration and covered with tears.

"Shannon," he said with a sigh.

"Screw you, Dean Steele!"

"Shannon," he said, rather firmly.

"Screw you, Dean!"

"Shannon," he said calmly.

"Screw you!"

"Shannon?" he said softly.

"What?" Her face was pouty.

"I'm wrong about this. I'm wrong to resent you for being a River Oaks princess. I'm wrong to blame you for not having other people's misfortune." He paused. "I'm ... kind of an jerk, basically. I'm sorry." She looked at him, softening visibly. "You're a good kid," he said. "A good person. There's nothing wrong with ... I'm glad you have nice parents who love you and give you things. Your mom and dad have earned what they have. You deserve everything you get."

"You don't believe that, Dean. You're just saying it to calm me down, but you don't believe I deserve to live in River Oaks and wear nice clothes and talk on my cell phone. I haven't suffered enough, or something."

"You're only sixteen, Shannon. You haven't had time to prove yourself yet. But I'll bet you're going to show the world that you deserve more than River Oaks. I'll bet you're going to show the world you deserve ... a castle in Spain. We just have to give you a little time."

"OK, Dean," she said, calming down somewhat, "But you have to promise not to make fun of me anymore, not to call me 'Precious' or 'Princess' or anything else if you don't really mean it."

Dean smiled gently at the girl. "OK, Precious, I promise." A grin slowly developed on her face. She gave him a hug. "You're my partner, Shannon," he said softly as they embraced. "That makes you a very special person." He paused. "And you are very precious to me."

"I love you, Dean," she whispered silently.

The Party

Millie reserved the Texas Ice Stadium for Shannon's seventeenth birthday party. Although Shannon knew of the party, she was kept in the dark as to what was to take place there. She only knew that elaborate plans were being laid. The last week was a fury of activity from which she was totally excluded.

The entertainment was a skating exhibition by some of the Skating Club students. It was staged as a reenactment of Shannon's skating history, with various girls acting out different stages of her career while the announcer narrated her development as a skater. Millie had written the script to include every embarrassing moment she could remember. Dean, who was sitting with the Foster family, disappeared at one point.

"And now, the high point of the evening," the booming voice from the PA system said, "A precision skating demonstration by veteran competitive figure skater, Dean Steele." Shannon rolled her eyes. She couldn't imagine what he would have worked up for her party, but she suspected she was in for some serious ribbing. "And now," the announcer said, "Here he is, 1991 USA national bronze medalist, and three-time southwestern regional senior men's freestyle champion, Shannon's pairs partner, Dean Steele!" Everybody clapped, as the spotlight trained on the opening at the end of the rink, but nothing happened. "Dean," the announcer said when the applause died down. "Where are you?"

"What?" came the reply from the unseen skater. He was wearing a wireless microphone.

"Dean," the voice said anxiously, "You're on!"

First silence, then "On what?" came the response in a stupefied voice.

"Your act! It's time for your act!"

"Uh, (hiccup) what act?" was the thick-tongued reply.

"Your skating exhibition. You're next on the program for Shannon's birthday party."

"Oh, that act!"

"Are you ready?"

"A pause was followed by, "For what?"

"For your act! Are you ready to skate your program?"

"Well, sure, (hiccup) I can do that!"

"Well, get on out there! Your music's half over already!"

"Look out! Here I come!" The audience fixed upon the entrance to the sheet. For a moment, nothing happened. Then Dean came flying out of the darkness at the other end of the arena, skating very fast backward. He was wearing a disheveled jacket and a beat-up hat sitting crooked on his head. He carried a wine bottle. Although he was skating rapidly backward, he was moving in the motion of walking slowly forward. Periodically he would hiccup, punctuated by a split jump.

"Dean!" the announcer said, alarmed, "Have you been dipping in the adults' punchbowl?"

"Heck no," he replied, "I'm way too big to swim in that little thing!"

"I mean have you been drinking the punch?"

Dean's face froze in a wide-eyed look as he passed in front of the stands. "I only had one," he said, holding up four fingers.

"One cup of punch?"

"Gallon, I think it was." He made a "big" gesture with his hands. "It was more than a quart, ... but less than a tanker truck."

"Well, Dean, you shouldn't skate if you've been drinking alcohol."

"It's OK, he said, "I'm very calm." He held out his hands to demonstrate how steady they were. Another a hiccup produced a split jump.

"Are you going to skate for Shannon?"

"Who?"

"Your partner, Shannon Foster!"

"Oh, I know her. She's that little ..." he made an hourglass figure with his hands.

"Dean!" the announcer interrupted, "Don't describe your partner over the PA system while you're drunk. It's just not a good idea."

"Righto!" he said, pressing his index finger to his lips.

"OK, then, what are you going to skate for us tonight?"

"Pears."

"But Dean, your pairs partner is up here in the stands. She doesn't even have her skates on!"

"No, not pairs, Silly. Pears!" He pulled two pears out of each pocket.

"Oh, you're going to skate ... pears."

"Absolit ... absolo ... I certainly am!"

"I'm going to juggle these four pears while scooting very rapidly across the frozen ice in a high rate of motion, while, at the same time ... skating very fast." He paused.

"I see."

"Did I mention speed?"

"Yes."

"Are you gonna watch?"

"I think we'll all be watching."

"Well, good. You can tell me how it comes out." He skated around the arena several times, waving the four pears in the air as if preparing to throw them up in the air.

"Dean, we're waiting. Are you gonna juggle those pears, or what?"

"I'm getting in the mood." As he passed in front of the stands, he slowed almost to a stop and started tossing one of the pears a few inches and catching it. "Pretty cool, huh?" he said, grinning widely as everybody clapped and cheered and laughed.

"Dean, I don't think that's really juggling."

"I was just getting warmed up!" he said defensively. Finally, he appeared to throw one of the pears very hard into the air. Then he threw the other three, one at a time, except he used sleight of hand and actually slipped them back into his pockets. He skated all around the ice as if waiting for them to come back down. Finally, he faked catching them, while actually pulling them out of his pocket again. The PA system made the whistling sound of a bomb drop each time. The crowd laughed and cheered. Then he made a pass by the bleachers actually juggling the four pears. The audience cheered wildly. "Now," he said, "I'm gonna do my jump."

"What kind of jump are you going to do, Dean, an Axel?"

"No."

"A Salchow?"

"Nope."

"A Lutz?"

"Huh-uh."

"Well, what is it?"

"A pear loop."

"But, Dean, you're skating singles tonight," the announcer said.

"No," Dean said, exasperated, "A pear loop," He held up two of the pears. He then jammed the two pears between his heels and blades and did a slow, clumsy single loop jump with them attached. After landing, he took a bow, but then pretended to lose his balance and started falling wildly. He skated across the arena in this continually falling position, waving his arms and thrashing about as if trying to catch himself. The pears on his skates made it look all the more ridiculous. As he approached the audience, he did a perfect double Axel. As he spun in the air, the two pears were thrown off his skates, and they went flying across the ice in different directions. He landed the Axel right in front of Shannon. In his recovery, he threw the two remaining pears at his partner.

146

They splattered against the Plexiglas shield as she and her parents ducked the flying fruit. "Oops!" he said, and skated off into the dark end of the arena.

"OK," the announcer said, "Are you through skating pears now?"

"Nope," he said. "Now I'm going to skate with a pair of girls!" He emerged with a six-year old girl skater in each hand. Each girl was wearing a special harness under her costume that allowed him to carry her like a briefcase. He skated around the arena, with the girls swinging randomly in the wind. He would occasionally raise one or both of them unceremoniously above his head. "Aren't they good?" he mused.

"But Dean," came the reply, "We haven't seen them skate."

He stopped and carefully placed his two little partners on the ice. They skated in a circle around him. He rotated slowly as they held his hands. "These kids can skate circles around me," he observed. Then he picked the two girls up again, placing one under each arm. "Now we're going to do a triple flip," he said.

"But Dean," the concerned voice replied, "A triple flip is a very dangerous jump. If you fall, those little girls could get hurt very badly."

"Not to worry," he said with a thick tongue. "I'm a trained proff ... pruff ... praff..." He paused. "I do this stuff for a livin'." The audience laughed. "Besides, there's lots more little girls where these came from."

"Someone call 9-1-1," the announcer said.

"Here goes!" Dean said as he approached the bleachers with the two little girls under his arms. Suddenly he skidded to a stop and set the two girls on the ice. Then the three of them took oversized coins out of their pockets and flipped them in unison. "Heads!" one girl yelled. "Heads!" cried the other girl. Dean looked at his coin and frowned.

"You lose!" the two kids yelled in unison. Then they took him by the hands and skated him out through the exit.

Dean then reemerged without the hat and coat and skated a brief but athletic program of jumps and spins that delighted the audience. It was a catalogue of figure skating moves, and the announcer called each one as it was done. It included all of the single, double and triple jumps, including the axel, and one each of the spins. It was done with a combination of grace and power that captivated the audience. He seldom took his eyes off his partner.

Finally, he took a bow to a standing ovation, and he blew a kiss to Shannon.

Shannon

"You're a wild man, Steele!" Shannon said as he rejoined her in the stands. "Pears skating? Only a twisted mind could come up with that!"

"Happy birthday, partner," he said.

She gave him a kiss on the cheek. "Thank you, Dean." She smiled softly, near tears. "You're the best partner a girl could ever have." After a pause, Shannon turned back to him and said, "You bastard! You laid those jumps out there like a gambler dealing a deck of cards. Your triples were better than your singles!"

"That's because I practice triples a lot more than I practice singles."

Millie

"Your program was just great!" Millie said when she finally got Dean to herself. I know you were skating it for Shannon, but I pretended you were skating for me. During your finale, I got so hot I thought I was going to get off right there at my daughter's birthday party!"

Dean smiled at her. "You're something, Millie," he said.

"I just love to watch you skate," she said. "It's my most serious vice."

The Paper

Leon Hale's column in Saturday morning's edition of the Houston Chronicle carried an account of the party.

> The hot ticket in the icy world of figure skating last night was the birthday party for Houston pairs skater Shannon Foster. Her parents, Fred and Millie Foster of River Oaks, hosted the frosty gala at the Texas Ice Stadium on the Gulf freeway. Just about everybody who's anybody on ice in Houston was there, including Kristy Yamaguchi and Tara Lipinsky who dropped by to deliver their well wishes. Several members of the Figure Skating Club of Texas skated their contest routines for the 'boots and blades' crowd. Shannon's pairs partner, Dean Steele, skated an inebriated comedy routine, skillfully juggling four pears and two little girls (not at the same time) while under the influence (or perhaps just pretending to be - I can't be certain). He then wrote a textbook on the ice with a routine that demonstrated every figure skating jump and spin there

is to the awed ice crowd. Shannon, the charming honoree, just turned seventeen on Thursday. Looking more like a beauty queen than a figure skater, she smiled and blushed as she greeted her friends and fans. It's too bad we didn't get to see her skate.

Chapter 20

A New Career

Janine was bubbling with excitement when Dean answered the phone.

"You won't believe it, Dean!" she said. "They want to take my picture. They want me to model bathrobes and sweaters for a Foley's catalogue. They're even gonna pay me!"

"I should hope so," Dean said. "Hey, that's cool. Just don't get so uppity you forget your old friends, now."

"Oh, Dean, you're so wonderful! I'm going to come over tonight and give you something really special … if that's all right."

"I believe I can just make that," he said. "But, uh, wait 'til I turn off the porch light, OK? I may have company this evening."

"Sure Dean. I'll be waiting."

The visit

Millie left about 9:30 and Dean turned off the porch light. Within minutes there was a tapping at the door. Janine came in beaming.

"You made me a model, you know that?" she gushed.

"No, God made you a model. I only told some guy about you."

"It's just one little job, but still, it's the most exciting thing I've ever done." She looked at him softly. "And I have you to thank for it."

"So, how are you going to show your appreciation, you little minx?"

The girl grinned. "I'm gonna give you the longest, sweetest blow job you ever had," she said, "Then I'm gonna lay down and let you fuck me 'til I come!"

"Sounds like a full evening," Dean mused. It was also exactly the right thing to top off his teasing encounter with Millie.

Smoochies

The next morning Shannon stopped by Dean's apartment. "You know what?" she asked.

"I couldn't guess," Dean replied in a bored voice.

"I finally got the brother I always wanted."

150

"That's great!" Dean said. "When can I meet him?"

"Next time you look in the mirror," she said, giggling.

"Oh, no, Kiddo," he said. "I'm just the skating partner, remember

"No, you're my brother. I just adopted you!"

"Does that mean we split the estate when Fred and Millie croak

"Sure, why not?" she said. "It'll be more fun to squander it together."

Dean looked at her and squinted. "Who are you?" he asked. "You look like Shannon Foster, but you're much too sweet and considerate to be that selfish little brat."

"This is the real Shannon Foster," she answered. "That other girl is my evil twin." She giggled.

"I see." He nodded his head slowly. "So, what do I have to do to get you as my partner? I'd trade her for you, even if you can't skate."

"Oh, I skate even better than she does."

"Great, where do I sign?"

"All you have to do is give me smoochies."

"OK, uh, but maybe you better go over what the standard 'smoochie,' actually entails for me, just to make sure I've got it straight."

"Sure. A smoochie is where you hold me in your arms, gaze longingly into my eyes, tell me I'm sexy, and kiss me passionately."

"I see. That's the standard issue smoochie?"

"Pretty much. You can add other stuff to it if you want to."

"Well, some of that I can do. But I'm afraid community standards prohibit a gentleman of my advanced age from 'kissing passionately' a young lady of your tender years."

"I won't tell if you won't." She grinned mischievously.

"Well, I'll tell you one thing. I'd risk the wrath of the citizenry if I thought it would make you act civil like this all the time."

"Guaranteed, Dean. Regular smoochies will keep me sweet as sugar."

"What's gotten into you, Shannon? Why are you pulling this smoochie stuff on me?"

The girl looked at him and inhaled. "I want to know what it feels like to be loved by a man. I need to know so I can act it out on the ice."

"You've dated guys before," he said. "Surely you know the routine."

"They're boys, Dean. Fumbling, bumbling boys. They can't even work their own zippers, much less mine. I've never been held by a real man. I need to know what that's like."

"You consider me a 'real man?'"

"You're the prototype, Dean. You're the magazine cover. You're the freakin' poster child for masculine. Everybody else is a Xerox copy!"

"You're not serious, Shannon. You're just tuggin' my twine."

"No, Dickhead. But I feel the transition coming on. The bitch-kid will be back any minute if you don't act fast!" Dean quickly considered the situation. He rationalized that her romantic maturity was important to their skating and that she needed to be able to portray a woman's responses on the ice.

"OK, Sweetcakes," he said. "One standard smoochie coming up!" He took her in his arms, looked into her eyes and caressed her cheek. "Your hair smells like wildflowers in the spring," he said, inhaling slowly. "Your skin is perfect, as smooth as polished marble, but so very, very soft." He tilted her head back and gently kissed her neck. "I love your ears," he said. "They're so cute I just can't keep my eyes off them." He exhaled hot breath into her left ear. "And your earlobes. I love the way they hang there like little candy canes on a Christmas tree, just waiting for me to nibble 'em off." His lips closed on her left earlobe.

"Oh, God, Dean" the girl gasped. "I've got goose bumps. This is so hot!" She sighed as he continued to manipulate the soft ball of flesh with his lips and tongue. Then he moved his face in front of hers. As he gazed at her, her eyes closed and her lips pouted. After an agonizing delay, he pressed his lips to hers. He held the kiss for a time, and then released his partner.

"Was that a smoochie?" he asked.

"Wow!" she said. "That was too cool!"

"So, does this mean you'll be civil from now on?"

"Sure, at least until I need another smoochie." She giggled. "I can't wait to tell the girls you ate my ear!"

"Shannon!" he challenged.

"Just kidding, Dean," she said. "Smoochies are a secret."

A New Job

Dean continued to use Janine to relieve the pressure Millie built up in him for another two weeks.

"Guess what, Dean," Janine said as they lay in recuperation from an intense sexual encounter. "I've got an offer for a new modeling job."

"Great!" he said, somewhat puzzled that she had waited so long to tell him. "What is it?"

"There's an agency that supplies runway models for fashion shows. They want me to join their troop."

"Sounds like big business," he said. "Why aren't you more excited about it?"

"It's... in Dallas. I'd have to move up there." She looked at him sheepishly.

"Dallas is cool," he said. "And modeling beats the Hell outta that typing job, right? So what's the big deal?" She turned a melancholy face to him. "You think you'll miss Houston?" he asked, somewhat puzzled. "You have a lot of friends here?"

"Just one," she said. "There's this guy who lets me come over and play with him sometimes. He's been real good to me, and I hate to leave him." She smiled sheepishly. "I give him something he needs." She giggled. Then the sad look returned.

"If you're talking about me, Miss Budding Supermodel, you're wasting your worry," he grinned. He wanted to make sure she felt no guilt about abandoning him. "I don't need any skinny kid hanging around here, always trying to get her hands in my knickers."

She laughed, then she sighed. "You sure, Dean? I hate to just walk out on you like that. Besides, I like being your … midnight girl."

"Janine, you have to do what's right for you. You don't owe me anything. I do enjoy the time we spend together, but you have to consider this career opportunity in Dallas." Instead of being relieved by gaining Dean's release, the girl's face wilted. Dean surmised that she would have been happier had he asked her to stay in Houston. "Look, Kid, your career is more important than us foolin' around. You have to think about the long term." He paused. "Go give it a shot in Dallas." He grinned. "If it doesn't work out, you can always come back with your tail between your legs and beg me for your old job back."

"Maybe I'm just being silly, Dean. I mean, they'll probably take one look at me and say, "Where's the girl in the picture? You're butt-ugly!" She looked at him. "If I stay here, I can go on being your midnight girl. I'm low-maintenance, Dean. You know that."

Dean realized he was being given another chance to talk her out of moving to Dallas. She would be happy to stay and be his whore if he wanted her. He decided that a bit of brutality was called for at that point.

"Well," he said, "Things are about to get real busy for me. I'm not gonna have much time for midnightin' anymore." He looked at her. "Besides, I think I probably need … something else."

An intense look of pain took over the girl's face. "I guess so," she said. "You can't waste your time on a tramp like me."

Dean was silent for a moment, giving the echo of her sad lament time to die out. He had to let her know that there was no reason for her to harbor any thoughts of hearts and flowers. She was his sex machine, not his life partner. After the sting of that realization had taken its course, Dean took the girl's face in his hands.

"Go to Dallas, Janine," he said. "Knock 'em dead. Make me proud of you."

She smiled weakly. "OK, Dean," she said. As they embraced, she was unable to hold back her tears. Dean was helpless to ease her pain. Then she dressed and left.

Dean didn't see Janine anymore. But he did occasionally receive, in the mail, a page cut out of a catalog with "That's me! Can you believe it?" scribbled on it. She was struggling to make good on her promise to make him proud of her.

Chapter 21

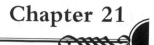

Indian Outlaw

"I need a favor," Dean told Willie.

"What you need, Dean?"

"Shannon and I will be debuting a new routine at TIS Friday night. We've never skated it in public before, and I'd like to run it up the flagpole before that." He paused. "Would you mind if we previewed it here on Thursday night?"

"That would be good, Dean, real good," Willie answered. "Can I tell people?"

Dean grinned. "It's not a secret, Willie," he said.

The Show

Shannon and Dean were getting ready to preview their routine at Willie's Ice Palace in South Houston. "Have you looked outside?" Shannon said excitedly.

"Yeah," Dean said, "It looks like a Mercedes dealership out there. The junkers that usually show up are having to park on the street."

"I think the whole FSCT crew is here," Shannon said.

Dean grinned. "Must be some big deal here tonight."

As Shannon and Dean warmed up on the ice they noticed a lot of the TIS regulars out there as well. Many of the FSC kids were there with both parents, which was a rarity.

"It's good to see the rich folks come down here," Willie said, "But I hope my place don't put 'em off none."

"Your place is fine, Willie," Dean said. "Let 'em get used to it."

The hockey buzzer went off. "All skaters please leave the ice," the PA system said.

Shannon and Dean skated out to center ice dressed in Indian costumes that Millie had engineered. They were made of white suede leather and ornamented with colorful patterns of beads. Shannon's outfit had a full skirt that came to mid-calf, and Dean wore long pants and a vest. They wore boot covers that looked like moccasin boots. Dean wore two stripes of war paint under each eye and a feather in his headband. Shannon had two braided pigtails and looked like an Indian princess.

One of Dean's co-workers at Accumedical Data Systems was a Cherokee Indian from Oklahoma. He had been a member of the Native American Students Association at Oklahoma State University, and he put Dean in touch with people who had videos of authentic tribal dances, such as the Apache war dance, the Zuni rain dance, and the Hopi snake dance. Dean had worked some of these moves into their routine.

The music was Tim McGraw's rendition of "Indian Outlaw," describing a brave who is half Cherokee and half Choctaw, and a maiden who is a Chippewa. It started with rolling thunder and a heavy beat of tom-toms in an Indian rhythm. They began to skate in steps derived from the tribal dance videos.

During the first verse Dean took an imaginary arrow out of an invisible quiver and fired it at Shannon from an unseen bow. The impact sent her into a sit-spin.

Shannon began the second verse skating close behind Dean, as if riding behind him on a pony. Then he pulled her between his legs and hoisted her overhead in a platter lift.

During the third verse Dean posed for the audience, Shannon skated up behind him and pulled at his costume, removing his long pants and exposing bare legs and suede shorts. Shannon skated away proudly waving the brave's britches like a flag.

During the chorus, Dean caught Shannon from behind, took back his pants and pulled off her long skirt as well, exposing a much shorter skirt and two shapely thighs. She feigned great embarrassment.

The remainder of the song was instrumental, with the heavy beat of tom-toms carrying it on strongly. Dean and Shannon skated facing each other in a rather suggestive chase. They were a few feet apart, with her stroking backward most of the time. Their faces wore intensely determined looks, Dean to get his hands on the maiden, and Shannon to preserve her innocence.

"Come here, Pocahontas," Dean said, grinning knowingly.

"Don't get any funny ideas, Tonto!" Shannon admonished, getting onto the role she was playing.

"You're gonna keep my big wigwam warm tonight," he said.

"Keep away from me, you horny old Indian, you!" Shannon said.

They continued to race around the arena, keeping up this playful pursuit, to the delight of the audience. After a while Shannon changed her attitude and skated dance steps affectionately with her partner for the rest of the song.

When the music stopped the assembly cheered. Both the poor kids and the affluent children poured out on the ice to congratulate Shannon and Dean.

"Your Indian dance is a big hit," Millie said when the two skaters made their way to the rail.

"Thanks, Mom," Shannon said. Dean smiled.

Shannon and Dean skated the Indian Outlaw number the following night at the Club Ice session at TIS. It was again very well received by an even larger crowd.

Hot Pants

After the session Shannon tromped into the girls locker room to take off her skates. Several of the other girl skaters were doing the same.

"We can ride my pony double," the girl at the other end of the bench sang a line from the song. She looked at Shannon and giggled. "Makes my little heart bubble," another added. More giggling. "Like a glass of wine." Now three girls were looking at Shannon and giggling.

"Do you have something to say, Caitlin?" There was irritation in Shannon's voice.

"Have you been riding his pony bareback, Shannon?" They giggled.

"Screw you, Caitlin!"

"Come on, Shannon. We're all friends here. Tell us what it's like to ride bareback with the Indian Outlaw." More giggling.

"Kiss my ass!"

"Ooh, Caitlin, you struck a nerve," Tissy said. "There must be something really hot going on here!"

"Shannon has hot pants for her partner," Tiffany said. They giggled.

"Bitches!" Shannon said, picking up her skate bag and walking out.

"Don't leave yet, Shannon," Tiffany said. "Tell us all about it!"

"Eat a bug, Tiffany!" she replied.

Dean

"I guess you know," Shannon said as she and Dean walked toward their cars, "All the jealous twits are giving me holy Hell about you!"

"I didn't know that," Dean said, with obviously pretended interest.

"Well, they are. They just say the tackiest things!"

"Well, what else are jealous twits good for?" Dean asked.

"Well this club has more than its share."

"I don't think you can ever achieve a measure of notoriety, as we have here, without evoking a jealousy response."

"They're just bitches, that's all."

"What are they sayin'?" His curiosity had been piqued.

"It's way gross, Dean. They say I'm 'riding your pony bareback.'"

"Riding my pony bareback?" he laughed. "How creative. They must have IQ almost equal to their age. They still sneak up behind me and yell 'rocket!' and wave their fists in the air and run away giggling. Or they mumble 'biggest block alive,' when they walk by."

"Gross! They say I have 'hot pants' for you." Shannon stopped and looked at him.

"What?" He sensed that her attention had suddenly focused on him.

"They say I have hot pants for you."

"OK, uh...," He seemed uncertain how to respond. "Do you?"

"Well, I wouldn't tell you, now would I?"

"Probably not," he said, matter-of-factly, pretending to understand this particular turn in the conversation.

"So?"

"So, what?" he asked, now in total confusion.

"So, what do you think about that?"

"About what?" Exasperation was creeping in.

"About me having hot pants for you?"

"Uh, well, I think it's...," He paused. "Why am I answering this?"

"Because it's important."

"Look, Shannon." He inhaled. "This is all our doing, here. We decided we were going to work this old man - young girl romance thing into our act. Now people are picking it up. What's the big surprise? If they didn't, that's when we'd be in trouble."

"You mean...?"

"Yeah. We skate, and sell the lust thing so well they start wondering if we're bouncing in the sack together. You think this is a bad thing?"

"Well...,"

"Look, we're not doing anything wrong, so it's just gossip. It has no basis in fact. So who gives a shit? Let 'em snicker. It keeps people interested in us, and in our skating. It'll fill up the cheap seats someday."

"Huh!"

"Yeah. Don't say 'Yes,' and don't say 'No.' Just keep 'em guessing. Make it a big mystery. 'Are they, or aren't they? Inquiring minds want to know!' It'll become the basic image of our act. But it'll spill over into our private lives too. We just have to deal with that. We're performers."

He paused. "We're celebrities now, Shannon. We don't have as much privacy as normal humans. It's the price you pay. But it's part of what we're trying to do here. So deal with it, Kid. OK?"

"Yeah, sure. I can do that!" she replied. "I'll just keep 'em guessin'"

"Well, don't overdo it. A full-page confession in the Chronicle would be a bit much."

"But you didn't answer my question."

"What question?"

"What would you think about me having hot pants for you?"

"I think it's...," He paused. "Ridiculous. I'm old enough to be your orthodontist, for Pete's sake."

The girl looked at him coolly. "But what if I did?"

"You're barely seventeen, Shannon. You wouldn't know from 'hot pants' if your Levis were on fire!"

Her eyes narrowed, and her lips pressed together. She looked at him for a moment, as if preparing to speak, then turned and walked away.

Chapter 22

Queen Jakes Knight

"We need to finalize your long program for Regionals and start thinking about a short program for Sectionals," Millie said through Dean's cell phone. "I'll be over to your place about 6:30. I'll come straight down from the office."

Realizing that was a statement instead of a question, Dean said, "OK." His last work session with Millie had been productive, but strangely uncomfortable for him. His unrequited sexual desire for the woman had proved to be an unpleasant distraction. "I should be able to control this," he thought. "She's just a woman, for Pete's sake!"

Ever since his first meeting with her she had never completely left his mind, Some part of his thoughts had been captured by her. Some small portion of his brain had become devoted to Millie Foster. She was never completely out of his mind. If she was nearby, he had some attention on her. Even if she was far away, she was not absent from his thoughts. He did not understand this. No other person had affected him in exactly this way.

Janine had provided some relief, but she was gone. He decided to force is mind to focus on the job at hand and, if he did think of Millie, it would be to admire her beauty rather than to lust after her body. "It's mind over matter," he told himself.

The Work Session

It was about a quarter to seven when Dean heard the Mercedes stop outside his apartment. Millie's high heel shoes made a clicking sound as they ascended the stairs. She knocked impatiently on his door. "I'm a little late," she said. "Sorry. There's just so much going on at the office, and the renovations at Bayou Plaza are falling behind schedule." She pulled some things out of the front closet and disappeared into the bathroom.

After what seemed like a long time, the woman who had arrived looking she just stepped out of a corporate board meeting emerged looking like she was ready for the red carpet at the Academy Awards. She wore a short, tight-fitting pale turquoise tank dress with slits on each side. The garment hugged her ample form from breast to waist, then flared, falling lightly over her well-rounded hips. The material, though opaque, was so light and thin as to suggest a silk scarf. The flared miniskirt only partially concealed the details of her derriere when she held still, but kept no secrets when she moved. Two thin straps reached over her shoulders and supported the scooped neckline that covered only the outer half of her breasts, leaving the soft skin of the inner portions exposed, almost to her navel. She wore a three-row rhinestone necklace with matching rhinestone teardrop earrings and a double-row rhinestone bracelet on her left wrist, and no belt at the waist. Her yellow-blonde hair was still amazingly fluffy after a day's work, and it formed a soft frame around her face. Her bare legs were supported by clear fashion slides with three-inch heels.

Millie and Dean chatted for a while, mostly about her frustrations at work, before addressing the skating programs. During the conversation Dean was able to concentrate, but he did pause on occasion to admire the radiant beauty beside him. He had to respect a lady who could do the woman thing so expertly. He couldn't imagine any way in which she could be improved.

The Encounter

They had been working for almost thirty minutes when it happened. Millie recognized the look on Dean's face almost immediately. Something had come over him. His gaze was intense. His mind was not in control of his body. Reason had abandoned his thoughts. Forethought and discretion were no longer a part of his reasoning.

Millie knew her time had come. Her patience had paid off. Her persistence had produced the desired result. She walked over and stood in front of him, making the object of his desire both clearly visible and readily available. They started at each other for a brief moment, and she crossed her wrists in front of her abdomen. Acting almost robotically, Dean reached up and slipped the thin straps off her shoulders. She shrugged slightly, allowing the loops to drop to her elbows. Then she crossed her arms and slipped them out of the straps. She paused only a moment before raising her arms over her head, Allowing Dean to slide the dress slowly down her body until it fell to the floor.

The woman stood in front of Dean for a long moment, wearing only her thong panties. Then he picked her up and carried her into the bedroom, where he deposited her gently but firmly on the bed. She raised her hips slightly as he slipped the G-string down her thighs and off over her feet. She watched as he peeled off his T-shirt and slipped quickly out of his pants. Then she placed her arms above her head and parted her legs as he lay down, moving between them.

They both were shocked by the intensity of the sensation when he entered her. Millie gave up a wide-eyed gasp and then lay back, submitting, with her arms above her head. Upon reaching full penetration, Dean paused for a moment and then began to move in long, slow strokes, savoring both the sensation and the sight of the situation. The vision of this powerfully sexy woman, laid out beneath him, completely under his control, yielding to his penetration, was overpowering.

Millie was quickly overcome by the feelings, and she responded with unfocused eyes and deep moans. Dean became invigorated, and he began to gradually increase his movements. There was a long period of increasing ferocity as Dean's motions and Millie's responses increased until the two lovers were engaged in a tumultuous frenzy of uncontrolled passion. Millie's body writhed and contorted to the point that only Dean's firm grip kept her under him. With his right arm encircling her neck and his left gripping her right hip, he thrust her with ever increasing force.

Millie's moans turned to screams as she neared her release. Dean was lost in the frenzy as his body, now operating completely free of his mind, exerted itself at full force. Then they stared at each other wide-eyed as the physiological sequence of climax events went into action. Millie's body tensed up as she gripped Dean's head with her arms. He tightened his grip on her body as his thrusts became more desperate. "Oh, God!" Millie cried out as sensation engulfed her. Dean voiced a long groan as his body forcefully gave up its precious DNA-bearing fluid. Millie stopped breathing, went completely rigid, and let out a long scream as her passion exploded.

Only slowly did they come down from the apex of sensation, leaving them both at last limp and gasping. A flood of relaxation engulfed them both as their once rigid bodies collapsed into a disorganized pile of flaccid limbs.

By the time Millie's breathing had returned to normal, she was asleep, or perhaps unconscious due to her ordeal. Dean, however, was wide awake and consumed by an overwhelming feeling of serenity and wellbeing. The sense of satisfaction he felt was almost frightening. It was the most calm and relaxed he had felt in months. He marveled at how the sex act could bring about such an improvement in his disposition. He had no worries or concerns. He couldn't remember any problems that he might have. He was at a loss to recall anything amiss in his life. He sat in the dimly lit bedroom, gazing at Millie's unconscious, but still beautiful form, amazed that she could bestow such serenity on him. He had never experienced that before.

It was most of twenty minutes before Millie's eyes began to open. The two lovers looked at each other for a long moment, engaged in a vague, silent communication. Finally Millie spoke. "Hello," she said, "I'm Millie Foster."

"Dean Steele," he replied, grinning. "Pleased to make your acquaintance." They smiled at each other softly. Then Millie closed her eyes, inhaled, and let out a long sigh. A grin took her face as she looked at her chambermate, preparing to speak. "In case you missed it," she said, "That was the absolute high point of my entire life." She looked away, then back. "Just so you know."

Dean was sitting up slightly in the bed, leaning back on a pillow against the headboard. With some effort Millie pulled her body up along his left side and began to stroke his chest with her left hand. They didn't say anything for a time. Conversation was unnecessary. They both contemplated the recent events in silence.

Finally Millie broke the stillness. "You were wonderful, Mr. Steele," she whispered. "Ten times better than my all-time best fantasy. Now I don't need to wonder what Heaven is like. I've been there."

"I once thought," Dean began, "That you were twice the woman of anybody I had ever met. But now I find your factor is more like ten."

"You like me, then?" she asked. "You consider me a worthy companion for your private chambers?"

"Oh, far beyond that," he replied. "Compared to this, all my previous experiences were little more than masturbation."

She snuggled against his shoulder. "I hate to say, 'I told you so,' but ..."

"Yes, you did mention it a time or two." They chuckled.

After a time she spoke. "Remorse, Dean? Is your guilt kicking in?"

"Actually I'm having trouble remembering why we shouldn't do this. I can't seem to force my thoughts onto any subject other than just how ... amazingly wonderful you are."

"Well, my witch's spell must be working as planned." She grinned.

"I feel like I've been brainwashed," he said. "I can't remember anything that happened before you showed up at the door tonight." Her grin widened. "I guess you gave me an overdose of endorphins."

"Of what?"

"The word is short for 'endogenous morphines.' It means chemicals your body makes that are analogs of the anesthetic, morphine. Having an orgasm releases 'em by the gallon."

"You mean we've been drugged?"

"Heavily ODed, by all outward appearances."

"Thank God for endorphins, then!"

"I feel so calm, and ... euphoric ... that I can't remember the last problem I had."

"See? I'm good for you!" She smiled softly.

"It sure feels like it!"

As they lay there quietly, Dean wondered what this new development would entail for the skating project. "I guess I'll figure that out tomorrow," he thought as he drifted off to sleep in Millie's arms.

Chapter 23

Big Girl

"OK, Kid," Dean said after one of their workouts, "What's going on with you?"

"What do you mean?" Shannon asked, showing some irritation.

"I see some disturbing trends here." He inhaled. "First I don't think you're really pushing in the gym. The amount of weight you handle isn't going up as fast as it should, and you do too many reps ... unless I stop you. You skimp on your supplements. You aren't jamming protein like you should be." He paused. "Do you have some kind of disagreement with your program?" The girl pouted but didn't answer. "Hello," he said, peering into her eyes. "Anybody home in there?" A snort was the only response he got. "Come on, Tiger. Level with your old partner, here. Let me know what dark secrets lurk behind eyes so bright." She looked at him, softening only slightly. "Come on, Sweetcakes. What sinister thoughts are rummaging around inside the pretty head?" Under pressure from his flattery, her grin was becoming difficult to suppress. "Surely a face like a china doll can't harbor a very horrible secret."

Unable to hold back any longer, the girl grinned and then looked at him with big round eyes. "I'm worried, Dean."

"About what, Princess?"

"That the judges won't like me."

"Why not?" was his incredulous answer.

"Because I'm too big! Everybody knows pairs girls are just these petite little things, and already I'm too damn big! No judge is ever going to give us good marks if I look like a cow out there!"

"Has anybody said anything about it?" he asked, sensing that she needed some counseling at that point.

"The girls at the rink laugh at me," she said. "They say I'm big enough to skate the boy's part. They joke about skating pairs with me!"

"Do you think they'll still be laughing when we medal at Nationals?"

"But will we, Dean? Can we ever win a medal in pairs if I'm not just some tiny little thing?"

"I hope this sport isn't so screwed up that we'd lose even a tenth of a point based solely on the girl's size. If it is, then I don't want to play in this sandbox anymore." Shannon blinked. "You know why I'm doing this, Shannon?" he asked with a sinister look on his face. "I never told you the real reason." Her eyes widened. "For me it's an ego trip. There's something I'm out to prove." He leaned close to her. "I want to show those idiots that I'm the only man in the world who can skate pairs with a full-size woman." He looked at her as if he had just revealed the secret of the ages. "There is no man alive on this planet who has my combination of strength and skating. I don't want to be just another figure skating medal winner. To heck with that! I want to be the only man in the history of the world who successfully skated pairs with a normal-size woman. I want to show it can be done." He had dropped into the persona of a politician making a dramatic speech. He paused to take a breath. "Don't you see? It's a place in history I'll hold for years! There's nobody coming up the ranks who can do it. I, Dean Steele, am the only one!" He dramatized the speech of a power-mad dictator.

Shannon watched through enlarged eyes as he threw his head back and closed his eyes for a dramatic moment. "The whole world is laboring under a misconception here. People wrongly believe that pairs girls are supposed to be tiny. It's a sinister plot that's been perpetrated by the boy skaters, because they're too lazy to lift a real girl. So they throw these midgets up in the air and say, 'Oh, isn't she cute, flying around up there?' And then everybody buys off on the bullshit and says, 'Oh, pairs girls are always so tiny!' Well, I'm gonna give 'em a wake-up call. I'm here to announce that pairs skating, properly done, involves a real woman, not just some tiny little girl. And the only logical conclusion that can possibly follow from that is that I, the real Dean Steele, am the only boy skater, in the world, qualified to skate pairs!"

"You're seriously full of shit today, aren't you, Dean?"

"Perhaps. But the weakness in my plan is… I need the right partner. If I did it with one of the rink pixies, it wouldn't work, comprendo?"

"Yes, Dean," she said, from beneath her brow.

"So, that's where you come in, Shannon Foster, beautiful muscle girl and expert skater. Do you follow my reasoning so far? Can you comprehend the essence of my evil scheme?"

"So, just how big do you want me to be, Dean?"

"You see that girl over by the calf machine? Julie?"

"She's a gorilla, Dean. Her knuckles drag."

"Right. Now, she's big enough, but she'd never be able to skate well enough. But then there's Foster! You already skate well enough. All we have to do is get you big enough!

"But, I'll be too heavy to jump!" she whined.

"Ooh," Dean mused. "There's less mass between your ears than I thought." He paused. "Fat and bone have to be lifted," he lectured. "But muscle does the lifting. Get the distinction here? If you could do doubles at 110, and you put on ten pounds of fat, you'd be doing singles, right?"

"Yeah," she said, in a "so what?" voice.

"But if you were doing doubles at 110, and you put on ten pounds of muscle, you'd be doing triples, comprendo?"

Her face twisted, reflecting her difficulty in formulating an objection. Finally she spoke. "But Dean, no judge is going to give us a medal if I look like a gorilla. They'll give 'em to those 'cutie-pie' little twits."

"There's an advanced principle of figure skating you need to be aware of here," he said. "It's called the 'screw-the-judges' hypothesis."

"Oh, so we sleep with the judges to get good marks? Is that it?"

"That's a different 'screw-the-judges' principle," he said, "And it might actually work better. But I'm talking about the one that says, 'Work up a good program and skate it well, and let the judges do whatever they want with it.' We skate to entertain. If we do that, we win, no matter how the judges mark their cards."

"But I'm gangly-looking! I'm not ... shapely, like the smaller girls."

"OK, look. It's the muscles that give the body 'shape.' Now if you pack a five-foot frame with normal size muscles, you get 'shapely.' But if you spread normal size muscles out over a five-foot-seven frame, you get ... gangly. So, what to do? You pack your frame with bigger-than-normal-size muscles. Then you get 'shapely,' in a full-size package."

"So, you want me to get big?"

"No, I want you to get huge! I want to feel the ground shake when you walk. Then, when I hold you up over my head, people will damn well know that Dean Steele means business when he lifts a girl! They'll realize that I, the amazing Dean Steele, am the only valid boy pairs skater the world has ever seen!" The orator was back.

"Does that mean I can eat ice cream?"

"No, Miss Piggy. We're talking muscle here, not fat. It's muscle that'll make you look sexy."

"You really want me to look sexy?"

"Yes, Dear Lady! I want you to be what those little nymphs and sprites can only promise to become. I want you to be flowering womanhood in full bloom, and I shall hoist you to the stars!"

"Uh, maybe you could just lift me over your head, OK?"

"Well, we can do it that way, if you prefer," he replied.

They laughed. Shannon felt better.

Chapter 24

Breakup

Millie showed up at Dean's apartment about 6:00 PM, still dressed for work. There was a brief embrace, a race for the bedroom, some frantic removal of garments, and an intense sexual encounter, followed by a brief nap.

"Isn't it time for us to start feeling remorse and regret, given this new development in our relationship?" Dean asked, after they awoke in an embrace.

"I wondered how long it would take you to get around to that," Millie sighed.

"Well, it probably does deserve some discussion," Dean said, "Given the risks." He paused. "I'd love to hear your thoughts on it."

"There are two kinds of sins, Dean," Millie began. "There are destructive sins and there are sins of disapproval."

"And how does that work, Your Reverence?" He was grinning.

"Well, destructive sins actually hurt people," Millie explained, ignoring his sarcasm. "They destroy life and property. But the other kind are sins only because somebody disapproves. They don't actually hurt anything. They just violate someone's moral code without actually doing any harm."

"I see. And which kind is our little sin?" Dean asked, already able to predict the answer.

"It's only a sin because of community disapproval. It actually harms no one. In fact, nothing is changed in the least by it"

"This is a lesser kind of a sin, then?" He was amused by her moralistic argument.

"If it is only a sin because of disapproval, and if no one who would disapprove knows about it, then it's not a sin at all!"

"Ah! So the only crime is getting caught, then."

"That's not what I said. I just said that it doesn't hurt anybody, and it draws no disapproval if nobody finds out, so it's the same as no sin at all."

Dean thought for a moment. "I think there's a third kind," he said.

Millie looked at him. "And what's that?"

"It's the kind of sin where you underestimate its harmful effects. It's a sin where you delude yourself into believing it isn't a sin, and then you suffer the consequences without ever knowing where they came from."

"Are you suffering consequences, Pretty Boy?" She was smiling.

"Probably."

"Like what?"

"I have to live with the guilt."

"And what does this guilt complex do to you, Mr. Morals?"

"It's hard to say. It builds up barriers between me and my partner and my sponsor. I can't be fully open with them. I have to be careful what I say. I can't leave any suspicious clues laying around."

"And you're suffering from this, Dean? You need to be closer to Shannon and Fred?"

"Barriers are barriers, Millie. Sooner or later they'll take their toll."

"Well, this thing between us has a life of its own, Dean. Even if you suffer from these 'barriers,' surely it's worth the price."

"That depends on what the full price eventually turns out to be."

"Well, it'll never come close to the good that comes out of our relationship," she opined.

"I hope so," Dean mused. "I sincerely hope so."

Janine

After dressing and refreshing her makeup, Millie was preparing to leave. "Well Dean," she said, "You're a lot more … responsive, since that little tramp is gone."

Alarms started going off in Dean's mind, but he maintained a calm exterior. "Uh … which tramp is that?" he asked nonchalantly.

"That little Wilson girl who used to leave her muddy footprints on your bedroom carpet."

"You know Miss Wilson?"

"We were never formally introduced, but I was nonetheless able to give her career a boost of sorts." A smug smile crossed her lips.

"What do you mean?" he asked. He was boiling with anger inside, while fighting to appear calm.

"Well, I just put in a good word for her with a friend who has connections in Dallas. It may not be the start of a stellar modeling career, but it got her out of your life. Besides, she'll do well in Dallas. There's enough sex, drugs and booze on Gaston Avenue[1] to keep her happy."

"So, what did you do, Millie, call in a favor from a friend?"

"Something like that. Just job offer enough to get rid of her."

"How did you know her, anyway?" he asked calmly. He was churning inside, but he had to hear the rest of her story.

"Don't be naïve, Dean. It didn't take me long to figure out you were getting your horns trimmed by one of these little tramps, and it wasn't difficult to find out who."

"Another PI?"

"Oh, no. Just a few discrete inquiries. You're a local celebrity, Dean. Your charming neighbors like to keep current on all the Dean Steele gossip. I made a deal with one of the girls who lives here to keep an eye on you. It didn't take long to get the rest of the story." She paused to give him a triumphant look. "Oh, don't worry. Your little whore didn't rat you out, but her girlfriends figured out she was involved in some kind of secret mission, and her trail led them to your door."

"So, you found out I was seeing Janine, and you got a friend to offer her a phony modeling job in Dallas?"

"You weren't 'seeing her,' Dean. That little tramp was simply draining your manhood every night. If she had any sense she would have charged you for it."

"How do you know she didn't?"

"Oh, she was only too happy to give it away! Being Dean Steele's secret sex toy was her greatest ambition in life. She'd come over here about midnight and do her thing, then slither away before daybreak."

Eviction

Dean had everything he needed. Millie's confession was complete. "All right, Madam, he said coolly. "Your invitation is hereby revoked. Now get your ass out of my house!" Millie looked at him in shock. "What makes you think you're so privileged that you can manipulate people's lives like that?"

"She's trash, Dean," Millie explained. "Surely you know those cheap sluts are a dime a dozen. She isn't ever going to be anything else. She'll fare no worse in Dallas than here."

"What about me? Maybe I valued my relationship with her."

"She was just blowing your horn, Dean! She was defiling you, stealing your essence. I did you a favor, believe me!"

"Last time I checked, this was still a free country. I never hired you to be my nanny, Millie."

"You're blinded by testosterone, Dean. You can't be expected to see things clearly where tramps and sluts are concerned. You need a cool head looking out for you."

"You have the key to your closet?"

169

"Yes, why?"

"Put it on the table over there. You won't be needing it anymore."

"Dean, calm down … please!"

"No. Millie, I don't plan to calm down until you're halfway across Houston." He opened her closet, rolled her dresses and shoes into a ball and tossed them to her. "And take this crap with you!"

"Dean, please!" she pleaded. "I did it for your own good. Don't let it upset you like this."

"Don't explain, Millie. Just take your stuff and get outta here!"

Seeing that she had no choice, Millie gathered up her things. "We'll talk about this tomorrow," she said. Then she left.

---

1. Gaston Avenue – a street in Dallas, Texas lined with apartment houses on both sides. Most of the tenants are young and single.

Chapter 25

The Call

"Let's do spins today," Dean said as they sat in the lounge at TIS before their afternoon practice.

"No spins," Shannon said, "I'm not in the mood."

"So, that's it?" he asked. "You come in here, reeking of bubble gum, with your dual parallel counter-rotating dog-ear ponytails swinging in the breeze, and say, 'No spins?' You expect me to put up with your cheap bullshit?"

"Of course," the girl replied flippantly.

"Well guess again, Precious, 'cause you got no score on round one. I really think it's important to practice spins. And besides, I really want us to show the world a good counter-rotating pairs camel spin."

Shannon reached into her purse. "Here's a quarter, Dean," she sneered, "Call someone who gives a shit!" An airborne twenty-five cent piece bounced off his chest.

The Call

When it stopped rolling, Dean reached down and picked up the quarter. He moved over to the pay phone in the corner of the room, lifted the receiver and dialed a number.

"Ellenton, Florida," he said. "The J. P Igloo Ice Sports Complex." He wrote down a number. Then he inserted the coin and dialed a number

"I'm calling for Nicole Bobek," he said after a pause. "Yes, Nicole Bobek. She should be on the figure skating sheet. Can you get a message to her please? It's important." Shannon eyed him suspiciously during the pause. "What? Oh, OK, good. Would you just ask her to call me? Yeah. Wave her over and tell her Dean Steele needs to talk to her as soon as she gets off the ice. It's important." There was a pause. "I know she's practicing. Just wave her over and tell her, OK? And give her this number. 281-...," Another pause. "OK, right. It's 281-555-7979. Dean Steele, got it? Yeah... Yeah... Yeah. Go tell her, OK? Thanks." He hung up.

"Very cute, Dean," Shannon said, "Pretending to call Nicole Bobek. I'll bet you were listening to the time the whole time. 'At the tone, the time will be...,' Sucko, Dean!" She gave him a bored and disgusted look.

The pay phone rang. "Uh, that'd be for me," he said.

"Wait a minute!" Shannon said. "I'll get it," she grinned. "You called one of those phone company call-back numbers, I know! It just waits a minute, and then it calls you back." She moved to the phone.

"Hello," Shannon said, glaring coolly at Dean.

"Hello," a woman's voice said. "Let me talk to Dean Steele."

"Uh, who's calling?" Shannon asked, somewhat shocked.

"Nicole Bobek," the voice said. "Go get him. I'm in a hurry." Wide-eyed, Shannon held out the phone for Dean.

"Hello?" Dean said into the instrument. "Oh, Hi, Nikki. Thanks for getting back to me. ... Oh, I'm good. How 'bout you? ... That's great. ... Yeah? ... Wow! I'll bet you really look good skatin' to that music." He paused for a while. "Hey, that sounds great. ... Listen, the reason I called..., uh, you know, you and I talked about it some a while back. I was wondering if you might like to get together and talk about ... you know, the possibility of maybe workin' up a number or two together. It's just an idea ... What? ... Yeah. ... Well, no, I only thought... Well sure. I think that'd be great. You really ...?" There was a pause. "Well, OK, sure. It's a deal. I'll fly to Tampa and rent a car." Another pause. "What? Well, yeah, I did have a partner. Yeah. But we broke up. Yeah. Well, it's kind of a long story. ... I know, but... Well, it's just that she turned out to be such a bitch, you know? Very immature. I couldn't deal with it. It just got to be just too much of a hassle, you know? That's all. Life's too short." He paused.

"Look, Nikki," he said, "I know you need to get back on the ice. I'll call you tonight, OK? After I set up my flight. When will you be home? ... OK, good. ... I'll call you then. ... Huh? Yeah, I will. ... Yes, I will. ... OK. ... Sure thing ... Bye. He hung up the phone.

Shannon

"So, that's it?" Shannon asked. "We've been broke up thirty seconds, and you've already got a new partner?"

"Supply and demand, Kid. I have that rare commodity in the figure skating marketplace - a Y chromosome."

"Is it that, or does 'Nikki' just have the hots for you?"

"She admires my skating," he replied, becoming deliberately evasive.

"Bullshit!" Shannon interjected. "You two would be disgusting!"

"We intend to project grace and dignity with our skating," Dean said.

"They'd have to post guards at the door. 'Under seventeen not admitted.' Even the construction workers would blush!"

"We'll skate the classic Russian ballet style."

"As if!" she hooted. "It'll be X-rated."

"It'll fill up the cheap seats."

"Sure, if that's what you want! A bunch of weirdoes getting their jollies watching you skate!"

"Uh, it works for me!" he said.

"Gross, Dean!"

"No, what we'll really have is judges giving us high marks."

Shannon looked at him. "OK, Dean. Who was that woman?"

"I thought you knew."

"No, you just called up some old girlfriend, and she played along with your little 'Nikki' joke."

"You wish."

"I know. The real Nicole Bobek wouldn't call you back. She wouldn't even remember you. All you did was dance with her once."

"You really believed me when I said that's all that happened?"

"Yeah. And you'd never be stupid enough to give me up anyway."

"Really?" He displayed exaggerated amazement at her statement.

"Sure. She doesn't have my potential." She gave him a cocky look.

"At least she practices!"

"Yeah, sometimes," she said, "When she's in the mood! Come on, Dean, admit it. You're lucky to have me. I'm your ticket to stardom."

"The Gods have smiled on me!" he mused sarcastically.

"Call 'Nikki' back and tell her to buzz off. Your career can't take the downgrade."

"Will you practice spins?"

"Yeah, if I ever need to," she answered, grinning.

"And will you always be a perfect angel and do exactly as you're told, without any protest whatsoever?"

"Get real, Steele!" she said. "This is still Planet Earth!"

He grinned. "OK, I'll call her, but it may break her heart."

"Shit happens," Shannon grinned. "She's bound to know that."

They practiced spins and lifts. "By the way," Shannon said as they walked out of the ice stadium. "Really. Who was that woman on the phone?"

"1995 US National Champion, Nicole Bobek," Dean said, solemnly. "That's my story, and I'm stickin' to it."

"Shithead!" Shannon laughed. She bumped him with her butt as they burst out into the warm Texas sunshine that saturated the parking lot.

That evening Dean's phone rang, "How'd I do?" a female voice asked.

"Oh, you were good, Diane[1]," he said. "She thought you were Bobek. Thanks for playing that for me."

"Anytime, Dean. It was fun. Bye."

Rules

"OK, Dean," Shannon said as they walked into the Foster living room that afternoon. Fred an Millie had not yet gotten home. "We need to be clear on what the rules are about how you can touch me and how you can't when we're skating."

"Ohoo, that sounds significant," Dean replied sarcastically.

"There are things about me you just have to know," she announced.

"A complex and mysterious personality," he mumbled.

"Of course you can touch me as required by any of the lifts and throws in the USFSA rule book. But you can't touch my breasts or my butt or the inside of my thigh."

"I hope I can remember all that. I'd hate to screw up and touch the wrong thing." He was becoming irritated.

"Well, just remember the rules," she said impatiently.

"I think we should use a simpler rule, just so I can remember it easy."

"Yeah? What's that?"

"It's the rule that says I can touch anything you've got, anytime I want, for any reason whatsoever, without permission and without apology."

"As if, Dean!" she said, disgustedly. "Like I would really allow that!" She peered at him from beneath raised eyebrows.

"I'm your pairs partner, Princess. It's my job to throw you up in the air and see that you don't bust your butt when you come back down. So I don't want to be encumbered by silly rules about which handles I can use to keep your tender young ass from impacting that cold, hard ice."

"Well, some places on my body are just simply off limits to you!" She took on a haughty air.

"You mean, I can't lick the back of your neck?"

"Are you crazy?"

Dean grabbed the girl, pinned her arms, lifted her ponytail, and ran his tongue slowly along the back of her neck. She squealed. "And what else, buns?" he grabbed her buttocks with both hands while she fought him. "Mighty meaty!" he exclaimed.

"Now, what was that about tits?" He grabbed her breasts and fondled them while she squirmed.

"And what else? Oh yes, pussy!"

"Don't you dare, Dean!" She glared at him.

He held her wrists behind her back with his left hand and gripped her pubis firmly with his right. She looked at him wide-eyed as he gave her most private area a squeeze.

"Now that we've been formally introduced," he said, "Maybe we can skate together." He released her.

"You're a despicable animal, Dean!" Her voice lacked conviction.

"Nobody's perfect," he replied.

Pouting, she glared at him for a time. "That was a terrible thing to do to me," she said. "It was crude and degrading." Her insincerity was poorly hidden.

"I guess you life is over now, for all intents and purposes," he responded.

"I'll never be the same, that's for sure," she said. "I've been ... manhandled!"

"I expect there'll be a lot more of that in your future, Lolita."

"What do you mean? You're gonna do it all the time?"

"No, but there'll soon be a whole bunch of puckheads lining up to 'manhandle' your precious bod. You'll be a 'hot property' if we ever start winning anything made out of metal."

"No Dean, that's not what you meant. You meant you're going to put your hands all over me like that all the time now. You're going to touch me in the most intimate places, and I won't be able to stop you. I'll just have to submit to it, like a helpless victim as your big strong hands explore my sensitive body all over." She looked at him wide-eyed.

Dean regarded the girl with a bored look. "Been readin' them trash novels again, Sweetheart?"

"No, I've been skating with a partner who's a dirty old man, and he can't keep his hands off my sexy young body. And he's so big and strong that I can't fight him off."

"I see. Well, just try to keep all those grimy handprints wiped off your ass. The judges might mark us down for that."

"You know what this means," she said after a pause. He merely looked at her. "It means I can grab you, anywhere I want to."

"We'll just wait 'till the need arises on that one," he responded, with a tone of warning.

"No we won't. If you can grab me, I can grab you. That's the rule."

"Democracy, equality, and fair play are no part of skating with Dean Steele, Kid. You been readin' the wrong rule book."

"No I haven't." She reached for his groin. He slapped her hand away before it landed.

"Shit, Dean! That's no fair!"

"The world isn't fair, Princess. Welcome to Earth, third rock from the sun." She looked at him, trying to figure out her next move. "Why don't we get off this particular topic?" he said. "It's taking us nowhere."

"You're right, Dean. We need to be working on our program. Enough of this horseplay. Let's get to work."

"Right!" he said, somewhat surprised by her sudden burst of maturity.

Sneak Attack

"Can you reach that green book up there?" she asked, pointing toward the top shelf of the bookcase. Dean pushed the nearby books aside with one hand and gripped the green one with the other. Shannon's move was swift and sure. She dived on him, wrapping her left arm around his waist, clutching his groin with her right hand, and giggling. It took him several seconds to dislodge her. She shrieked when he finally threw her off.

Shannon came up with a sly, satisfied grin on her face. "Gee, Dean," she teased him, "That was a handful!"

"You're a bitch, Shannon, and a sneaky one at that."

"You may be stronger than I am, Mr. Muscle Man, but I'm trickier. You'll never be safe around me, either!"

"I guess we'll both just live in fear, then," he responded.

"This is too cool, Dean," she said, recovering her composure. "You grabbed my box, and I grabbed your dick. I can't wait to tell the girls!"

"That would be particularly unwise, Shannon." He stared at her firmly.

"You should have seen your face! It was classic," she giggled.

"I'm pleased you were entertained," he said coolly.

"Grabbing Dean Steele's dick is more than just wholesome entertainment," she said. "It's a conquest!"

"Oh, you think you deserve a medal for that program?"

"Absolutely! I'm now a member of that select group of several thousand women who've had your dick in their hands!"

"Lucky you," he mused. "But your numbers may be a bit high."

She grinned triumphantly. She was pleased with herself.

---

1. Diane Sutton, a friend of Dean's. She will pop up later in the series.

Chapter 26

Jenny's Problem

Jenny's Confession

Shannon caught Dean in the parking lot at TIS. "Dean," she said cautiously. We need to talk to you. Her friend, Jenny Turlington, stood beside her with a worried look on her face.

"What's up, ladies?" he asked.

"I think we need your help. Jenny does, I mean."

"OK," he said. "What's the problem?"

"Jenny's in trouble, kinda." Shannon's face was twisted with trepidation.

"What kind of trouble?" He looked at the other girl.

"I kinda screwed up," she said.

"Are you pregnant?"

"No," she said, "I don't think so."

"Well, you just answered my second question. You got yourself nailed?"

"I think so."

"You don't know?"

"I'm not sure." She was near tears.

"Tell him what happened, Jenner," Shannon said.

"He'll kill me, Shan!" she said.

"He won't kill you, Jennifer!" Shannon scolded.

"I won't kill you, Jenny," Dean repeated.

"You tell, him, Shannon," Jenny whined. "I just can't!"

"OK," Shannon said, "She told her parents she was…"

"I speak English, Shannon," Dean interrupted. "I don't need a translator." He turned to Jenny. "What happened, Honey?"

The girl looked at him with anguish in her eyes. "There was this party," she said. "It was at your apartment house. One of the guys I met at the pool when I was over there with Shannon invited me."

"You went to a party at the Piccadilly Apartments?" Dean asked.

The distress on Jenny's face gave her answer. "I just thought it would be fun, you know? I thought it was just a party."

"Did your parents allow this?"

"No. I told them I was spending the night with Brittany." She took on a sheepish look.

"I see," Dean said.

"Go on. Tell him," Shannon prompted.

"Well, I went in and met some people and talked for a while, and that's all I remember. I woke up about midnight with a headache."

"They probably drugged you."

"I guess so. I went out like a light."

"Probably GHB."

"What?" Shannon asked.

"Gamma-hydroxybutyrate. The papers call it the date rape drug."

"Oh. Well, go on, Jen. Tell him."

"Well, when I woke up, they started telling me how wild I was. This one guy had pictures of me. Awful pictures." She began to cry. "It was terrible. I was dancing on the bar, and taking off my clothes, and having sex with guys, and having sex with girls." She began to bawl. "And I don't remember any of it!"

"OK, Jenny. Listen to me carefully. Do you feel like you've had sex? Weren't you a virgin before? Can you tell if you've been penetrated?"

"Well, I don't feel any different down there, but I was all gooey when I woke up."

"Were you sore or bleeding or anything?"

"No."

"OK, I expect they just poured Wesson oil on you."

"You don't think they screwed her?" Shannon asked, her face twisted in disbelief.

"Those guys are total assholes, but they know it's twenty-to-life for forcible rape. Having sex with a woman who is unconscious or incapacitated is forcible rape in Texas, and she's also underage. Surely they wouldn't take that chance."

"They didn't screw me?" Jenny asked.

"I can ask around, but I seriously doubt it."

"But those pictures…,"

"Probably faked. They could have posed you with a guy, or a girl, while you were unconscious. And on the ones where your face doesn't show, it could have been another girl taking off your clothes."

"They'd do that?" Shannon asked.

"At the drop of a hat," Dean replied. "Degrading young girls is great sport for them."

"But why go to all that trouble?"

"Well, first they convince her she's already done it once, then it'll be easier to convince her to do it again, voluntarily. It usually works."

Jenny's face showed puzzlement as she tried to understand what had happened to her. "So they didn't screw me? I didn't really do all that stuff?"

"Probably not. I expect they just knocked you out, undressed you, and had great fun making all those pictures with your unconscious body. Then they showed you what a slut you are so you'd be more likely to actually do it next time. Did they invite you back?"

"Yeah. This weekend."

"Well, they're hoping you'll do it for real this time. They're trying to make a party girl out of you."

"You mean, I didn't really do all those terrible things?"

"Most likely not. First off, if you don't remember anything, you were probably unconscious the whole time. If you had been awake enough to dance on the bar, you'd have some recollection of it."

"Oh, my God!" Jenny said.

"And second, a dozen people would risk serious jail time if your tender young bod had been violated. I expect you were the victim of a cruel practical joke."

"Oh, my God!" Jenny exclaimed as she grabbed Dean in a fierce hug. "Thank you, Dean."

"Don't be too quick to celebrate, Jenny," he said. "I haven't scolded you for going to that party yet. And they still have some pretty naughty pictures of you."

"What are we gonna do, Dean?" Shannon asked, "Can you go beat him up, or something?"

"I think we should be a bit more subtle than that," he said, "But I do think we should do something to get those pictures back."

"What's the plan" she asked.

"Let me noodle on it. I'll ask around about the party and see what I can find out about what happened, and who has the pictures."

"Dean," Jenny said, looking into his eyes, "I'm sorry I did such a bad thing. I should have listened to you. It was just stupid of me to go to that party by myself."

"Live and learn, Jenny," he said. "It could have been a lot worse."

The Hack

Shannon and Jenny arrived at Dean's apartment just after lunch the next day. He had found out that Sam Anderson had hosted the party. "What are we gonna do, Dean?" Shannon asked. "Break into Sam's apartment?"

"No, just his computer," Dean replied. "A bit of discrete hacking."

"This is too cool!" Shannon said. "How do you do that?"

"With a Trojan horse. A little program called 'Back Orifice' - a favorite among hackers. It lets me get into this computer from the outside anytime I want to, in case Jenny decides to attend another party."

"Back Orifice?" Shannon asked. "Sounds nasty!"

"Yeah. It was developed by an anonymous group of programmers who call themselves 'The cult of the dead cow.' They refer to this program as a 'remote administration tool,' but it's really just a hack. It lets me control his computer from mine."

"You mean, you're a hacker?" Shannon asked. "You're gonna open up his computer to the whole world? Cool!"

"Not really. He already had one gaping hole open. His port 139 was wide open to the world, thanks to Microsoft. I closed it for him so no other hacker can get in and find out he's been infected.. He's a lot safer now than he was before. I'm the only one who'll know which port to use to get in with Back Orifice."

"What's a port?"

"It's like a door. His computer has sixty-five thousand of 'em, and I'm leaving just one of 'em unlocked. Nobody could get in unless they had Back Orifice and knew which one of his sixty-five thousand doors was unlocked. They'd also have to know the internet address of his computer. All in all, not very likely. I'm the only hacker he needs to worry about now."

"Can't he find this orifice thing on his computer?"

"A good virus checker would find it, but, let's see here," Dean used the Back Orifice program to connect over the Internet to the computer in apartment 117, and he opened its "Start" menu. "Yes he has VirusScan on his machine." He launched the program. "But it was last run…, five…, six months ago. And it hasn't been updated since it was installed,… let's see…, over a year ago. So it wouldn't find this newest version of Back Orifice anyway. Besides, even if he did find it, he'd just think it came in with some of the porn he downloaded from the internet."

"Umm, so, what can you do with this horse thing?"

"Any damn thing I want to! I can take control of his computer any time of the night or day. I can read his mail, delete his files, or just give him a little 'kiddie porn' and then call the cops. What … ever!"

"Damn! How did you get that Orifice thing installed on his computer anyway?" Shannon asked. "Did you sneak into his apartment while he was at work?"

"No," Dean said. "Sam had installed a porno search program on his computer. It was supposed to get him into a lot of the pay sites for free, but he couldn't make it work, so he asked me to fix it for him. He was overjoyed when I got it working. I neglected to mention that I left his back door open."

"Why did you do that?"

"I figured it was a fair trade. I locked out a million other hackers and let myself in. Besides, he owed me for fixing up his free porn program, and I had a hunch it might come in handy some day"

Dean did a search on Sam's computer for image files with the letters "jen" in the name, and quickly located the directory where the pictures of Jenny were stored. He displayed them one at a time. "Is this you?" he asked the embarrassed girl. "Nice bod!"

"Ooh, gross, Jenner!" Shannon said. Jenny blushed.

"OK," he said as he displayed a picture of Jenny nude with a naked guy on top of her., "See here? You're clearly unconscious. And here." He brought up an image of her with a girl's head between her legs. "They turned your face away so it wouldn't be obvious you're out cold." He paused to bring up another image. It showed her head, from behind, buried in a man's crotch. "They just propped you up with your face in this guy's lap. And this one, dancing on the bar. It doesn't show your face. It's one of the other girls who's built kinda like you are. See? She has a tramp stamp tattoo on her lower back. You don't have one of those, do you?"

"That bitch!" Jenny said. "She's wearing my clothes!"

"Not for long, Jenny," Dean said. "They seem to be coming right off."

There were other images of Jenny in equally compromising positions, but each one could be seen to be faked. "Are you gonna erase 'em?" Shannon asked.

"No, I'm gonna scrub 'em." he replied.

"I thought all you have to do is drag 'em to the trash can."

"No, 'cause you can always get 'em back from the trash."

"Oh, so you have to empty the trash, right?"

"No, even that doesn't get rid of the data. It just marks the files as deleted. They can still be recovered, at least up until that same part of the disk gets used to save another file."

"So, what's scrubbing?"

"It goes in and writes garbage on the disk where the picture was stored. There's nothing left. Even the FBI can't get it back."

"Are you gonna keep a copy for yourself?" Shannon asked.

"Of course," Dean said, grinning. "I like good porn as much as the next guy." Jenny blushed. He copied the files that actually contained pictures of the girl to his hard drive.

"OK," Dean said, "He has the Norton utilities on this machine, but he didn't install the file scrubber. I suspect he just used the default install procedure, and the scrubber wasn't included in the installation." He opened the installation log file in the Norton utilities folder. "Yep," he said, "Standard install. I'll just install the scrubber, and he'll never notice that it wasn't in there from the beginning." Dean ran the installation program. Then he used the file scrubber to remove the files that contained actual pictures of Jenny.

"Now," he said as the girls watched intently, "I'll replace the missing files with garbage files that have the same file names. I have some random noise images here. When he can't display the pictures, he'll just think the files somehow got corrupted. Just one of the many mysteries of Microsoft Windows."

"What are you doing now?" Shannon asked after a pause.

"I'm resetting his clock to the day of the party. I don't want the new files to have today's date on them. He'd know something was fishy. I'll put it back to the right time when I'm finished."

"Oh," Shannon said.

Grateful Girl

"Dean," Jenny said after Dean disconnected from the other computer. "You really did a nice thing for me today. I mean, you really got me out of a mess. I was so scared. I thought I had done all those terrible things, and I was just ruined, and you found out I didn't, and you erased those awful pictures. I'm really glad for what you did, and I'm so terribly sorry I didn't listen to you and went to that party." She grabbed him in a bear hug, sobbing softly.

"Are you gonna have sex with her, Dean?" Shannon asked quietly.

"What? I thought preserving her virginity was the game here, not bustin' it."

"Come on, Dean. You saved her ass today. She's really grateful to you now. She owes you a big favor. You can have her." The two girls looked at him expectantly.

"And what about you." he asked.

"I get to watch!" she said. "I'll be real quiet."

"OK, so I make love with the grateful young lady, here, while you watch. Is that the plan?"

"Yeah, cool!" Shannon said, Jenny looked at him with large, soft eyes, but said nothing.

"Come on, Dean. She's crazy about you. She thinks you're the right guy to get her cherry. Go ahead. She's seventeen already. It's her time."

Dean looked at Jenny. She offered only an embarrassed smile.

"Go on, Jenner, tell him. You have to tell him, for Pete's sake!"

"Dean, You're so cool," she said, "And I really like you a lot. If you want to kiss me and stuff, I think it'd be really nice."

"Are you sure, Honey?" he asked. "You know what you're saying?"

"Yeah," she said sheepishly. "I know."

Dean took the girl in his arms and engaged her in a passionate kiss. She sighed and began to melt visibly. Shannon watched intently as Dean's hands moved upon the girl's body. He continued to kiss and caress her for a time, then he broke it off.

"OK, ladies," he said. "That's enough excitement for one day. We've committed computer fraud, and we're gettin' close to statutory rape, here. Why don't we celebrate our successful criminality with banana splits all around? I'll buy."

Shannon

"Damn," Shannon said later when they were alone, "I thought sure you were gonna bang Jenny right there!"

"You're a freak, Foster," he replied. "Has anyone ever pointed that out to you before?"

"You had her, Dean. She melted like a snowball in Hell. You coulda had her for sure!"

"With you watching, right?"

"Hey, I wouldn't tell anybody."

"You really think I'm stupid enough to screw one underage girl while another one witnesses the felony?"

"You don't trust me?"

"You could say that, yeah!"

"Bummer, Dean. I thought we were better friends than that."

"Shannon, it's just too weird, don't you get it? Too damn weird!"

"I know it looks that way. I mean it would to our parents and stuff. But she likes you. She's ready. She wants you to get her cherry. She told me so. And you're such a stud anyway, always porkin' somebody, so what's the big deal?. And I wouldn't tell anybody. So, what would it hurt?"

"OK, Shannon. I give up. I can't possibly make you see how bizarre it is, and what a mistake it would be, so I'll just hush. Now let's get off that topic, shall we?"

"Fuddy duddy!" Shannon said. "I can't see what's the big deal. What's one cherry, more or less, to Dean Steele?" Dean let out an anguished groan. "OK, so if you're not gonna screw her, why did you kiss her all up and stuff?"

Dean sighed. "I just let her thank me. She needed to give expression to her gratitude. It just wasn't necessary to pop her cherry."

"You just let her thank you? Dean! She liked it more than you did!"

"She gave me something personal, Shannon. It was a kind of payback. If she liked it, well, that's just a bonus."

"You could have made a woman out of her, Dean."

"She's already a woman. I could have committed a serious crime."

"Hey, you're already a hacker. Why not a rapist too?"

"Well, when you say it like that …"

They laughed.

Chapter 27

Reconciliation

Dean ignored Millie for two days after he threw her out. Finally she managed to get him alone. "Are you still stinging from the tragic loss of your little playmate?" she asked.

"Do you still see the world's population as merely puppets on your string?"

"I was only looking out for you, Dean," she lectured. "That girl was no good for you. Someday you'll see that."

"I just thought I was entitled to make my own mistakes. Isn't that how we learn?"

"Some mistakes are better avoided," she explained. "You could catch something hideous."

"Stay out of my private life, Millie"

A mischievous smile took her face. "Actually," she said coyly, "I was thinking about barging boldly back into your 'private life,' ... this evening about 8:15." She regarded him with raised eyebrows. "I've misbehaved badly, and I deserve to be punished."

"My cat-o-nine-tails is at the cleaners."

"Surely you have some instrument of torture that can instill discipline in one so vile as me."

"Not even the dungeons of London during the inquisition had such tools."

"But you have to try, Dear Boy," she cooed. "You simply can't let this breach of etiquette go unpunished." She looked at him with an innocent grin. "I'll come over at 8:15, I'll bring my spare dresses. They're all freshly cleaned and pressed. You'll give me my closet back, and you'll make me pay dearly for my inexcusable behavior."

"You've lost your closet privileges, Millie."

"But it's so convenient to have a place to keep a few nice comfortable outfits so I can wear them when we work together. And we do need to work together, don't we Dean?" She batted her eyelashes.

By now they both realized that her punishment would be merely having to beg her way back into his life. Dean enjoyed making her plead for the privilege of teasing him, and Millie enjoyed the process of talking him into his sensual enslavement. "Will you be nice?" he asked.

"Of course I'll be nice!" she said. "I'll look nice. I'll smell nice. I'll be nice and soft to the touch. Now nice do you want?"

"It doesn't sound like you've learned you lesson, here," he observed. "I see precious little regret or remorse."

"Sure I have," she replied. "I've learned that I require Dean Steele's company on a regular basis. "I've learned that I have to be very soft and tender around you. I've learned that I can make you melt me like butter on hot toast."

"And that you can get away with murder if you put on a short skirt and twitch your ass?"

"Oh, I've known that for twenty years." she grinned. "Now, ... what must I do to get an invitation to visit the lion in his den this evening?"

Dean figured he had made his point. The damage was done, as far as Janine was concerned, and there was some truth to what Millie had said. Perhaps Janine was no worse off. Whether a typist at a modeling agency in Dallas or at an insurance firm in Houston probably made little difference. "OK, Millie, you win. All you have to do is write a five-page essay on 'Why I will not mess with other people's lives anymore,' contribute a million dollars to the River Oaks Home for Hopelessly Tacky Young Women, and do 500 hours of community service at the South Houston Rescue Mission for Horny Perverts."

"I'll get right on it," was the snappy reply. "But first, I'll drop by your place this evening for some retribution directly from the injured party himself." She paused. "I have to make up for your loss."

"To the extent that you're a qualified substitute," he added, taking the opportunity to sting her once again.

"Ha!" she exclaimed. "Her only assets were a distinct absence of morals and an acute lack of class. She's no match for me in skill at being a woman."

Dean grinned silently. Though Janine was a competent chamber mate, she was no match for Millie in the arena of overall womanhood.

Millie's Return

There was a knock at Dean's door. Millie stood there, loaded down with items of apparel. "I brought a few extra things," she announced. "I think you'll like them." Dean rolled his eyes and stepped aside. She arranged her things in his closet. "My key, please?" she said, holding out an upturned palm.

Dean opened a drawer and gave her the key. "Thank you, Sir," she grinned. "Now, if you'll just give me a minute to freshen up ..."

After a while she emerged with a thin, clingy, almost transparent white minidress desperately hugging her voluptuous form. "Now," she said in a businesslike tone, "Where is that aspiring young skater who needs my assistance?"

"Right over here, Madam," Dean replied. Millie grinned. Dean rolled his eyes. He was amazed at her ability to do whatever she pleased and get away with it.

Somewhat to Dean's surprise, Millie spread out the charts for one of their routines and began to pour over the sequence of steps. "You want to do that ... now?" Dean inquired, somewhat surprised that sex was not first on her agenda.

"Of course! We have to have this thing ready for Club Ice on Friday."

Dean sighed as he studied her well-formed derriere, poorly hidden by her short, tight, clingy minidress. Since this would be their first time together in several days, Dean would have preferred to put teasing before skating, but she seemed to be focused on choreography. He resigned himself to work on the routine. As they worked over the sequence of steps carefully laid out on the chart, Millie moved seductively from one sexy pose to the next. Her actions were more suited to a glamour photo shoot than a choreography work session. He found it difficult to keep his focus on the boring work of planning the routine. Admiring her sexy beauty was far more interesting.

Millie kept her attention on the chart, while Dean's attention focused gradually on the attractive woman in his presence. Soon he didn't give a damn about which steps came before which jump. At one point she bent over the table facing him, and her top fell open, revealing her bulging boobs fighting for freedom from the scanty bra trying desperately to restrain them. Later she reached across the table, pressing the soft, thinly covered flesh of her breasts into his left cheek.

"Millie," he said at last, "Can't we postpone the jumps and spins until afterwards?"

"After what?" she blinked.

"After I fuck your brains out!" His exasperation finally surfaced.

"Dean," she scolded, "We're working on a skating project here. We're not going to drag sex into it and mess everything up. Now just keep your mind on the matters at hand."

"What?" he exploded. "After all that ... soap opera we went through ... you're saying we're not ... involved anymore?"

"What's done is done, Dean. The important thing is that we stick to the skating now. We have too much at stake to let our personal feelings interfere." She paused to place one of her 4-inch black patent leather heels on the seat of the chair she stood beside, and to place her left hand on her left thigh and slide it up to rest on her waist, exposing her hip. "I hope you have intelligence enough not to put this thing at risk by getting emotionally involved."

Dean exhaled a long sigh. "I thought we have evaluated those options and decided that gratifying our animal lust was more important than home, family, and the USFSA."

"We were fools, Dean. We made a mistake. We can't let that happen again."

"OK," he said, "We'll work on the routine. I just hope you won't be distracted by eight inches of dick inside you while you work!"

"Dean, stop it! I know you have … needs, but just don't think about it. Keep your mind on the routine."

"With you bent over like that, in that little dress made out of … cigarette smoke? Get real, Millie!"

"Dean!" she said sternly, "Just sit down and help me with this sequence. And don't even think about having sex, because I've decided that's out of the question. We have to be responsible adults here."

"This 'change of heart' of yours comes a bit too late, Millie, and I suspect the Ice Queen is up to her old tricks." He inhaled and walked calmly over to the front door of his apartment. He took the key out of the deadbolt and moved back over to Millie, visibly sliding the key into his pocket. "I don't know what kind of a game you're playing, Ms. Foster, but the doors are locked, and you're gonna get fucked at least twice before you get out. The rent on your closet is due, and you shall pay handsomely."

"Get serious, Dean. We have work to do."

"I am serious, as you shall soon see. And I'm not inclined to play along with your bullshit. Skating is now over; sex is now on. I do not take your objections seriously. My forgiveness comes at a price."

"Dean, please! Don't be this way!"

"Are you wearing pants, Millie?" he said, placing his hands on her thighs and slipping her hem up to her waist, exposing an extremely brief thong G-string. "Just barely," he observed. "I think you can get by without this little thing." He started slipping them down her thighs.

"My God, Dean, stop that! I'm a married woman!"

He slipped the straps off her shoulders, sending boobs bursting out of her extremely brief bra. "Dean, Please!" she pleaded. "Don't do this!"

He tasted her nipples for a time, then slipped her dress down her legs and onto the floor. "Dean, please!" she protested. "Get a grip on yourself. Don't put everything at risk like this!"

Her tiny bra still clung to her waist as he laid her rather forcefully on the black leather couch and positioned himself between her legs. "Dean. please, no!" she pleaded as he unhitched his belt. "No, stop!" she moaned as he entered her slowly but forcefully, and began to move slowly inside her.

"No," she said softly several times as their passion built toward a climax. She bit her tongue to stifle the word, "yes," and forced the word, "no," out between her teeth. "No," she said one last time as his release commenced, followed closely by the beginnings of her own. Soon they were both gasping and moaning in a violent vortex of lust that left them both dazed.

"What was that all about?" Dean mused as his head slowly cleared.

"You took me by force, Dean Steele!" his chambermate announced. "Do you know how many times I've laid in front of the TV with a vibrator between my legs, watching you skate and hoping that you would someday take me by force?" She sighed. "This is the absolute apex of my entire life!"

"All this ... 'we can't' bullshit was ... just so I'd ... rape you?"

"It was wonderful! Far better than I ever imagined. You were so powerful, and I was so helpless! God, that was great!"

Dean realized that, after this reignition, the affair would now continue. With the relationship thusly reaffirmed, the die was cast. There was no going back. Once or twice could be "slipsies," but this made it an affair. And with the need so strong, and the experience so rewarding, for both of them, he knew it would continue. The question was no longer, "Should we or shouldn't we," but rather "How do we keep it a secret?"

In a sense, the pressure was actually less than before. There was only one thing to worry about now: how to keep anyone from finding out that they were involved. Though no picnic, this was less stressful than negotiating Millie's seductive tactics and his unrequited lust for her. At least the air was clear now. They were involved. They would simply add a few discrete sexual encounters to their weekly schedule. He heaved a sigh of relief.

Chapter 28

The Grandmother

Dean and Shannon went to Dallas for a two-day pairs clinic held at the Dr. Pepper Center. After the clinic they packed up the Mustang and headed home.

"Where are we going, Dean?" Shannon asked as the Mustang turned north on Central Expressway. "Houston is south!"

"I need to stop by and see an old friend," he replied. They pulled in to the parking lot of a nursing home.

Ellen

"Dean!" the old woman said as they walked into her room. "I hoped you'd drop by to see your old grandma."

"Wouldn't miss a chance like this," he replied, grinning. He gave the frail lady a kiss. "This is Shannon, he said. "She's my skating partner."

"So this is the girl! My, she's a pretty one! I'll can tell she's a dancer."

"Pleased to meet you, Mrs. Comwell. Dean's told me all about you!"

"Oh, call me Ellen, and don't you believe him! He's still mad because I wouldn't let him have a motorcycle when he was twelve!" They laughed.

"I brought you something," Dean said, "A little update for the book." He took several plastic sheet protectors out of his briefcase and inserted them in a notebook binder that was labeled, "Ellen Comwell - Who I Am."

Shannon took the book from Dean and began to leaf through it. "This is so cool!" she said. "Your whole life is in here. It has pictures and everything! Look! Here's Dean when he was a skinny kid. Oh, and that's your brother, Jamie! And your parents." Dean and his grandmother chatted while Shannon studied the book. "Did you make this for her Dean? It looks like it was done on a computer."

"Yeah, but it's still under construction. I have some more stuff that ought to go in there, thanks to you."

"It's so cool! Whenever somebody comes to see you, you can just show it to 'em, and they instantly know all about you!"

The Grip

Dean and his elderly companion looked at Shannon in silence. There was a subtle sadness in their eyes. Suddenly an icy fist closed around Shannon's heart. Her throat tightened up and she began to shake. Gasping, she struggled to her feet and made her way out of the room. She stood in the hallway, shaking and sobbing, for a long time.

It took the better part of ten minutes before Shannon could regain her composure, replace her smile and resume her sunny disposition. At last she went back in the room. She chatted with Dean and Ellen for about ten minutes. She particularly enjoyed Ellen's stories of Dean's childhood.

Mr. Mayfield

At one point Dean asked his grandmother, "How's your boyfriend?"

"I don't have any boyfriend!" she asserted.

"Mister Mayfield?"

"Oh, him! I don't see him much, anymore."

"I think I'll go check on him." Shannon accompanied Dean down the hall. "Knock, knock!" he said as he entered the room. They saw an old man, clad in pajamas, lying on the bed. He obviously had been crying. "Mr. Mayfield!" Dean said. The old man did not respond. Dean touched him. "Mr. Mayfield!" The old man looked at Dean but said nothing. "Do you remember me?" Dean asked in a very loud voice.

"What?"

"Do you remember me?" he said, even louder.

"Yeah. You're Ellen's boy."

"Where is your hearing aid?"

"Susan took it."

"Was it broke?"

"No. She just don't want me to have it."

"Where are your glasses?"

"She took them too."

"What about your clothes?"

"She got 'em."

"Mr. Mayfield has two daughters," Dean explained. "The other daughter put his wife of 52 years in a nursing home across town, and Susan put him here. The separation almost killed 'em both. He's very hard of hearing and doesn't see well. She didn't let him get a hearing aid, even though the Veteran's Administration would pay for it. She wouldn't even get him a pair of glasses. She left him here with only pajamas to wear."

"That sucks!" Shannon said.

"So, time before last when I was here, I bought him a hearing aid, and a pair of reading glasses. I even checked with his doctor and got her approval. I also brought him some street clothes. Now it seems his daughter doesn't like the idea." Dean sighed. "He's a sweet old man, and Ellen used to chat with him a lot, after he got his hearing aid."

Dean turned back to Mr. Mayfield. "Are you sure Susan took your hearing aid away from you?"

"Yes she did. Said she don't like me accepting charity from strangers!"

"OK," Dean said. "I'll take care of it." He went to the nurses' station. "Mr. Mayfield had a hearing aid." he told the nurse on duty. "What happened to it?"

"Oh, his daughter took it away from him! She was adamant about it. I told her his doctor had approved it, but she wouldn't hear of it!"

"Thanks," Dean said. He returned to Ellen's room and dialed 911 on her phone. "No emergency," he said, "I'd like to report a felony theft. What number should I use?" He dialed the second number. "Felony theft report," he said. "The item is a man's hearing aid." He gave his name and Ellen's address. "The suspect is one Susan Mahoney. I'll give her address and description to the responding officer. Thanks."

Dean and Shannon chatted with Ellen for about fifteen minutes, and there was a tap on the door. A uniformed Dallas Police Officer stuck his head in. "Come in, Officer," Dean said. "I made the call." The policeman sat down and reported in on his handheld radio. Dean described the situation to him. "I bought the hearing aid," he summarized, "And I loaned it to Mr. Westfield. It's my property, and the nurse at the desk saw his daughter, Mrs. Mahoney, take it."

"Some people!" the officer mused. "My daddy died when he was fifty-one. If he was alive now, I'd sure take better care of him than that!" Dean nodded his head. "This address is on my beat. I'll pay the woman a visit. If she gives me any trouble, I'll handcuff her and take her downtown! That old man will get his stuff back. I'll see to it!"

"Thanks," Dean said. "Let me know if you need anything else from me. I'll file charges if necessary."

"Someone will be in touch," the officer said as he left.

Shannon and Dean said goodbye to Ellen and left. They rode in silence for a while. Finally Shannon spoke. "That book," she said. "It wasn't for visitors, was it, Dean? You made it for her."

"Sometimes she loses track," he replied. "It helps her keep things straight."

"Alzheimer's, right?" Shannon's eyes became watery. "How often does she read it?"

"Used to, she would just check it every once in a while, to remind herself of something. Nowadays she reads it every morning and refers to it several times a day."

"And, what if she hadn't read it this morning?"

"It varies, but there's a good chance she wouldn't have known who I am." He paused. "As bright and alert as she is, if her memory was OK, she could still be living at home."

"That's just so sad!" Shannon said as tears ran down her cheeks. "That poor woman!"

"Well, at least she had the opportunity to get old."

"Like your parents didn't? And your brother?" Dean was silent. Shannon was silent. "I'm glad you took me with you, Dean," she said at last. "I got to meet your grandmother!" They smiled at each other warmly.

The Call

A few days later Dean got a call on his cell phone. "This is Officer Garcia, Dallas PD," the caller said. "Is this Mr. Steele?"

"Yes, Officer Garcia. How are you?"

"Fine. I called to let you know we recovered your stolen property."

"Great!" How did it go?"

"Well, I responded to the location and contacted the suspect. At first she denied it, but when I said we had witnesses, she got rowdy and started yelling. I cuffed her and put her in the patrol unit. Then her daughter came out and calmed her down. Finally she agreed to take your property back to the nursing home. I told her she would have to give it to me or she was going to jail. She did, and I took it to Mr. Mayfield myself. I warned her that this call will go on the record, and if we ever get another complaint, she's going to jail." He paused. "I don't know if that will do any good with people like that, but it was the best I could do."

"I think you did a great job. Officer Garcia. You made the point. I'll let you know if she ever misbehaves again."

"Well, I just don't understand why some people don't take good care of their parents."

"Me neither."

"Good day, Mr. Steele."

"Goodbye. Officer Garcia."

Chapter 29

The Fall

Dean and Shannon skated an exhibition at the Aerodrome in Sugar Land, Texas. It was an informal event put on by the Iceland Skating Club primarily to let their skaters preview their competitive programs. The event had grown to the point that members of other clubs would participate as well. Foster and Steele were not yet ready for prime time, but they felt confident enough that they agreed to perform a simple pairs routine for the local skating people.

There was an ice cut before the performances started. Then one young girl lost her hairpiece during her routine, but finished it anyway. She picked up her ponytail and two other skaters scanned the ice for bobby pins that she might have shed.

Shannon and Dean were a bit nervous, but they both calmed down during the first minute of their routine. They were skating competently, but without great precision and polish.

At 2:45 into the routine Dean swung Shannon up and over his head in a hand-to-hand lift. She came to rest supported by his right hand at her pubis. Initially their left hands remained clasped for stability, but as the move unfolded they released their grip. Shannon gracefully spread out her arms and legs in different directions in the star position as she floated nine feet above the ice. Dean rotated slowly on his right outside edge with his right arm vertical, palm up, and his left arm extended to the side.

The one-handed star lift was one of the most crowd-pleasing moves they knew how to do. They had practiced it enough that the execution was becoming both smooth and graceful. Dean started off skating forward on both feet as he swung the girl into position on the pedestal he made for her. As she got into the star position he began to turn slowly while still moving at good speed across the ice. The gathering of skaters and parents watched in amazement as Shannon's formidable body swung gracefully into position above Dean's head and then floated like a balloon across the arena. Supported only by one of Dean's arms, she gave the impression of flying.

The lift was planned to go for two revolutions with Shannon in the air. At one and a half revolutions, with Dean skating backward on his right outside

194

edge, a gorilla reached up from inside the ice and grabbed his right ankle in a vice-like grip, pinning his skate firmly to the ice. His momentum carried the rest of his body and his partner onward, and he immediately began to fall backward. It took only one tenth of a second for his center of mass to move away from his support line, turning him, and his partner, into helpless projectiles in the arena.

At two-tenths of a second into the fall he felt Shannon's weight disappear from his arm. By three-tenths she was no longer in contact with his hand, now sailing unsupported through the air nine feet above the frozen surface. He rotated his head so he could keep her in sight as she floated away from him. Millie grabbed Fred's arm in a grip that would later produce a bruise.

Dean's body continued to rotate as he fell backward. He strained to reach for his partner, but she continued to drift away from him, like an errant satellite in an abortive space shuttle docking maneuver. His body gradually became more horizontal as Shannon's momentum carried her forward without much loss of altitude. The firm grip on his right boot pulled hard at his leg as his right shoulder moved toward the ice.

Dean hit the ice on his right side, with his right arm still extended above his head, reaching in vain for his partner who was now several feet in front of him. The impact forced the air from his lungs and snapped his head down against his shoulder. Shannon, meanwhile, had begun to rotate and was now face-up, still about three feet off the ice, but descending rapidly. Her right skate was first to hit the ice, then her left, followed by her right arm, then her right hip and right shoulder. She bounced and began to roll across the cold surface, eventually coming to a stop lying flat on her back. Dean had bounced sharply on impact, and he came to rest face down on the ice.

Pain shot through Dean's body as he tried unsuccessfully to refill his emptied lungs. Gasping for air, he raised himself up and began crawling across the ice toward the spot where Shannon lay in a motionless heap. Many agonizing seconds passed as Dean struggled with his journey. Shannon was unmoving, and her face was turned away from him. Her arms and legs lay scattered about in an arrangement suggestive of the crumpled frame of the Hindenberg[1] after its disaster.

The audience watched in shock, not knowing what to do. Two of the parents in the crowd were medical doctors, but they hesitated for several seconds as the transformation from spectator to participant slowly took place.

When Dean finally reached Shannon's unmoving carcass he gently turned her head toward him. Her eyes were closed and there was no sign of life on her face. He struggled to raise himself into a sitting position beside her. She looked almost peaceful, breathing slowly and deeply.

One of the girl skaters stepped through the gate and raced toward the two fallen bodies at center ice. Upon arrival she merely stood there with her hands on her knees, but this was sufficient to prompt one of the doctors to begin moving toward the opening in the boards.

Dean cautiously lay Shannon out on her back and then cupped her face in his hands. "Shannon," he said gently, to no response.

Moving cautiously across the ice in street shoes, the doctor finally reached them. He pulled one of the girl's eyelids open, exposing an unfocused stare. Then he looked at Dean. "Lay down," he said. "Breath slow and deep." Dean did not comply. The doctor turned his attention back to Shannon as a groan escaped her lips. Her eyes opened but did not focus on anything.

"Shannon," Dean said.

"Shit!" the girl blurted. "We fell down!" Her eyes closed in a grimace.

Dean gave the doctor an inquiring gaze but received no response. The second doctor arrived and began to examine Dean. Soon Millie arrived, after abandoning her high heel shoes at the rail and navigating the ice in stocking feet. A few moments later Fred arrived, carrying Millie's shoes.

After a few minutes Dean was breathing comfortably, and Shannon was awake and talking. The two doctors had ordered stretchers, but the two skaters would not wait for them.

"Are you OK, Kid?" Dean asked.

"Yeah, I guess so," she replied. "Where did you land? I didn't see you anymore."

"Somewhere back over there," he replied. "Is anything broke?"

"No," she said. "I fell forever. I had loads of time to tuck and roll." She looked at him. "Are you hurt?"

"Probably not," he replied.

"What happened down there?" she asked.

"I hit something," he said.

Back in her shoes, Millie bent down beside them. "You hit this," she said, holding up a bobby pin. "See? Here's where your blade bent it."

Millie and Fred helped Dean and Shannon walk off the ice. On the way to the door Millie stopped Walt Mason. "I want you to get a copy of every video tape of that fall for me," she said.

"Right!" he replied.

Millie's advice

"Mom," Shannon said, three days later, "Dean's gone all weird on me."

"What do you mean, Honey?" Millie asked.

"I mean, it's like he can't lift me anymore. You've seen the tapes the last few days. He looks awful out there. And I can't even get him to practice a star lift."

"Is it because of the spill you took?"

"I guess so," she replied. "Ever since he's been just ... too weird."

"I'll talk to him, Honey," the woman said.

"Dean," Millie said, smiling tenderly, "Are you OK?"

"Yeah," he said.

"Shannon says you haven't wanted to do lifts since y'all's fall."

"We've had other things to work on," he answered.

"You need to climb back on the horse that threw you, Cowboy." He inhaled to say something, then arrested his thought. "Dean," she said softly, "Tell me what's bothering you."

"I'm fine, Millie."

She looked into his eyes. "What happened out there, Dean? Something has changed. What did it?"

"Nothing's changed, Millie."

"OK then, just tell me about the fall."

"I'd rather not," he said.

"In that case, I insist," she said. "Humor the Ice Queen." She softened. "What really happened in that split second?"

Dean stared off into space. "It was strange," he began. "One second I had her ... in perfect control. And in an instant she was gone. She just disappeared, like God had reached down and snatched her away from me. And then I saw her floating away through space, like an astronaut without a tether, and I couldn't reach her. It was a helpless feeling. She just kept drifting away from me." Millie remained silent. "And then the ice came up and smacked me. Damn it hit me hard!" I couldn't focus my eyes or my thoughts, and I couldn't breathe."

"Did you tuck in for the fall?"

"Yeah, as well as I could."

"I've seen the tapes, Dean. You were still reaching for her when you hit. That's why you broke a rib."

"Do you have a lecture for me, Millie?"

"How did you know? Of course I have a lecture for you, you hard-headed little shit!" Dean inhaled in preparation for the onslaught. "In some falls you can catch her," Millie began. "You know that. In other falls, like this one, you have to separate. There's no way you can break her fall out of a star. She has to do it. You have to disconnect, and you only have a split second to decide." She paused. "Pairs skating is dangerous, Dean. You know that, and Shannon knows it. It only looks like a walk in the park." Another pause. "You can't skate caution, Dean. It just doesn't work."

"One reason Shannon is developing so well as a pairs skater," she continued,"Is that she's absolutely fearless. Even after this fall, she just got up and went right back at it." She looked at him. "You have to do the same thing, Dean. You have to be just as fearless as that girl. But you have to be unafraid for two people, yourself and your partner. You have to be willing to put yourself at risk, and you have to be willing to put her at risk too. You have to take chances with her life, Dean. There's no other way to play this game. You have to just believe that when she falls, and you can't catch her, that she'll land on her feet. If you don't, we're just wasting our time here."

Dean sighed. He had no response. "You used to be fearless, Dean. Wild and free. You need to be that way again, even if it means Shannon could get hurt."

"But she's so helpless up there," Dean said." As soon as her blades leave the ice, she's completely at the mercy of what I do with her."

"No, she's not, Dean. She's like a cat. She can jerk and wiggle and get herself in position to land. You saw it on the tape. You hit harder than she did... because you were still trying to catch her. She just put her wheels down and landed and rolled. You should have done the same."

Dean sighed. "I used to collect videos of skaters' falls and collisions. One thing I remember about the pairs' falls is that the guy never lets go of the girl. She usually hits flat on her tummy because he's still holding her hands up in the air. I used to watch those tapes and yell, 'Let the bitch go, Asshole!' I guess Shannon and I need to practice disconnecting when a fall starts."

"Do whatever you have to, Dean. Just put that arrogant, devil-may-care fire back into your skating. We'll never get anywhere without it."

"Uh ... I don't believe I've ever had a mother ask me to risk her daughter's life before."

"You've never skated pairs before." Millie grinned, "And you've never worked for the Ice Queen. She's a very hard mistress!"

"OK, Your Highness," he said. "I'll subject your daughter's fragile frame to sudden icy impact at every opportunity from now on."

"That's my boy!" she said, smiling at him.

Shannon

"Your mom wants me to risk your life," Dean said as they walked into the Texas Ice Stadium.

"She hates me," Shannon replied, grinning, "What can I say? She can't deal with me being foxier than she is."

"You get half as 'foxy' as the Ice Queen, and then we'll talk."

"Better wake up and sniff the java, Dude! I'm already there."

"What I'm saying is ... if we're ever gonna impress anybody with our skating, I'm gonna have to take chances with your precious young bod. There could be more falls like the one in Sugar Land."

"I'm young, Dean. I bounce. You're old. You break. Don't worry about protecting me. Look out for your own ass!"

"Falls aren't the only danger, Miss Smartass. You could get punched by a pissed-off partner."

"That's 'Miss Bitch' to you, knave! 'Miss Sexy Bitch.' And don't you forget it!"

"We've got to do something about your attitude," he mused. They went into their locker rooms chuckling.

---

1. The Hindenburg – German airship that crashed and burned in New Jersey on May 6, 1937.

Chapter 30

Queen's Dance

As Millie's 39th birthday approached, Dean convinced her to skate with him to make a video for the party that Fred was planning. They worked for two weeks in a closed rink while Shannon was in school. The final two days were for the taping. Shannon was excluded, along with everyone else but the TV crew. Millie had a special costume made, and the video crew recorded several sessions, mainly using a steadicam setup on the ice. Dean also wore a bicycle helmet fitted with a small camera for some of the shots. When the time for the event came, Fred rented the ballroom at The Houstonian Hotel for the party.

The Preview

Dean drove to the video lab in the Mustang.

"You wanna see it?" Bruce Lane asked.

"Sure," Dean replied. "Is it good?"

"Well it oughta be. I had 24 gigabytes of high resolution digital video to work with. I had three camera angles of at least six instances of every move, and about a dozen of that last one. So I had plenty to work with."

"Good," Dean said.

"But it may be a bit too strong for a birthday party," Bruce added.

"What do you mean?"

"Well, I basically pulled out all the stops. Let's just say, it ain't subtle!"

"In what way?"

"The MPAA would give it an 'X' rating. I've seen porn that's less … provocative."

"Does it make Millie look good?"

"Oh, yeah!" His head bounced up and down vigorously and his eyes were wide. "Oh, yeah!"

"Then you did it, Dude." Dean slapped him on the shoulder.

Bruce loaded the video onto a playback machine and ran it for Dean on a 38-inch studio monitor. "Remember," he said, "It'll come across a lot stronger on a big projection screen." The two men watched in silence as four and a half minutes of images and sound unfolded.

"Yes!" said Dean, as the last image faded out, pumping a clenched fist, "Yes! The man is a genius!"

The Party

Dean drove to The Houstonian by himself. He reluctantly gave Matilda to the valet parking attendant and went inside, looking for the ballroom. He wore a dark gray suit, though most of the men there were wearing tuxes. Shannon spotted him and began dragging him around from guest to guest, introducing him to old family friends.

After the guests had all arrived and had a chance to snack and drink for a time, Fred, acting as emcee, showed a video that traced Millie's life, mostly skating, from childhood. It included both her victories and her falls. The audience was amused, and Millie was embarrassed, both according to Fred's plan.

Suddenly the arena went dark. A fireworks explosion rattled the ballroom windows as a huge TV screen lit up with a spinning 3-D logo that said "Millie 2000." The new video began with slow motion close-ups of skates being tied and skate guards going on over glinting silver blades. The camera followed the skates at a low angle as they strode in slow motion across the black rubber toward an opening in the boards. It saw the guards come off and the skates step out onto the ice, and it followed at ice level as they stroked away toward the center of the arena.

The audience was gripped by the power of this presentation. The music boomed through the cavernous ballroom. Onscreen the camera slowly pulled back to show Millie in a dramatic opening pose. She was truly regal looking in a pale purple costume with flashing rhinestones and purple skate covers. Her hair and makeup were immaculate. There was an audible gasp from the audience. This was clearly the prelude to something spectacular.

The first minute showed Millie skating gracefully to precisely timed music. The camera shots varied from full length to extreme close-ups, and the lighting was dramatic. Every move showed grace and beauty.

Then the camera moved back. Sitting at ice level, it slid left until a black boot came into view in the foreground. Slowly pulling back and up it revealed a man, Dean, standing erect, with Millie still skating in the background. After a moment he pushed off and began skating toward her.

He stopped at center ice and stood motionless, as the woman skated. Millie continued skating, apparently not noticing him. Finally she skated up to him and stopped, facing him. Dean bowed slowly and deeply. In a dramatic moment the two skaters faced each other, motionless and expressionless. The audience sensed a silent exchange. Then Dean extended his hand.

Expressionless, Millie paused, regarded him, then pushed off backward and resumed her solo skating. Dean remained motionless at center ice as she glided and spun.

The audience was held in a iron grip as the drama unfolded on the giant screen. Again Millie skated up to Dean and stopped, regarding him. Again Dean extended his hand. Again Millie paused, as if considering his offer, then pushed off and resumed skating alone.

Later Millie again skated up to Dean and stopped in front of him. Again he extended his hand. After a dramatic pause, she took it.

The two skaters glided away into an ice dance routine that brought synchronized oohs and gasps from the assembly. At first she was cool and aloof, allowing the man to hold her only at arm's length while they skated. But as time went on, she softened, finally flowing like honey across the ice as Dean held her in his arms.

Eventually she surrendered completely, melting into Dean's arms like butter on hot toast. She allowed him to lift and carry her across the ice. Her poses during the lifts became more sensual as the program unfolded. Eventually she opened herself completely to her newfound partner, allowing him to hold and carry her as he pleased, opening her arms and legs to him freely, her face expressing total surrender and idyllic bliss. She pressed herself against him in the close dance holds, and she gazed longingly into his eyes as they waltzed face to face.

Throughout the program Dean's face was rarely seen, either falling outside the shot or submerged in shadow.

The climax came in the form of a one-handed star lift, shown in slow motion. Dean took her left hand in his and placed his right hand firmly under her short skirt. She sprang, and he pulled, until she was horizontal overhead. Then she released his left hand and assumed a graceful star pose. For long moments they glided across the huge TV screen. The camera cut between medium, long and close-up shots, revealing every nuance of this difficult move. Millie's face was sublime, and her body divine. Dean was strong, solid, and relaxed as he supported the Ice Queen on her nuptial flight.

Finally the lift came to an end. Dean slowly lowered the woman's voluptuous body to the ice. The camera revealed every detail of the landing, which evolved smoothly into a long graceful embrace, turning slowly as they flowed across the white expanse. Millie appeared drained, but enraptured, caught up in the afterglow of a romantic experience.

Gradually Dean bent the woman down until she came to a stop resting on one knee on the ice. Then he released her, turned his back, paused, and slowly skated away. Millie raised her arm to him with a pained and confused look on her face, but he disappeared into shadow. She slowly regained her composure, got up and resumed skating as she had in the beginning. The music swelled, and the camera pulled back, back, back as the screen faded slowly to black.

When the lights came on, most of the women were wiping their eyes, and the men were shaking their heads in wonder. Both the figure skating veterans in the crowd and Fred's ice-naïve business associates were equally moved by the emotion they had seen played out on the giant screen. Millie was aghast and speechless. Shannon was open-mouthed. Fred was wide-eyed in shock. Dean grinned quietly to himself. "Yes!" he whispered to himself, "Yes!"

Nobody said anything for a long time. They looked at each other in open-mouthed amazement, as if to say, "Did you see what I just saw?" Most eyes were either moist or actively draining water.

Finally Fred walked over and took Millie in a loving embrace. The spontaneous applause that broke out turned into a tearful standing ovation.

After that embrace the guests were released from the grip of the video and again free to think and talk. A steady stream of people came up to Millie with variations on "I had no idea ...!" Millie was fighting back tears most of the time.

Shannon pushed her way through the crowd to her mom. She grabbed the woman by the shoulders and said "Mother, you are beautiful. Just so beautiful!" Millie hugged her tightly as they both sobbed.

Alone in a corner, Dean pulled out his cell phone and dialed a number. "You did it, Dude," he said when Bruce Lane answered. "You blew 'em away. Your show was a smash!"

"It wasn't... too intense?" Bruce asked.

"It may have been. Everyone here is still in a state of shock."

"Are they pissed?"

"Pissed is not the word. Flabbergasted is more like it. But flabbergasted in a good way."

"How did Mrs. Foster take it?"

"The Ice Queen can't keep her hankie in her purse."

"How about Mr. Foster?"

"Fred's all soft and cuddly," Dean answered, "Extremely proud of his beautiful wife."

"Shannon?"

"Haven't seen the Princess yet. That'll be interesting."

"Well, I was just hoping I wouldn't be ostracized by the Houston business community over this thing. If it had gone the wrong way...,"

"I think you better order yourself a 55 gallon drum of midnight oil, Buddy. Everybody's gonna want your services now. 'Make my wife beautiful,' will be the marching orders."

A few minutes later Shannon walked up to Dean and regarded him solemnly from beneath raised eyebrows. Her head was cocked to the right, her lips pursed. Dean squelched a friendly greeting when he saw her demeanor, holding short to see what kind of mood she was in.

"You did that, right?" She asked coolly. "That was your routine."

"It was a joint effort," he replied, noncommittally.

"Bullshit!" she snapped. "It had Dean Steele fingerprints all over it." The girl looked at him intensely, "She weighs one forty, Dean," she lectured him. "You could have pulled a muscle doing that star!" Without giving him a chance to reply she turned and walked away.

"Wuhh!" Dean said under his breath.

Dean spent most of the party standing alone in the shadows, except for the occasional congratulatory encounter with a guest. Most of the guests were family friends whom Dean didn't know. They would smile at him and then strike up a conversation with someone else. It was Millie's night. Shannon was being with her family. She didn't drag Dean around the room anymore, showing him to everybody like she usually did. She just glanced at him occasionally out of the corner of her eye, as if keeping track of his whereabouts without approaching him.

Willie, looking out of place in a business suit, walked up beside Dean and stood silently for a while. "You seem to be on the outside, looking in, young man," he commented at last.

Dean chuckled at the remark. "I got what I wanted tonight," he replied. "I may be the happiest guy here!"

"Well, you sure aren't gettin' much credit for your work," Willie said.

"That's the plan," Dean said. "Everything is right on schedule."

"If you say so. But it's a party, and nobody's talking to you."

Dean turned to look at the aging black man. "You're talking to me," he said. Willie smiled and Dean embraced him in a hug. "Thanks for being there," Dean said.

"I've always got a lot more out of Dean Steele than I ever put in." Willie replied. Shannon caught the brief embrace out of the corner of her eye. No one else noticed.

The Day After

The next day was Sunday, and there was nothing planned for the skating team of Foster and Steele. On unplanned days like this Dean normally called

204

Shannon with some idea they could work on together, some suggestion to get together and go see something. Today he didn't. Partly to let her be with her family, and partly because she had so coolly ignored him at the party the night before, he avoided dialing any of the Foster numbers. Instead he washed his motorcycle. He also installed Mathematica 3.0 on his computer and figured out how to use it to solve systems of simultaneous linear equations.

About 3:30 PM he heard a noise outside. The front door was unlocked, and Shannon walked into his apartment without comment. She got a drink out of his refrigerator.

"Good afternoon, Miss," he said. After taking a swig, the girl looked at him with the same face he had seen the night before. "What?" he said sternly. "What?"

"What, what?" she replied in an icy, aloof, "I don't know what you're talking about" voice.

"What the Hell is wrong with you, Foster? What are you doing in my apartment? And what's eatin' your ass so bad?"

The girl sat down on the couch, folded her arms and crossed her legs. "I'm not sure, exactly," she informed him, looking at him at first, then looking idly away.

"Well, is there someone you can ask? Consult an on-line information service, or a 1-900 psychic help line, perhaps?" While trying to be understanding, he was having great difficulty suppressing his frustration.

"My phone didn't ring today," she said. "Was that you?"

"Uh, yeah, that must have been me not calling."

"Why not?"

"It's Sunday. We have the day off."

"You usually call me on Sunday."

"I got the impression you wanted to be with your family this Sunday."

"What gave you that idea?"

"It's your mom's birthday."

"The party was last night."

"But the birthday is today. I figured the Fosters would do the family thing today."

She sat silently for a moment. "I saw you hug Willie last night."

"He's just a friend," Dean replied. "We're not romantically involved."

"Yeah?" she said, ignoring his joke. "You hug all your friends?"

"At ten, two and four," was the answer. "But you're not pissed because I hugged Willie."

"I didn't say I'm pissed."

"You didn't say you aren't."

"I'm just in a funny mood, OK?" came the snippy reply.

"I've seen funny moods, Puddin'," he said, "And that's what this isn't!" She looked away. "Come on, Brat," he said, deliberately pushing her most sensitive button. "Spit it out! Your asshole is so tight, only dogs can hear you fart"

"I don't know!" she snapped. "I've just felt like shit ever since last night, that's all."

"You seemed to be having a good time at the party."

"I was, I mean, I did. I loved it. But for some reason, I'm all nervous and upset. And I'm pissed as Hell at you! I know you're an asshole; I just can't put my finger on exactly why."

"Well, let's see, does it, perchance have something to do with ... the video?" he asked, as if taking a wild guess.

"It might."

"So tell me about the video."

"It was good. It was real good. It was ... so damn wonderful! I can't believe my mom was so beautiful. She ... she just ...", Shannon couldn't finish her sentence. Dean remained silent as the girl struggled to sift through her thoughts.

"I mean I knew mom skated, OK? Like, she was with the Ice Capades and stuff. But before last night ... I never saw ... I never thought ...," She shook her head. "God, she was ... so ... beautiful!" Tears welled up in her eyes as she looked desperately at Dean. "I don't think I can ever be that beautiful," She began to cry. "I can't be as beautiful as my mom was up there, and she's thirty-nine!" she sobbed in despair. Silent, Dean allowed the girl's pent up emotion to flow out of her. Slowly her sobbing subsided and her thoughts began to move on.

"And that routine. God, I never saw anything like that before! It made her ... so ... beautiful. So .... feminine. So ... damn ... sexy." Her teeth were clenched and her words were punctuated with rage. Then she glared at Dean. "And it was your routine, wasn't it?" He did not reply.

"You did that to her. You made her skate that way. You made her look that way. You made her so ... damn ... beautiful!"

"Is that what pissed you off?"

"No. I don't think so. I mean ...," She took a breath and exhaled. "Yes, dammit! Yes! You made my mother look like ... Peggy Fleming! And I hate her for it, and I hate you for it!" She fumed as tears of anger filled her eyes.

"I know this sounds bad," she said, holding up a palm. "I know I should be glad if my mom gets to be glamorous at her birthday party." She paused to sniff. "But I hate it! I can't help it. And I hate you for doing it to her!"

"Why?" Dean asked.

"Because …," She pumped her hand up and down as she thought about it. "Because it's …," she shook her head.

"Why?" Dean asked again, quietly.

"I just think it's …," She fell silent.

"Why?" Dean asked, almost whispering.

"Because," she said as the answer began to crystallize in her mind, "Because you did it for her!" Her voice broke up as she cried and spoke at the same time. "You did it for my mom, damn it, not for me! You're my skating partner, Dean Steele! And you made my mother look like Dorothy Hamill. You're supposed to do that for me!" Her sobbing resumed, punctuated with grunts of anger.

"I work my ass off skating with you, Dean Steele, all day every day. I do everything you say. I eat vegetables. I take seven hundred vitamin pills. I take dance lessons. I lift weights. I forgot what ice cream tastes like, for Pete's sake!

She paused to think. "Shit, there isn't any Shannon Foster left anymore. There's only Dean Steele's trained seal who follows him around like a retarded puppy dog, doing whatever he says." She paused. "But I do it because you say you can make me look beautiful on the ice. I do it because you say you can make me look sexy." She paused to blow her nose.

"So what happens?" she continued. "You take my mom … my fat, 39-year-old mother, who eats like a pig, and smokes like a train, and drinks like a fish, and you spend two weeks with her. And you make her into this … this … gorgeous ice goddess who just takes everyone's breath away when she skates!"

"And I'm sittin' there thinking, 'Hullo! … Excuse me? … I'm the skating partner here. Remember me?' And everyone's just going goo-goo over the fabulous Millie Foster. And I'm thinking, 'But wait! She's just the ice mom. She just buys the ice and washes the socks. She's not the skater anymore. That was ages ago. It's supposed to be my turn!'"

Shannon paused to wipe her nose. She glared at Dean. "You gave my mother what you were supposed to give me, you asshole!" Then she fell silent, finished for the moment.

"Shannon," Dean said quietly. "Last night … wasn't your night. It was Millie's night. You have lots of 'Shannon nights' in front of you. But that … that was the last 'Millie night' there will ever be. She's thirty-nine. That was her swan song. That was 'adios' to youth and beauty."

Shannon's eyes gradually widened as his words slowly came home to her. "Oh, Dean!" she said. "Oh my God! I'm such a bitch!" She began to cry anew. Her sobbing became convulsive as it took control of her body. She held out her arm in a weak invitation, and Dean responded with an embrace.

"Poor Mom," she sobbed. "All she can ever have is that video tape. Just a memory of the one last time she was ever beautiful." Dean held the sobbing girl until she was totally drained.

Finally the sobbing subsided and Shannon began to return to normal. "Oh, my God," Shannon said, clutching for her purse. She pulled out her cell phone and pressed one button.

"Mom?" She said. "Mom, you're beautiful and I love you very much."

"What? No, Mom. Just listen. You're beautiful, and I'm so proud of you, and I love you very much."

"Nothing. Nothing. I just wanted to tell you you're the best mom a girl could possibly have. OK? Yes. All right. Bye." She put the phone back into her purse.

"There's a situation you aren't aware of," Dean began, speaking in a somber, mysterious tone. "There's something … you don't know."

"What is it?" Shannon asked.

"Well," he began, "You know that before they ever put a man on the moon, NASA fired a lot of test rockets, right?"

"Uh … yeah," the girl replied, somewhat puzzled. "I know that."

"And then they sent chimpanzees up into space before they tried it with human astronauts, right?"

"So?"

"Well that's what you saw last night. That video was a test rocket. And your mom was the chimp who rode in it."

"Mom's a monkey?" She wrinkled her lip in confusion.

"In a sense. But the good news is, the test flight was a success. We put Millie in orbit. Now we can get on with the program of putting Shannon on the moon."

"You mean … you were just practicing with Mom?"

"In a way. It's the first chance I've had to produce a complete, finished program. You and I are still laying the groundwork for our skating. Millie's birthday party gave me a chance to take a routine all the way through to completion. It was a dress rehearsal for when you and I do it for real."

The girl's face brightened up as she contemplated what her partner was saying. Then it fell again as she looked into his eyes. "But, Dean, can I ever be as beautiful as Mom was last night?"

"I've worked that out," he said, "And my calculations predict you'll be more beautiful than your mom by a factor of … 6.2."

"Really?" she gasped. "More beautiful that Mom was?"

"Hey, if I can do that with a 40-year-old housewife who eats like a pig …,'

"And drinks like a fish," Shannon finished his sentence for him.

"Then just imagine what I can do with a smart seventeen-year-old who skates and dances and works out with weights every day!"

"Awesome!" she said.

"It is. The sky's the limit!"

Shannon's head was reeling with visions of phenomenal performances and adoring audiences. After a while she looked at Dean. "That was a wonderful birthday gift you gave Mom. Nobody else could have given her anything so neat."

"Most of the credit goes to Bruce and his video crew."

"No, you thought it up. You designed it. You worked in all those sexy moves that made her look so … damn … good! I still can't believe my mom was so … damn gorgeous! Every man there wanted her. I'll bet there were a hundred woodies!" Dean grinned with embarrassment. "You know," she said teasingly, "It looked like you and Mom were just about to go at it right there on the ice. If I didn't know better, I'd think you two really had the hots for each other."

"That's why it's called 'acting,'" he said.

"Well, it was pretty convincing. The way you two looked at each other, I thought you were gonna rip each other's clothes off. And on that star lift! I could almost hear her having an orgasm!"

"See? It is possible to build emotion into a skating program."

"Are we gonna do that?"

Dean's face transformed into an evil grin. "What you saw last night was the tip of the iceberg," he said. "You ain't seen nothing yet!"

"So, when we perform, We're gonna have sex on the ice in front of twenty-six thousand people?"

"Five nights a week, when we're on tour," he replied.

"Cool! She said.

Millie

It was almost eleven when Dean heard Millie's Jag drive up. She knocked, rather than coming in. She stood at the door wearing an elegant black outfit, waiting to be admitted.

"I hope it's not too late," she said. "I waited 'til Shannon got back home."

"No, come in," he said.

"I came over to thank you personally for making that video," Millie said after perching herself primly on his sofa, "And to apologize."

"Apologize? For what?" He asked, puzzled.

"I acted the perfect bitch last night. I ignored you completely. And so did my little bitch of a daughter, I might add." She moved closer to him. "I should have given you credit publicly for making me look so good. Hell, you were the star of the evening, not me."

"I'm glad you didn't," Dean said. "The party was perfect the way it went."

"But why wouldn't you want to get credit for the magnificent job you did making that video?"

"If you had thanked me, you would have thanked everybody else who helped out on it. It would have turned into an academy awards ceremony with you as the emcee, and that would have just diluted the impact the video had on the crowd. The point of the thing was to present Millie, the beautiful skating star. Passing out kudos would have just watered down the effect it had on everybody, and it wasn't necessary." Millie squinted, analyzing him. "I got my thrills just standing around watching how it affected your friends," he continued. "A lot of people who thought they had you figured out got a wake-up call. They were totally amazed by this new aspect of Millie Foster they had never imagined before. It was comical. I was royally entertained."

"You really mean that, don't you, Dear Boy? You're not just saying it to make it easy on me after I treated you so tacky."

"I was happier than a pig in a mud hole watching your old friends fawning over you like you were some movie star. It meant that the video worked. I made them feel that."

Millie looked at him and shook her head. Then she spoke again. "I guess you think I don't realize what you really did," she said, resuming her regal perch on the sofa.

"What's that?" Dean asked.

"You gave me back my dream. You let me live out my fantasy … one of them at least. That video was magnificent."

"Well it was mostly you. I just …,"

"Hush!" Millie stopped him with an upheld palm. "Save the bullshit, Dean Steele. It was you. It was all you. I just stood where you told me. And yet I was the one who looked good!" She regarded him with raised eyebrow. "You're very tricky, Mr. Dean Steele. Very clever, very sneaky, working behind the scenes, manipulating me, playing me like a fiddle."

"But I can see right through you," she continued. "I know how you work. If you want me to be aloof and distant when I skate with you, you say something you know will piss me off. But if you want me to melt in your arms, you turn on the charm and get me all hot and bothered right there on the ice. You give me that look, or that special squeeze. Or you press against me and breathe in my ear. damn, you get me so hot! It's a despicable way to treat a lady." She grinned. Dean was embarrassed that she had so accurately pegged his technique.

"You know, don't you, that over two hundred people watched me lusting after you last night. Now all my friends know how hot I get for a certain boy skater."

"They saw the lust, Millie, but I think they assumed you were acting the part."

"They're fools if they think that! Any idiot can see that woman is crazy about that mystery man in black." She looked into his eyes. "Dean, I love you. You're a wonderful man. And I just want to fuck you to death!"

"What a way to go!" Dean smiled.

"Anyway, it worked," she said. "You did what you came to do."

"And what was that, Ms. Foster?"

"You plotted to make a 39-year-old ice mom realize she could have been a figure skating star. With the right partner and choreography, Millie Foster could have been a headliner in the Ice Capades. I know that now. If I can look that good at thirty-nine, I could have been an international star at twenty-two."

"You make it sound like a modern tragedy."

"Oh, my heavens, no!" she said. "I've got the life I want. I don't need that pro skating business. Six performances a week. Rushing all over the world just to skate the same program for another bunch of paying strangers. Putting up with a dozen ten-gallon egos in a one-gallon bus. I wouldn't trade places with Michele or Tara or Kristi, or anybody else in the pros. I've got Fred and Shannon and my career. Everything I want ... even including one muscle-bound boy skater." She looked at him intensely.

"But I always thought it was because I couldn't make it on the ice. That I just didn't have what it takes to be a figure skating star. Last night you showed me I was wrong. I am what I am because I chose to be, not because I couldn't have had the other. You gave me that realization, and I love you for it. Nobody has ever done anything that nice for me before."

She eyed him as a hungry lion regards a newborn lamb. "And I swear, I'll make it up to you, Dean Steele. Somehow I'll find a way to repay you. I'll give you love, money, sex, be your slave, whatever you want. But, by God ... I'll find a way!"

Dean was at a loss for words. His only recourse was to change the subject. "What did Fred think of the video?"

"It made him horny. He jumped me like a big green frog as soon as we got home. Practically ripped that expensive dress right off of me. I got almost no sleep last night. He was a pimply-faced teenager again."

"Sounds like ole Fred owes me more than you do," Dean said, grinning as he tried to visualize Fred in a green frog suit.

"You know, don't you, Dear Boy, that I pretend he's you when we make love? I have a pretty vivid imagination in the dark. I can almost see you lying there – feel you on top of me."

Dean looked away, his face pained. "A deep ocean of secrets is a woman's heart[1]," he said. Millie took his cheek in her hand and turned him back to face her.

"Hey, Cowboy. Don't worry about that little ole thing. Our marriage has never been better since you dropped into my life. You keep my hormones stirred up all the time, and I take it out on ole Fred. I keep his horns trimmed real short, and he can't wipe that silly grin off his face."

Dean softened. "OK," he said.

"Sometimes I wake up from a dream about you," she said, looking down at her hands and grinning sheepishly. "In the darkness I give Fred the working over that I always fantasize giving you. It's not the real thing, but it sure is fun."

"What does Fred think about that?"

"About waking up at 3:00 AM with his beautiful wife blowing his horn? I can't say I've heard him complain!" They laughed. They sat in silence for a time, enjoying the moment.

"Oh shit," Millie said at last, standing up. "It's after midnight. Fred will be watching that video with a hard-on, and wondering where I am."

Dean smiled and shook his head. "Come here, Ice Queen," he said. "I'm gonna give you a hug."

"Oh my God," she said, grinning. "Is this what I think it is?"

Dean took the woman in his arms in a tight embrace. He kissed her neck and nibbled her left earlobe. His left hand ran slowly up the inside of her left thigh as he exhaled warm air into her ear. "Oh, you animal!" she sighed.

Dean closed his lips on hers and slipped his tongue between her parted teeth. She pressed it between hers and the roof of her mouth and sucked it gently. His hand moved up her abdomen, and slipped under the waistband of the black bikini panties she wore. "Oh, you bastard!" she moaned.

Moving from one side to the other across her stomach, his hand gradually worked the silk undergarment downward. Millie trembled as she felt herself being slowly and torturously undressed. He continued this slow teasing motion until the black silk had reached mid-thigh. "Don't stop, Dean" she pleaded in a weak whisper. "Don't stop now."

He placed both hands on her bare buttocks and pulled her against him. A massive bulge in the front of his pants pressed into her abdomen. She moaned as he kneaded her buttocks with his hands and pulled her pubis back and forth against his bulge.

"Touch me," she whispered, opening her thighs. "Touch me."

Finally Dean stopped the seduction and ended the embrace with a tender kiss on the forehead. Millie looked at him with a desperate question on her face. His calm countenance answered in the negative. There was no time for a sexual encounter this evening. She took a deep breath and exhaled a sigh. "Well, if you won't do it with me," she teased him, "You could at least pull up my panties!"

"I'd rather watch you do it," he replied, grinning slyly.

Millie lifted her skirt, exposing her soft mound of fur. Almost as slowly as he had worked them down, she pulled her panties back into position. Her face held a seductive look and her hips gyrated as the garment worked its way slowly back home.

"I just wanted you to see what you're missing," she said, before allowing her skirt to fall back into place.

He acknowledged with a grin and a nod. "Give my best to Fred."

"Oh, he'll get my best, about five minutes after I get home!"

Millie picked up her purse. "Do you have a towel I can sit on going home?" she asked coyly. "I'd hate to mess up the leather seats in the Jag." She grinned mischievously and winked.

Dean raised his eyebrows in a 'shame-on-you' pose. Then he blew her a kiss. He watched the woman's ass sway as she walked down the stairs. He watched her legs as she got into the white XJ-S. He watched the Jag's taillights until they disappeared.

"Damn, what a woman!" he mumbled to nobody

---

1. From the movie "Titanic."

Chapter 31

The Raid

Dean spotted the unmarked police car in the parking lot by its tiny hubcaps and several short radio antennas. As he walked by the office he heard the manager say, "Apartment 117." He recognized Sam Anderson's apartment number. "Here's the warrant," one of the three burly men in business suits said.

Dean was not surprised that Sam had been caught up in a vice investigation, given his rather careless use of drugs. He moved quickly to his apartment and sat down at his computer. He once again used the Back Orifice hacking program to connect to Sam's computer. He downloaded an application called "Diskwasher" onto Sam's machine and installed it. The program erases files and folders and overwrites them with random garbage, leaving no trace that they ever existed. Then it erases itself when it finishes.

He opened the "Delete list" window on Diskwasher and selected the three Back Orifice files that gave him access to Sam's computer. Deleting these would remove all evidence that the computer had ever been hacked.

Then he opened the "Pictures" folder and selected the sub-folder named "Janine" and the one marked "Jenny." Even though he had previously replaced the pornographic pictures of the two girls with garbage files, a few recognizable pictures of them remained. He didn't want either of them to be dragged into a vice investigation. He would delete all evidence that they had ever been involved with Sam.

He also selected the "Kids" folder where Sam kept a few kiddie porn pictures. Dean thought that the people who take indecent pictures of children, and those who distribute them, should be punished. But the guy who, perhaps out of curiosity, has a few such pictures on his computer should not be the target of law enforcement. The politicians, in their zeal to get re-elected on a hot emotional issue, had pushed through hysterical legislation that targets the mere possession of child pornography. It's too easy for a hacker to put kiddie porn on some unwitting victim's computer then give the police an anonymous tip. Sam might go down for illegal drugs, assuming the cops had evidence on him, but not for possession of kiddie porn.

The window on the screen said, "Click OK to wash." Dean moved the mouse pointer to the "OK" button. As his finger hovered over the left mouse button, the words, "obstruction of justice," popped into his mind. It would be untraceable. There would be no evidence on the computer that he had ever been there. He thought about Janine, out of her mind on drugs, getting screwed by two or three guys for the benefit of Sam and his camera. He thought about Jenny, barely seventeen, stark naked, and totally unconscious, with her head propped up in a woman's crotch so Sam could take a picture.

He clicked the "Back" button and removed the "Kids" folder from the delete list. Then he clicked "Finish" and "OK." As the manager's master key opened the door to Sam's apartment, the list of deleted files scrolled quickly across Dean's screen, disappearing without a trace. He flushed the disk cache to remove the last vestiges of his visit, and then he gave Sam's machine the command to "Shut down Windows." Finally he broke the connection between the two computers for the last time. As the police officers entered the apartment, Sam's computer quietly turned itself off.

About half an hour later Dean was looking out his front window, and he saw one of the police officers carrying a computer out to his car. Shannon, who had been reading a magazine on the couch, came over and looked out. "What's that guy doing?" she asked.

"Just taking out the garbage," Dean replied. "Just getting rid of some of the Piccadilly trash."

Chapter 32

Epilog — The Future

Shannon is now seventeen and is showing signs of maturing. She and Dean have performed to rave reviews in Baton Rouge and Austin in addition to their home club. They are developing a unique style that shows great promise with audiences.

Dean and Millie are now involved. They must manage their risky affair so as not to let it interfere with the skating project. Dean cannot let his guilty secret undermine his relationship with his skating partner or raise the suspicions of his sponsor. And he cannot allow the demanding Mrs. Foster to distract him from preparing for the upcoming contests.

Next Shannon and Dean will enter the series of contests that lead up to the US National Championships, the World Championships, and eventually the Olympics. The first is Southwest Sectionals in Denver, followed by Midwest Regionals in Detroit and Nationals in Cleveland.

Will they be able to hold their own against the established pairs teams? How will the judges at these higher-level contests respond to their unconventional style? Will they be able to keep their cool under the intense pressure of national and international competition? What new challenges will they face competing in this rarified atmosphere? What tactics will be used against them in contests where so much is at stake?

Now that Millie has "conquered the Ice Man," will she settle down to a convenient routine for their liaisons, or does she harbor deeper desires that will soon demand satisfaction? Have her demands on Dean now been satisfied, or is she just getting started? She is a jealous woman. Will her possessiveness cause upsets that threaten the skating project?

The more time Shannon spends with Dean, the more her emerging sexuality focuses on him. Has her curiosity been satisfied, or is she just getting started? As her womanly charm develops, will it become a distraction for Dean? Will she be at all reluctant to use her budding sensuality on her skating partner?

And what of Sarah Steed, Dean's former fiancé, his friend, Diane Sutton, and the model, Janine Wilson? Have we heard the last of them?

Book Three takes the story through the upcoming contests and a number of off-ice adventures as well.

Kent Castle
Houston, Texas
July 4, 2014

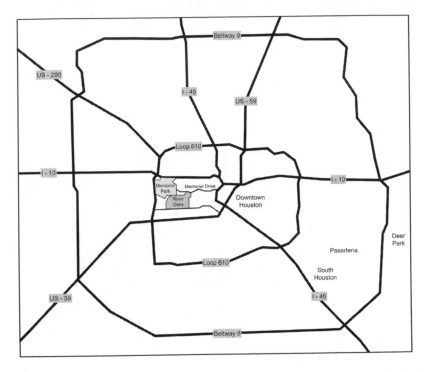

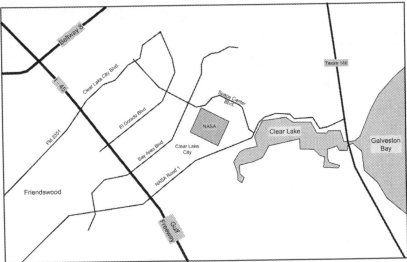